THE HAL

It is that subtle scar of evil on the face of innocence, or a nightshade shroud on the body of
normality. It can provoke primitive savagery from
the civilized, or mete out just deserts to the depraved.

It is the signature of the masters . . . and it will
be found branded onto each of these tales of
nightmarish wonder.

"MEMORABLE, ATMOSPHERIC TALES."
—*Publishers Weekly*

THE MAGAZINE OF
Fantasy & Science Fiction

- Eleven-time winner of the Hugo Award for Best Science Fiction Magazine or Best Editor
- *F&SF* has published more Nebula Award-winning stories than any other publication
- Established in 1949, *F&SF* is the original publisher of SF classics like Daniel Keyes' *Flowers for Algernon*, Walter Miller's *A Canticle For Leibowitz* and Stephen King's *The Dark Tower*

"The genre's most literate magazine."

—*Booklist*

"One of the three best in the world . . . It has remained since 1949 a leading magazine with high literary standards."

—*Science Fiction: An Illustrated History*
by Sam J. Lundwall

ABOUT THE EDITORS

EDWARD L. FERMAN, publisher of the Magazine of Fantasy and Science Fiction for twenty years, has edited many anthologies, including most recently *The Best From Fantasy and Science Fiction: A 40th Anniversary Anthology*. ANNE JORDAN is the magazine's former managing editor.

High Praise For
THE BEST HORROR STORIES FROM THE MAGAZINE OF FANTASY AND SCIENCE FICTION

"Well-written tales . . . Contains something that many horror anthologies don't—interesting stories that go beyond simple splatter."

—*Dallas News*

"HORROR FANS, TAKE NOTE! . . . This excellent collection presents a selection of the finest horror tales to appear from the 1950s until today. . . . Hauntings, vampires, the yeti, human sacrifice, and (yes) even the driver's test can all be found in this volume of horror."

—*Ft. Pierce News Tribune* (FL)

"Good reading for mature horror fiction buffs. . . . The contents . . . attest their source's high entertainment standards."

—*Booklist*

"Noteworthy. . . . This collection . . . pleases through both its quality and its range."

—*Kirkus Reviews*

The Best Horror Stories from
The Magazine of Fantasy & Science Fiction—
published by St. Martin's Press

VOLUME 1
(edited by Edward L. Ferman and Anne Jordan)
VOLUME 2
(edited by Edward L. Ferman and Anne Jordan)

VOL. 2 THE BEST HORROR STORIES

FROM
THE MAGAZINE OF
Fantasy & Science Fiction

Edward L. Ferman
and Anne Jordan, Editors

ST. MARTIN'S PRESS / NEW YORK

Volumes 1 and 2 of this series were first published in one volume, under
the same title, in hardcover and trade paper by St. Martin's Press.

THE BEST HORROR STORIES FROM *THE MAGAZINE OF FANTASY AND SCIENCE
FICTION*/VOLUME 2

Library of Congress Catalog Card Number: 88-1987

ISBN: 0-312-91603-5   Can. ISBN: 0-312-91604-3

Printed in the United States of America

St. Martin's Press hardcover edition published 1988
St. Martin's Press trade paperback edition published 1988
First St. Martin's Press mass market edition/January 1990

10 9 8 7 6 5 4 3 2 1

CONTENTS

INTRODUCTION

I love horror stories and always have. I love shuddering with fear yet knowing I am safe. When I was a child almost anything could frighten me. At the age of six, I crouched, enthralled and terrified, under a gum-studded movie seat and peeked out at *King Kong*. At eight years old, my sister and I cowered together on the couch sharing the measles and, with shivers, E.C. Comics' *Tales From the Crypt*, *The Vault of Horror*, and *The Haunt of Fear*—the good old horror comics that so frightened *parents* they were removed from the newsstands. My first encounter with real written horror stories came when I snuck a book of my father's, *The Ghost Story Omnibus*, into my bed for late-night, flashlight reading. And now, as an adult, it has been my joy as an editor and an aficionado to read the superb horror stories published by *The Magazine of Fantasy & Science Fiction*. The stories contained in this collection, both Volumes 1 and 2, are the cream of these stories.

A horror story must be carefully crafted. It is built like a house of cards and, with one slip on the author's part, the whole thing can come tumbling down, the credibility of the story shattered. In the horror story it is the reality rather than the fantasy contained in the story which is important. If we cannot believe in the reality of the monster, or the haunted house, the story becomes a mere collection of words, often with an unintentional element of absurdity mixed in. At the age of six I could believe in King Kong because I was uninitiated and undiscriminating about the world. Today the movie and its massive protagonist seem artificial and contrived. I can no longer believe in the awkward, puppet-like antics of that great gorilla and, in many ways, they are humorous.

Reality is the key ingredient in the stories in this collection. Russell Kirk's "Balgrummo's Hell," for example, has an old-fashioned flavor to it. It uses many of the conventions of the traditional Gothic horror story, yet it is thoroughly believable. I, for one, would not like to find myself alone in Balgrummo Lodging. Nor would I wish to be with Ellen, Lisa Tuttle's character, in "Bug House," a very *creepy* tale.

We are able to believe in these stories, however, because we can believe in the actions of the characters that these authors have so skillfully created. The characters are the eyes for the reader, viewing and interpreting events. If we cannot believe our "eyes," we cannot believe in the events which take place. Once again, the reality of the story tumbles down.

The authors included in this collection are first-rate and able to do what winning horror story writers should: scare you half to death with their realities. Pamela Sargent's "The Old Darkness," included here, will send your electric bills sky-high trying to avoid that fear. For those preferring a bit more science and science fiction mixed with their horror, Michael Shea's "The Autopsy" provides that—and more.

All the stories included here are outstanding not only for the skill each writer has shown, but also for their ability to send us back to that almost primeval fear we shivered with, crouching beneath the movie seat. Captured here are eleven worlds of fear peopled by those things that haunt our souls and make us shudder in the dark. Enjoy them; they're only stories, after all. Or are they reality?

—ANNE DEVEREAUX JORDAN

GLORY

RON GOULART

What would a horror anthology be without a vampire story? "Glory" *is* a vampire story, but of a very different sort than those usually seen in horror anthologies, and it's a work typical of the mordant style of Ron Goulart. He (as with many of the writers in this collection) published his first science fiction piece, "Letters to the Editor," in *F & SF* and since then, happily, has been a regular contributor. His tales often employ the traditional themes and motifs of science fiction or horror but with satiric twists that create an irresistible zaniness. "Glory" is a story of the movie industry. Film companies are continuously reviving old films; film stars of yesteryear regain popularity, and both movie houses and television indulge in an orgy of movies featuring these stars. In "Glory" one such "revival" leads to very . . . *draining* . . . consequences.

O ne of the most puzzling mysteries in the entire history of Hollywood was finally solved only a few weeks ago. And had things gone just a shade differently, the truth about what really happened to one of the brightest, loveliest motion picture stars of the thirties would have been revealed to the world. That didn't quite happen, though, and this is why.

Dennis Hoff had been sitting in his undersized office in the middle of the Golem Brothers Talent Agency, located just beyond walking distance of Wilshire Boulevard, on that particular hot, hazy Tuesday afternoon. He was a plump, pink man of thirty-eight with not enough hair.

"She's perfect for the part, Joel," he was saying into his phone.

"I admit, Den, she *looks* like a hooker. But when she read for me, she fluffed her lines."

"That was only in your office, Joel. On camera, trust me, Mindy can deliver. She's terrif—"

"Den, it takes a special talent to futz up a line like, 'Oof!' But I am still interested in . . . Who's the girl you sent me for *Nun with a Gun?*"

Hoff glanced toward his narrow doorway and saw a friend of his hesitating on the threshold. He nodded at him to wait a minute. "That was Lindy. Yep, she's exactly right for—"

"Why don't you give them distinctive names? Mindy, Lindy, they all sound—Got another call. Get back to you, Den."

Hanging up, Hoff grinned. "On the brink of placing two of my clients with Konheim Productions. C'mon in."

Jack Wilker was a modest-sized, dark-haired man in his early thirties. He almost always wore faded gray warm-up suits like the one he was decked out in today. Tucked up under his arm was a scruffy attaché case. "Smoking is going to kill you."

"It's not me who smokes, you know, old buddy. It's the

Golem brothers, both Nat and Larry," he said. "You look less gloomy today."

Taking a deep breath, Jack entered and sat opposite the desk. "I'm going to break out of the hack novelist ranks. No more books in the Spykiller series. . . . I can say goodbye to *Bombs in the Bahamas, Guns in Guatemala, Bazookas in Brazil.*"

The phone rang.

"Excuse me, Jack. Hello? Nothing just yet, Ernie. But, trust me, Vegas is very, very interested. The only thing that's making them a bit uneasy is the way you bill yourself. 'The Grand Old Man of Salsa,' Ernie, they think is a put-off. Remember I did tell you we might have to come up with something peppier? Okay, think about it all, and I'll get back to you. Right now I've got Boz Eager here in my office to sign his contracts for that new cable series, *Gay Cop.* So, *vaya con Dios*, old buddy."

"You're going to get struck by lightning someday," suggested Jack.

"Naw, only lies'll get rid of Ernie Caliente. Have you ever tried to book a seventy-six-year-old marimba player?"

"Not since college."

"A pain in the toke." Leaning back in his chair, he made a small, sad sound. "So why the elation?"

"Nonfiction."

Hoff watched him for a few seconds. "That gets you excited?"

Jack slapped his attaché case on his lap. "You know that Capricorn/AA is planning a twenty-five-million dollar movie about Glory Sands, the sexy blond actress who vanished without a—"

"I've been trying to interest Blummer over there in Mindy Mandrake for the past three—"

"I thought her name was Lindy?"

"That's Lindy Landfill."

Nodding absently, Jack continued, "Okay, what I've been

working on is a bio of Glory Sands. Her disappearing without a trace back in 1937 is one of the most puzzling mysteries in the entire history of Hollywood." Chuckling, he opened the case. "Yet nobody's done a book on her glittering yet tragic life in years. So I figured I'd put together a proposal and sell the book for a nice five-figure advance."

"Not a bad notion. Is that what's got you so buoyed up, the notion of doing—"

"Better than that, Den." He thrust a hand into the attaché case. "No, I made a discovery late yesterday at a secondhand bookshop down in Oil Beach. Place has a whole damn wall of movie stuff and related crap. Fairly cheap." He produced a slender, weathered, leather-bound volume and held it up, hand jiggling slightly. "Do you know what this is? This is Peter Yarko's last diary."

"That's exactly what I was about to guess. Who the hell is Peter Yarko?"

Jack's head tilted back, eyebrows climbing. "You mean you're trying to get Lindy Landfill a part in *The Glory Story*, and you don't even know—"

"Mindy Mandrake."

"And you don't even know who Yarko was?"

"Hey, I live right here in the present. Only hicks from the sticks play Hollywood trivia, old buddy," said Hoff. "I have to think about current talents like Ernie Caliente, Boz Eater, Lin—"

"Peter Yarko was the director of *The Devil Is a Blonde*, *Blond Explosion*, *The Blond President*, and—"

"Ah, proving blondes do have more fun." Then Hoff snapped his fingers. "I remember now; he's the Polish gink who arrived out of nowhere with Glory Sands in tow in the early thirties. Directed her in her first few pics, got screwed by MGM and tossed out. Sure, Victor Yarko."

"Peter Yarko." Jack eased the thin, musty book open. "I don't know how this ended up in that particular bookstore. The point is, nobody's apparently read it ever, beyond the title page. *My Diary. Vol. 33/P. Yarko. 1937.*"

"How much'd you pay for that?"

"Twenty bucks."

"You consider that cheap?"

"Just hush a minute and listen to—"

"Yarko disappeared about the same time she did, didn't he? Right, the movie's going to imply he murdered her in a fit of jealousy and joined the Foreign Legion to—"

"Spanish Civil War. Yarko quit Hollywood, went to Spain to fight on the Loyalist side, and was killed within a few weeks." Jack was leafing through the foxed pages of the old diary as he spoke. "Glory Sands had disappeared without a trace three days before he took off for Spain. By the time anybody thought to question him, Yarko was long gone."

"And he left a big Hollywood-Moorish mansion up in Beverly Hills," remembered Hoff. "Sure, all his nitwit relatives fought for years over who owned it, and it's been sitting empty since the seventies."

"Listen to this final entry. 'Wednesday, March 3, 1937. They took Glory away from me, and that was wrong. Yet I now realize it was also wrong of me to have unleashed her and brought her here to America. But that's been mended, and now, thanks to Tumly, she rests under an eternal spell and the world is safe again and MGM can take a hike. The secret room beneath my wine cellar shall be her last resting place, and never again shall she rise from her coffin. . . .'"

"Tumly," muttered Hoff, stroking his pudgy pink chin, "Tumly. Sure, that must be Byers Tumly. He's still working the occult dodge. Eighty-some years old. I booked him on *Odd, Isn't It?* a couple years back when those pinhead shows were pop—"

"Den, you're missing the point." He rose up excitedly, and his attaché case plumped to the floor, spilling copies of his Spykiller novels to the thin rug. "See, I've solved the damn mystery that's baffled the world for half a century. I know where her body is, I know who put it there, and I figure I can get at least fifty thousand as an advance."

"Sit." Hoff made a lower-yourself motion with his right

hand. "You have completely, old buddy, missed the real and salient point of all this."

"It's that I can now write the first complete biography of Glory Sands," said Jack, grinning. "I can become a literary lion, a Pulitzer Prize contender, and a fellow who isn't always three and a half months behind in his alimony payments to not one but two former wives. With an advance in the neighborhood of fifty thou, I can—"

"Fifty thou is jelly beans," the pudgy talent agent informed him. "We can make millions on this."

"How? Sell my book to Capricorn/AA as a source of—"

"We sell Glory Sands herself to them, schmuck."

Jack blinked. "Why would they want a corpse? The publicity value of a dead body doesn't seem to me to—"

"She ain't a corpse, ninny." Grunting, he reached out to grab the mildewed diary from his friend's grasp. "Listen attentively now. '. . . An eternal spell . . . never again shall she rise. . . .' You're supposed to have a way with words, yet you didn't tumble to the obvious and glaring nuances herein. Glory Sands *isn't* dead; she only sleeps. She's down there under that deserted manse in a state of suspended animation. Like Sleeping Beauty and other comatose ladies of lore and legend."

"I suppose you could interpret the—"

"Attend to me, lad," ordered Hoff, tapping the open pages of the Yarko diary. "This director gink had her put into a trance. Don't ask me why, but that's what the guy did. After all, there were some strange folks in Hollywood even back then. Motives don't matter. Important thing is, she can be revived."

"Who's missing nuances now? It says *eternal* spell, and that—"

"Byers Tumly," Hoff shut the book. "Byers Tumly is alive at this moment, even as we speak, and you sit there like a lunk missing the hotdamn point. Byers Tumly, a crackerjack mystic with the powers of black magic at his command, lives with his sappy granddaughter in Pasadena."

"So?"

"What Tumly can do, Tumly can undo."

"Reverse the spell?"

"Yes, indeed, old buddy, reverse the spell and bring her back to life."

Jack scratched his armpit. "In a way, that'd be great," he said finally. "What I'm saying is, she'd certainly be a good source of information for my biograph—"

"What is Blummer over at C/AA looking for, yearning for, beating the bush for? He's been turned down by Cybill Shepherd and couldn't cut a deal with Meryl Streep. He's seriously contemplating, in the vein of Selznick's hunt for a suitable Scarlett O'Hara, a nationwide search for an unknown to portray Glory Sands upon the silver screen."

"Wait now. We can't do that."

"Why not, pray tell?"

"It's too unusual and strange, for one thing. What I'm saying is, if Glory Sands does awaken from this trance, she's still going to look exactly like she did fifty years ago," said Jack. "Either that or she might be a wrinkled-up mummy who—"

"You still don't comprehend what I intend."

"And how could we explain her to people? Tell them the truth, and they'll suspect either a hoax or they'll be scared off. I don't imagine Blummer at Capricorn/AA is anxious to hire a reanimated corpse to—"

"We aren't going to let anyone know she's really Glory Sands."

"Then how can I finish the biography or—"

"You don't. Not until after we sell her to Blummer to play herself in the bio-pic." Hoff bounced in his chair as he explained this. "No, we market her as an amazing Glory Sands lookalike. A young and talented newcomer who was born—destined, if you will—to play this role. We introduce her to Blummer—hell, she's a cinch to land the role—and then he promotes her like crazy. As her managers, we get a handsome percentage of everything—her salary, the poster money, the advertising loot, the whole flapping casaba. Twenty percent of millions is going to be a lot more than a paltry advance from some Manhattan book—"

"She might not go along with the idea."

Hoff scoffed. "Hey, this is what I do for a living, amigo," he reminded Jack. "I thrive on selling half-wits inept and malformed actors and actresses that they really have no earthly use for. I can sure as heck, trust me, persuade Glory Sands to pretend to be a gifted unknown."

"And suppose, once we pry open the coffin, she's a little wizened-up mummy?"

"Then I'll get her a job with Ernie Caliente." Hoff rose up. "Let us, however, look only on the bright side. We are, old buddy, on the brink of great things."

A gust of hot night wind came rushing across the weedy back acre of the walled-in Yarko estate. It caught hold of Byers Tumly, inflated the heavy plaid overcoat the frail old mystic insisted on wearing, nudged him over a long-dead hedge, and dumped him into a dry fish pond.

"Indeed . . . hum hum," he murmured, sprawled face-down next to a broken stone cherub who was clutching a gulping dolphin. "I am . . . don't you know . . . beginning to remember. This pond, yes . . . used to be fish in it."

Jack caught the wizard's thin arm and yanked him to his feet. "I don't know much about occult ritual," he said to Hoff, who was carrying a large flashlight and a satchel full of rattling tools, "but shouldn't our mystic be sober for this?"

"He is sober."

"Hum hum . . . Peter Yarko . . . remember the night well . . . wind in the willows . . . cast a spell . . . ancient runes . . . Calabar . . . Egbo . . . Nyamba . . . indeed, indeed."

"He's tipsy." Jack guided him around a marble faun and toward the dark, sprawling mansion.

"He's merely old."

The wind came skimming across the sharply slanting tile

roofs, twisting the lame weathercock, making rude, raspy sounds.

"Age doesn't smell like an old bar rag."

"Whatever was the reason for casting the spell? . . . paid me handsomely . . . hum hum . . . Sign of Solomon . . . salamander . . . Obambo."

"It'd be encouraging if he could recall why Glory Sands is sealed up in the bowels of this—"

"The diary already explained all that, old buddy. Yarko was ticked off at her, so he had our wizard here put her into a trance."

"C'mon, Den, every time you get mad at a lady, you don't call a sorcerer to—"

"*I* don't, true, but I don't happen to be a brooding, tormented artist like Yarko." Hoff halted in front of the boarded-up rear door of the deserted house.

". . . better off this way," muttered old Tumly, swaying as the wind whipped around him. "Make world safe for . . . democracy . . . something like that . . . Nergal . . . Astaroth . . . Moloch."

After setting his satchel carefully on the mossy ground, Hoff extracted a crowbar. "First thing to do is get rid of these boards." He started to do that.

"This is what's popularly called breaking and entering," mentioned Jack. He was clutching the ancient sorcerer, to keep him from blowing away.

"You can tell the cops it's research for your next crime novel," said Hoff, ripping away another old board. "But I really doubt they pay any attention to this pile any longer."

The nails shrieked as he pulled them free. Downhill somewhere a lone hound commenced howling forlornly.

"A bad sign," observed Tumly. "Perturbed spirits prowl."

Jack asked him, "You sure you have no idea why Glory Sands was—"

"It'll come back to me." He chuckled in a rusty way. "Yes . . . hum . . . this excitement is good for me. Gets the brain to clicking along once again. . . . Sitting in Pasadena can be . . . Do you have any idea how many game shows there are on television?"

"Must be about—"

"There," announced Hoff. "All the boards are down. Now I'll pick the lock."

"You know how to do this sort of thing?"

"Well, it ought to be relatively simple, shouldn't it? Thousands of people who never even graduated from high school become burglars." He squatted before the tarnished doorknob.

"Yes, I remember this house," said Tumly, wrapping his large plaid overcoat tighter around him and venturing along the dusty hallway. "It didn't smell so strongly of rot and decay then."

The long corridor, paneled with dark-stained wood and floored with dusky mosaic tiles, was thick with the odors of mildew and neglect.

Hoff played the beam of his light ahead, touching the carved panels, the wrought-iron wall lamps, the serpentine pattern in the tiles. "What a setting," he remarked. "This must inspire the creative writer in you, Jack."

"Inspires me to want to get clear before the cops find—"

"This way." Tumly was pointing to their left. "There's a stairway off yonder kitchen . . . hum hum . . . I'm remembering more by the minute. Yes, she lies down below."

The old wizard lurched, tottered, and caught hold of a dusty wine bottle on one of the racks that filled the damp, stone-walled room. "Hum, yes. It's coming back to—"

Jack made a grab for his sleeve. "This is not time to go guzzling—"

"I'd never touch port." Tumly caught hold of the bottle by its neck, pushed it downward. "This particular bottle happens to be a concealed lever, young man."

A rumbling started up across the shadowy wine cellar.

Gravelly noises came rattling up from below. Next came an echoing, bumping thump.

"He *is* remembering rightly." Hoff turned the beam of the flash onto the twisting stairway that was showing now in the large rectangle that had opened in the floor.

The coffin was down there, a heavy thing of bronze. It rested on a low stone pedestal, gobs of scarlet sealing wax dabbed around the edges of the domed lid.

Hoff hurried across the chill stone floor and knelt next to it. "This hasn't been futzed with," he said. "Meaning Glory's still inside."

"This is going to make a great chapter in my book." Jack approached the bronze coffin. "Yeah, and I can spin off lots of articles too. Slick magazines first, then supermarket tabloids."

The old mystic shuffled over. "Things are growing ever clearer," he assured them, poking his knobby hands into the pockets of his immense overcoat.

"And Glory Sands is really inside there?" Jack asked him.

"Helped deposit the lady within it myself." Tumly had located a magnifying glass with a bit of fuzz sticking to its lens. He made a slow circuit of the coffin. "Hum hum. . . . Yes, to be sure . . . simple enough restraining spell . . . yes." From another lumpy pocket he brought forth a fat black candle. "Stick this on that shelf over there, young man, and light it."

Jack obliged, nose wrinkling at the acrid smell the sputtering candle produced. "Can you—"

"Quiet, please." Tumly had straightened up, and there was a small skin-bound volume open in his quivering hands. "Beelzebub . . . Beelzebub . . . Beelzebub."

Shivering, Jack took a few backward steps.

The old sorcerer continued on, mixing Latin with incantations in even older, deader languages.

Five long minutes passed.

Then the thick globs of crimson wax sizzled and started

melting. Clotted streams of red dribbled down across the bronze sides of the heavy casket.

"Now, be quick, lift the lid free," Tumly ordered.

Hoff took the far side, Jack the other. Grunting, they managed to lift it up and away.

While they were leaning the lid against the stone wall, a satiny rustle sounded within the open casket.

A very pretty blond young woman in a white satin evening gown sat up in the casket and looked around at the three of them.

"Ah, yes," said Tumly. "I remember now why we sealed her up. She's a vampire."

Hoff, grinning broadly, came into the cottage out of the fuzzy glare of the afternoon. "Absolutely great," he announced, waving the manila envelope he held aloft in his pudgy right hand. "I picked up the contact prints of the pics we had Orlando of Hollywood shoot a couple of nights ago, and they're completely sensational. She looks, specially in that slinky satin dress she was interred in, just like Glory Sands."

"She *is* Glory Sands." Jack was sitting in his favorite, and only, armchair and gazing into his small, empty fireplace. "She was hidden away under Yarko's place because of her vampire ways. But now you've stuck me with baby-sitting a potential kill—"

"C'mon, she agreed to downplay that stuff," the agent reminded him. "Glory's as eager as we are for a new career in—"

"Also, Den, I don't see why we had to spend so damn much on those photos."

"Because, old buddy, we are going first cabin on this whole venture. We're going to sell that platinum bimbo as—"

"Not so loud," cautioned Jack in a lowered voice. "But what I'm talking about is, I have to pay rent on this place, and I've had to shelve my bio so—"

"What are you so uneasy about? She can't hear us." Hoff settled into the wicker sofa with his broad back to the view of the overgrown yard outside. "Vampires sleep by day, don't they?"

"Nertz," observed a feminine voice from the next room.

"Apparently that isn't always so." Jack nodded toward the doorway of his kitchen.

"Well, then that's even better for us. That way we won't have to con Blummer into filming *The Glory Story* entirely at night."

"You bozos really hand me a laugh." The lovely blonde, wearing one of Jack's candy-striped shirts and a brand-new pair of designer jeans, came into the parlor holding a fat bologna sandwich. "Where'd you get your facts about vampires anyhow, from some B-movie starring that dippy Hungarian hophead who went flapping around in a cape? Jeez." She perched on the arm of Jack's chair, one pretty leg swinging out and tapping the base of his old floor lamp. "Vampires have been getting a bad press for . . . Hey, are you sure dames wear this kind of slacks nowadays? They're so tight my fanny's going to sleep."

Watching her, Hoff nodded approvingly and chuckled. "Perfect, she's perfect. That sassy 1930s patina will knock Blummer and his toadies on their respective tokes."

After taking a bite of her sandwich, Glory said, "This bologna sure as heck doesn't taste like the bologna I remember."

"Fifty years," reminded Jack, "have passed since you last tasted—"

"Darn, I never figured bologna would change." Sliding off the chair arm, she crossed to the window. "Smog, huh? It sure does a swell job of mucking up the air. Don't you ever have your shrubs trimmed, Jack? I had two Japs who did—"

"How'd you like to see your pictures, Glory?" Hoff was shaking the proof sheets from the envelope. "You look great."

"Cameras love me," she explained, biting into her sandwich. "Even in Paris in the 1870s, I—"

"Whoa now," cut in Jack, "you were alive in the 1870s?"

"Why the heck do you think I became a vampire in the first place, sweetheart?" She turned to face him, wiping a speck of mayonnaise from her dimpled cheek. "Immortality. Sure, I was born in Lisbon . . . that's in Portugal . . . in 1726."

Hoff lowered the photos to his lap. "Glory, we better not mention that fact to anybody else, okay?"

"You think I'm a dope? I mean, honey, I want to start making dough again more than you guys even." She gave Jack's small forlorn parlor a disdainful look. "I sure don't want to live in this cracker box much longer."

"Exactly. And as soon as I sell you to Blummer, we'll start looking at mansions in Bel Air," promised the agent. "That's the sort of setting Gloria Sanctum needs."

"Jeez, what a dippy name." The reanimated actress lowered herself to sit on the bare hardwood floor, leaning her slim back against the built-in bookshelves. "I know I can't call myself Glory Sands anymore, but—"

"Gloria Sanctum has a certain flair," Hoff assured her. "And preserves your initials."

"I never even much liked Glory Sands. That was Yarko's idea," she said, shaking her lovely head. "Imagine that bum having a spell put on me and dumping me in his darn basement."

"Apparently," said Jack, not quite looking at her, "he was concerned about your vampire activities and—"

"Hell, no. I think he just wanted to give MGM the finger." Finishing her sandwich, she licked her fingers. "Yarko exaggerated things, like most creative bozos."

"Are you suggesting," said Jack, "that you really weren't much of a practicing vampire?"

"Look, sweetheart, once in a while I did maybe drain some sap of his blood," she admitted, smiling attractively. "I mean, you're a vampire and that's what you do, you know? But I was discreet and I didn't do it often. Rarely with anybody in show business."

"So there's really not that much to worry about," said Hoff.

Very gracefully the blond actress stood up. "Let me see the pictures, Denny."

"To me, Glory . . . Gloria, rather. Better get used to using your new name." He handed her the sheets. "To me, Gloria, the shots of you smiling right into the camera are the best."

She studied the shots. "My left profile isn't bad either," she remarked. "Being buried for fifty years hasn't really hurt my looks any."

"Gloria, you're as lovely now as—"

"Hey!" After staring out the window, Jack hopped up and ran for the door.

"What's wrong, old buddy?"

"Somebody outside, peeking over my hedge at us."

The two men ran out into the hedged-in yard. But there was no one out there now.

"You get a look at him?" asked Hoff.

"Not really, but . . . It was a guy . . . and there was something vaguely familiar about him."

"Hey, you two," called Glory, "come on back in here and let me tell you which ones of these we're going to use."

Jack tossed another shovelful of dirt aside. "What was it you were going to tell me when you first got here, Den?"

"Huh?" Hoff was thumbing through the notebook he'd found in the pocket of the dead man sprawled on the garage floor. "Oh, yeah, good news. Blummer was very, very impressed with the glossies of Glory . . . Gloria. He wants her to come in and read on Monday. It's a sure thing, far as I can tell."

The grave was getting deeper. "Don't you think maybe this is a snag?"

"How so?" Hoff shut the notebook.

"You were paying attention when I explained to you that I found this guy out behind my cottage a couple hours ago, at sundown? What I'm saying is, he was killed by a vampire."

"Well, any half-wit can see that," said the agent. "He's got those two puncture marks in his throat, and he's been drained of his blood."

"Glory did it."

"Call her Gloria."

"Gloria. Glory. She admitted as much before she locked herself in the bedroom."

"Let her sulk for a while; that's okay."

"But she—"

"He's got only himself to blame, old buddy." Hoff slapped the notebook against his thigh. "This is Walt Downey, a free-**lan**ce writer for *The National Intruder*. He's also the very same chap you spotted prowling amongst your shrubbery a few days ago."

"A reporter? Damn, that means—"

"A *free-lance*," cut in Hoff. "Nobody knows what he was planning to write about next. Seems he was interviewing Tumly for some other article, and the old gink let slip a reference to us and Gloria."

"What sort of reference?"

"Sort of to the fact that we'd brought her back from the grave. Keep digging, will you?"

"That's splendid. Glory's resurrection's going to become a mass media event."

"Downey had only, according to his notes, begun to investigate. He wasn't yet sure if we had Glory Sands or were simply cooking up a hoax for publicity purposes," said Hoff. "Fortunately for us, she got him just in time."

"It's murder."

"Not necessarily. The fact she's a vampire would make a good defense," the agent said, watching Jack work on the reporter's grave. "Sure, she can plead she couldn't help herself. But it'll never come to that. We bury this gink and—"

"Making us accessories."

"From what I can learn out of his effects, old buddy,

Downey had no near kith or kin. Even the *Intruder* won't miss him, since most free-lance writers are expendable," said Hoff. "Let's, therefore, strive to look only on the bright side. Think about what our share of her salary of, say, four hundred thousand dollars per picture is going to be. And keep digging."

Glory took another sip from her glass. "Phooey," she remarked. "This stuff sure doesn't taste like orange juice."

"Let's get back to the issue." Jack was seated across his small lopsided breakfast table from her.

" 'Made from concentrate.' Whatever the heck that might be. I mean, how dippy can you get?" She clicked the glass down. "You got fresh oranges out the kazoo all around here, and you dumbbells—"

"About Downey."

"Who?"

"The reporter you got rid of the other night. We really have to talk about—"

"Jeez, are you still squawking about that? Denny didn't think it was all that important."

"Glory, I have a small-garage. If you keep on—"

"The guy was poking his nose into our business, wasn't he?"

"Having all your blood drained from your body isn't quite the punishment that fits that particular—"

"Okay, okay, swell. Don't keep nagging, okay? I'm doing the best I can," the blonde told him. "I just wish we'd get that contract signed so—"

"Blummer was favorably impressed with you when you read for him, according to Den."

"Blummer, what a twerp," she said, tangling her fingers in her silky hair. "You know what he used to be? A certified public accountant. That sure isn't my idea of a mogul. And that dippy director . . . what's his name?"

"Piet Goedewaagen."

"He's younger than I am," she said, frowning. "Younger than I'm supposed to be, I mean. He passed out cold before I even got to the second page of my dumb scene."

"Goedewaagen has a drug problem, I hear."

"He fell off his darn chair. Plunk on the rug."

"Let the producer worry about him. You—"

"Woody Van Dyke never fell off his chair. When we shot *Blonde Fever* up at Catalina in thirty-five, he—"

"How often are you likely to attack people?"

"¿Quién sabe? as they say in Tijuana." She shrugged gracefully. "It sort of depends on my mood and whether I'm bored or not. Sometimes, you know, I just get the urge."

Jack took an unenthusiastic bite of his cold toast. "Glory, could—"

"Call me Gloria. We don't want to spoil—"

"Killing people is going to spoil things a lot sooner than my calling you the wrong name," he said. "Now, when you were here before, back in the 1930s, about how often did you attack—"

"Not all that much. It fluctuated."

"Can you give me a ballpark figure? What I'm asking is, how many victims did—"

"Oh, less than a hundred."

"A hundred?" He dropped his toast.

"Less than, I said."

"Ninety?"

"Give or take."

"How'd you keep people from finding out that—"

"Yarko took care of most of that," answered Glory. "Seeing that they got buried or lost in an out-of-the-way place. And sometimes I'd go after a nobody down on Skid Row."

"You were in Hollywood from 1933 to 1937." He eased a small calculator out of his jacket pocket. "That's four years. So we divide ninety victims by four, and we get . . . oy! . . . 22.5 per year."

"That's a cute gadget. Can I see how it—"

The phone sounded out in the parlor. "You can fool with

it. Here." Tossing her the pocket calculator, he sprinted
into the next room. "Hello?"

"We're on the real brink now, old buddy. I just got a
call," said Hoff.

"I'm not hearing you too clearly. What's that noise in
the background?"

"Marimba music." The agent raised his voice. "Blummer
just phoned. Wants me over at C/AA in one hour. I smell
six figures in the offing."

"Listen, Den," said Jack, hand masking the mouthpiece.
"If we unleash this creature on the world, we're going to
be responsible for at least 22.5 deaths per year for—"

"Ernie, that's *bastante*, old amigo. I like the new act,
and, trust me, I'll book you at someplace terrific. Now get
the hell out of here. Adios," Hoff was saying. "Okay, Jack,
you—"

"Twenty-two point five. That's the number of victims we
can count on each year that she's still aboveground." Jack
glanced at the kitchen doorway. "So what we have to do,
we have to get Tumly and seal her up again under—"

"Can't get Tumly."

"You didn't book him off in the boondocks someplace?"

"The poor old gink passed on."

"That's . . . wait a second. How?"

"What?"

"How'd Tumly come to die?"

Hoff coughed. "Don't scream and yell when I fill you
in."

"Never mind. I know. His daughter found him sprawled
out someplace with all the blood missing from—"

"Granddaughter, it was, who found the poor soul."

"Yeah, and Glory was gone the night before last," he
said in an intense whisper. "Wouldn't explain where
she'd—"

"Let's keep looking on the bright side," said Hoff. "When
I next visit your place at dusk, I have no doubt that I'll have
a very nice contract close to my girlishly pounding heart."

"No, nope. You have to get another sorcerer then. He can put—"

"Where am I going to get a sorcerer?"

"You're a goddamn talent agent. Go find one. And quick. If you can find an eighty-year-old salsa player, then—"

"Calm yourself. Put Glory on the phone," requested the agent. "I'll impart to her all the good things that are in the offing, and use my considerable powers of persuasion to convince her to lay off her hobby for a while. I'll get her to promise she won't do anything to futz up her budding career."

"Vampires," said Jack, "don't keep promises."

Hoff arrived at dusk, his stride slower than usual. His pudgy body had a mournful sag. "Idiots," he said as he stepped into the parlor. "I should have remembered that this is Hollywood."

Jack was in his favorite armchair, surrounded by shadows.

"I go over to see Blummer," continued the unhappy agent. "I am ushered into his vast Capricorn/AA office. And what does that nitwit tell me?"

Jack didn't respond.

"He tells me," said Hoff, "they've decided they don't want Glory to play Glory Sands in their movie. And why? I'll tell you why. She's not right for the part."

Jack didn't respond.

Slowly Hoff crossed the dim room. "Well, don't be gloomy, old buddy. I'll come up with a new way to sell her to somebody." He reached out and clicked on the floor lamp next to the chair.

That was when he saw the marks on Jack's throat.

BUG HOUSE

LISA TUTTLE

American-born Lisa Tuttle resides in England and is both a journalist and story writer. She was one of the early members of the Clarion Writers' Workshop and, in 1974, won the John W. Campbell Award for best new science fiction writer. Although she has written numerous impressive science fiction stories, Ms. Tuttle excels in the contemporary horror tale and in her ability to terrify readers. "Bug House" is a particularly creepy and effective chiller.

The house was a wreck, resting like some storm-shattered ship on a weedy headland overlooking the ocean. Ellen felt her heart sink at the sight of it.

"This it?" asked the taxi driver dubiously, squinting through his windshield and slowing the car.

"It must be," Ellen said without conviction. She couldn't believe that her aunt—or anyone else—lived in this house.

The house had been built, after the local custom, out of wood, and then set upon cement blocks that raised it three or four feet off the ground. But floods seemed far less dangerous to the house now than the winds, or simply time. The house was crumbling on its blocks. The boards were weatherbeaten and scabbed with flecks of ancient gray paint. Uncurtained windows glared blankly, and one shutter hung at a crazy angle. Between the boards of the sagging second-story balcony, Ellen could see daylight.

"I'll wait for you," the driver said, pulling up at the end of an overgrown driveway. "In case there's nobody here."

"Thanks," Ellen said, getting out of the backseat and tugging her suitcase after her. She counted the fare out into his hand and glanced up at the house. No sign of life. Her shoulders slumped. "Just wait to be sure someone answers the door," she told the driver.

Trudging up the broken cement path to the front door, Ellen was startled by a glimpse of something moving beneath the house. She stopped short and peered ahead at the dark space. Had it been a dog? A child playing? Something large and dark, moving quickly—but it was gone now or in hiding. Behind her, Ellen could hear the taxi idling. For a brief moment she considered going back. Back to Danny. Back to all their problems. Back to his lies and promises.

She walked forward again, and when she reached the porch she set her knuckles against the warped gray door and rapped sharply, twice.

An old, old woman, stick-thin and obviously ailing, opened the door. Ellen and the woman gazed at each other in silence.

"Aunt May?"

The old woman's eyes cleared with recognition, and she nodded slightly. "Ellen, of course!"

But when had her aunt grown so old?

"Come in, dear." The old woman stretched out a parchment claw. At her back, Ellen felt the wind. The house creaked, and for a moment Ellen thought she felt the porch floor give beneath her feet. She stumbled forward into the house. The old woman—her aunt, she reminded herself —closed the door behind her.

"Surely you don't live here all alone," Ellen began. "If I'd known—if Dad had known—we would have . . ."

"If I'd needed help I would've asked for it," Aunt May said with a sharpness that reminded Ellen of her father.

"But this house," Ellen said. "It's too much for one person. It looks like it might fall down at any minute, and if something should happen to you here, all alone . . ."

The old woman laughed, a dry, papery rustle. "Nonsense. This house will outlast me. And appearances can be deceiving. Look around you—I'm quite cozy here."

Ellen saw the hall for the first time. A wide, high-ceilinged room with a brass chandelier and a rich Oriental carpet. The walls were painted a cream color, and the grand staircase looked in no danger of collapse.

"It does look a lot better inside," Ellen said. "It looked deserted from the road. The taxi driver couldn't believe anyone lived here."

"The inside is all that matters to me," said the old woman. "I have let it all go rather badly. The house is honeycombed with dry rot and eaten by insects, but even so it's in nowhere near as bad shape as I am. It will still be standing when I'm underground, and that's enough for me."

"But, Aunt May . . ." Ellen took hold of her aunt's bony shoulders. "Don't talk like that. You're not dying."

That laugh again. "My dear, look at me. I am. I'm long past saving. I'm all eaten up inside. There's barely enough of me left to welcome you here."

Ellen looked into her aunt's eyes, and what she saw there made her vision blur with tears.

"But doctors . . ."

"Doctors don't know everything. There comes a time, my dear, for everyone. A time to leave this life for another one. Let's go in and sit down. Would you like some lunch? You must be hungry after that long trip."

Feeling dazed, Ellen followed her aunt into the kitchen, a narrow room decorated in green and gold. She sat at the table and stared at the wallpaper, a pattern of fish and frying pans.

Her aunt was dying. It was totally unexpected. Her father's older sister—but only eight years older, Ellen remembered. And her father was a vigorously healthy man, a man still in the prime of life. She looked at her aunt, saw her moving painfully slowly from cupboard to counter to shelf, preparing a lunch.

Ellen rose. "Let me do it, Aunt May."

"No, no, dear. I know where everything is, you see. You don't. I can still get around all right."

"Does Dad know about you? When was the last time you saw him?"

"Oh, dear me, I didn't want to burden him with my problems. We haven't been close for years, you know. I suppose I last saw him—why, it was at your wedding, dear."

Ellen remembered. That had been the last time she had seen Aunt May. She could hardly believe that woman and the one speaking to her now were the same. What had happened to age her so in only three years?

May set a plate on the table before Ellen. A pile of tuna and mayonnaise was surrounded by sesame crackers.

"I don't keep much fresh food on hand," she said. "Mostly canned goods. I find it difficult to get out shopping much anymore, but then, I haven't much appetite lately either. So it doesn't much matter what I eat. Would you like some coffee? Or tea?"

"Tea, please. Aunt May, shouldn't you be in a hospital? Where someone would care for you?"

"I can care for myself right here."

"I'm sure Dad and Mom would love to have you visit . . ."

May shook her head firmly.

"In a hospital they might be able to find a cure for you."

"There's no cure for dying except death, Ellen."

The kettle began to whistle, and May poured boiling water over a teabag into a cup.

Ellen leaned back in her chair, resting the right side of her head against the wall. She could hear a tiny, persistent, crunching sound from within the wall—termites?

"Sugar in your tea?"

"Please," Ellen responded automatically. She had not yet touched her lunch and had no desire for anything to eat or drink.

"Oh, dear," sighed Aunt May. "I'm afraid you'll just have to drink it plain. It must have been a very long time since I used this—there are more ants here than sugar grains."

Ellen watched her aunt drop the whole canister into the garbage can.

"Aunt May, is money a problem? I mean, if you're staying here because you can't afford—"

"Bless you, no." May sat down at the table beside her niece. "I have some investments and enough money in the bank for my own needs. And this house is my own too. I bought it when Victor retired, but he didn't stay long enough to help me enjoy it."

In a sudden rush of sympathy, Ellen leaned over and would have taken her frail aunt in her arms, but May fluttered her hand in a go-away motion, and Ellen drew back.

"With Victor dead, some of the joy went out of fixing it up. Which is why it still looks much the same old wreck it was when I bought it. This property was a real steal, because nobody wanted the house. Nobody but me and Victor." May cocked her head suddenly and smiled. "And maybe you? What would you say if I left this house to you when I die?"

"Aunt May, please don't . . ."

"Nonsense. Who better? Unless you can't stand the sight of it, of course, but I'm telling you, the property is worth something, at least. If the house is too far gone with the bugs and the rot, you can pull it down and put up something you and Danny like better."

"It's very generous of you, Aunt May. I just don't like to hear you talk about dying."

"No? It doesn't bother me. But if it disturbs you, then we'll say no more about it. Shall I show you your room?

"I don't go upstairs anymore," May said, leading the way slowly up the staircase, leaning heavily on the banister and pausing often in her climb. "I moved my bedroom downstairs. It was too much trouble to always be climbing up and down."

The second floor smelled strongly of sea damp and mold.

"This room has a nice view of the sea," May said. "I thought you might like it." She paused in a doorway, gesturing to Ellen to follow. "There are clean linens in the hall closet."

Ellen looked into the room. It was sparely furnished with bed, dressing table, and straight-backed chair. The walls were an institutional green and without decoration. The mattress was bare, and there were no curtains at the french doors.

"Don't go out on the balcony—I'm afraid parts of it have quite rotted away," May cautioned.

"I noticed," Ellen said.

"Well, some parts go first, you know. I'll leave you alone now, dear. I'm feeling a bit tired myself. Why don't we both just nap until dinnertime?"

Ellen looked at her aunt and felt her heart twist with sorrow at the weariness on that pale, wrinkled face. The small exertion of climbing upstairs had told on her. Her arms trembled slightly, and she looked gray with weariness.

Ellen hugged her. "Oh, Aunt May," she said softly. "I'm going to be a help to you, I promise. You just take it easy. I'll look after you."

May pulled away from her niece's arms, nodding. "Yes, dear. It's very nice to have you here. We welcome you." She turned and walked away down the hall.

Alone, Ellen suddenly realized her own exhaustion. She sank down on the bare mattress and surveyed her bleak little room, her mind a jumble of problems old and new.

She had never known her Aunt May well enough to become close to her—this sudden visit was a move born of desperation. Wanting to get away from her husband for a while, wanting to punish him for a recently discovered infidelity, she had cast about for a place she could escape to—a place she could afford, and a place where Danny would not be able to find her. Aunt May's lonely house on the coast had seemed the best possibility for a week's hiding. She had expected peace, boredom, regret—but she had never expected to find a dying woman. It was a whole new problem that almost cast her problems with Danny into insignificance.

Suddenly she felt very lonely. She wished Danny were with her, to comfort her. She wished she had not sworn to herself not to call him for at least a week.

But she would call her father, she decided. Should she warn him against telling Danny? She wasn't sure—she hated letting her parents know her marriage was in trouble. Still, if Danny tried to find her by calling them, they would know something was wrong.

She'd call her father tonight. Definitely. He'd come out here to see his sister—he'd take charge, get her to a hospital, find a doctor with a miracle cure. She was certain of it.

But right now she was suddenly paralyzingly tired. She stretched out on the bare mattress. She would get the sheets and make it up properly later, but right now she would just close her eyes, just close her eyes and rest for a moment. . . .

It was dark when Ellen woke, and she was hungry.

She sat on the edge of the bed, feeling stiff and disoriented. The room was chilly and smelled of mildew. She wondered how long she had slept.

Nothing happened when she hit the light switch on the wall. So she groped her way out of the room and along the dark hall toward the dimly perceived stairs. The steps creaked loudly beneath her feet. She could see a light at the bottom of the stairs, from the kitchen.

"Aunt May?"

The kitchen was empty, the light a fluorescent tube above the stove. Ellen had the feeling that she was not alone. Someone was watching. Yet when she turned, there was nothing behind her but the undisturbed darkness of the hall.

She listened for a moment to the creakings and moanings of the old house, and to the muffled sounds of sea and wind from outside. No human sound in all of that, yet the feeling persisted that if she listened hard enough, she would catch a voice. . . .

She could make out another dim light from the other end of the hall, behind the stairs, and she walked toward it. Her shoes clacked loudly on the bare wooden floor of the back hall.

It was a night-light that had attracted her attention, and near it she saw that a door stood ajar. She reached out and pushed it farther open. She heard May's voice, and she stepped into the room.

"I can't feel my legs at all," May said. "No pain in them, no feeling at all. But they still work for me somehow. I was afraid that once the feeling went they'd be useless to me. But it's not like that at all. But you knew that; you told me it would be like this." She coughed, and there was the sound in the dark room of a bed creaking. "Come here, there's room."

"Aunt May?"

Silence—Ellen could not even hear her aunt breathing. Finally May said, "Ellen? Is that you?"

"Yes, of course. Who did you think it was?"

"What? Oh, I expect I was dreaming." The bed creaked again.

"What was that you were saying about your legs?"

More creaking sounds. "Hmmm? What's that, dear?" The voice of a sleeper struggling to stay awake.

"Never mind," Ellen said. "I didn't realize you'd gone to bed. I'll talk to you in the morning. Good night."

"Good night, dear."

Ellen backed out of the dark, stifling bedroom, feeling confused.

Aunt May must have been talking in her sleep. Or perhaps, sick and confused, she was hallucinating. But it made no sense to think—as Ellen, despite herself, was thinking —that Aunt May had been awake and had mistaken Ellen for someone else, someone she expected a visit from, someone else in the house.

The sound of footsteps on the stairs, not far above her head, sent Ellen running forward. But the stairs were dark and empty, and straining her eyes toward the top, Ellen could see nothing. The sound must have been just another product of this dying house, she thought.

Frowning, unsatisfied with her own explanation, Ellen went back into the kitchen. She found the pantry well stocked with canned goods and made herself some soup. It was while she was eating it that she heard the footsteps again—this time seemingly from the room above her head.

Ellen stared up at the ceiling. If someone was really walking around up there, he was making no attempt to be cautious. But she couldn't believe that the sound was anything but footsteps: someone was upstairs.

Ellen set her spoon down, feeling cold. The weighty creaking continued.

Suddenly the sounds overhead stopped. The silence was unnerving, giving Ellen a vision of a man crouched down, his head pressed against the floor as he listened for some response from her.

Ellen stood up, rewarding her listener with the sound of a chair scraping across the floor. She went to the cabinet on the wall beside the telephone—and there, on a shelf with the phone book, Band-Aids and light bulbs was a flashlight—just as in her father's house.

The flashlight worked, and the steady beam of light cheered her. Remembering that the light in her room hadn't worked, Ellen also took out a light bulb before closing the cabinet and starting upstairs.

Opening each door as she came to it, Ellen found a series of unfurnished rooms, bathrooms, and closets. She heard no further footsteps and found no sign of anyone or anything that could have made them. Gradually, the tension drained out of her, and she returned to her own room after taking some sheets from the linen closet.

After installing the light bulb and finding that it worked, Ellen closed the door and turned to make up the bed. Something on the pillow drew her attention: examining it more closely, she saw that it seemed to be a small pile of sawdust. Looking up the wall, she saw that a strip of wooden molding was riddled with tiny holes, leaking the dust. She wrinkled her nose in distaste: termites. She shook the pillow vigorously and stuffed it into a case, resolving to call her father first thing in the morning. May could not go on living in a place like this.

Sun streaming through the uncurtained window woke her early. She drifted toward consciousness to the cries of sea gulls and the all-pervasive smell of the sea.

She got up, shivering from the dampness which seemed to have crept into her bones, and dressed herself quickly. She found her aunt in the kitchen, sitting at the table and sipping a cup of tea.

"There's hot water on the stove," May said by way of greeting.

Ellen poured herself a cup of tea and joined her aunt at the table.

"I've ordered some groceries," May said. "They should be here soon, and we can have toast and eggs for breakfast."

Ellen looked at her aunt and saw that a dying woman shared the room with her. In the face of that solemn, in-arguable fact, she could think of nothing to say. So they sat in a silence broken only by the sipping of tea, until the doorbell rang.

"Would you let him in, dear?" May said.

Ellen rose. "Shall I pay him?"

"Oh, no. He doesn't ask for that. Just let him in."

Wondering, Ellen opened the door on a strongly built young man holding a brown paper grocery bag in his arms. She put out her arms rather hesitantly to receive the groceries, but he ignored her implied offer, walking into the house and around her to the kitchen. There he set his bag down and began to unload it. Ellen stood in the doorway watching, noticing that he knew where everything went.

He said nothing to May, who seemed scarcely aware of his presence, but when everything had been put away, he sat down at the table, taking Ellen's place. He tilted his head on one side, eyeing Ellen. "You must be her niece," he said.

Ellen said nothing. She didn't like the way he looked at her. His dark, nearly black eyes seemed to be without pupils—hard eyes, without depths. And he ran those eyes up and down her body, judging her. He smiled now at her silence and turned to May. "A quiet one," he said.

May stood up, holding her empty cup.

"Let me," Ellen said quickly, stepping forward. May handed her the cup and sat down again, still without acknowledging the young man's presence. "Would you like some breakfast?" Ellen asked.

May shook her head. "You eat what you like, dear. I don't feel much like eating . . . there doesn't seem to be much point to it."

"Aunt May, you really should eat."

"A piece of toast then."

"I'd like some eggs," said the stranger. He stretched lazily in his chair. "I haven't had my breakfast yet."

Ellen looked at May, wanting some clue as to how to treat this presumptuous stranger. Was he her friend? A hired man? She didn't want to be rude to him if May didn't wish it. But May was looking into the middle distance, indifferent.

Ellen looked at the man. "Are you waiting to be paid for the groceries?" she asked.

The stranger smiled, a hard smile that revealed a set of even teeth. "I bring food to your aunt as a favor. So she won't have to go to all the trouble of getting it for herself in her condition."

Ellen stared at him a moment longer, waiting in vain for a sign from her aunt, and then turned her back on them and went to the stove to prepare breakfast. She wondered why this man was helping her aunt—was she really not paying him? He didn't strike her as the sort for disinterested favors.

"Now that I'm here," Ellen said, getting eggs and butter from the refrigerator, "you don't have to worry about my aunt. I can run errands for her."

"I'll have two fried eggs," he said. "I like the yolks runny."

Ellen glared at him but checked herself. He wasn't likely to leave just because she refused to cook his eggs—he'd probably just cook them himself. And he *had* bought the groceries.

But—her small revenge—she overcooked the eggs and gave him the slightly scorched pieces of toast.

When she sat down at the breakfast table, Ellen looked at him challengingly. "I'm Ellen Morrow," she said.

He hesitated just long enough to make her think of asking him his name more directly; then he drawled, "You can call me Peter."

"Thanks a lot," she said sarcastically. He smiled his unpleasant smile again, and Ellen felt him watching her throughout the meal. As soon as she had finished eating, she excused herself, telling her aunt that she was going to call her father.

That drew the first response of the morning from May. She put out a detaining hand, drawing it back just shy of actually touching Ellen. "Please don't worry him about me, Ellen. There's nothing he can do for me, and I don't want him charging down here for no good reason."

"But, Aunt May, you're his only sister—I have to tell him, and of course he'll want to do something for you."

"The only thing he can do for me now is to leave me alone," May said.

Unhappily, Ellen thought that her aunt was right—still, she could not leave her to die without trying to save her. Her father had to know. In order to be able to speak freely, she walked past the kitchen telephone and went back to her aunt's bedroom, where she was sure there would be an extension.

There was, and she dialed her parents' home number. The ringing at the other end of the line went on and on, until she gave up and called her father's office. As she had already half suspected, the secretary told her that her father was on one of his fishing trips—absolutely unreachable for another day or two. But she would leave word for him to call as soon as he got in.

So it had to wait. Ellen walked back toward the kitchen, her crepe-soled shoes making almost no sound on the floor.

She heard her aunt's voice saying: "You didn't come to me last night. I waited and waited. Why didn't you come?"

Almost without thinking, Ellen stopped out of sight of the doorway and went on listening.

"You said you would stay with me," May continued. Her voice had a whine in it that made Ellen uncomfortable. "You promised you would stay and look after me until the time comes."

"The girl was in the house," Peter said. "I didn't know if I should."

"What does she matter? She doesn't matter," May said sharply. "Not while I'm here, she doesn't. This is still my house and I . . . I belong to you, don't I? Don't I, dearest?"

Then there was a silence. As quietly as she could, Ellen hurried away and left the house.

The sea air, damp and warm though it was, was a relief after the moldering closeness of the house. But Ellen, taking in deep breaths, still felt sick.

They were lovers, her dying aunt and that awful young man.

That muscular, hard-eyed, insolent stranger was sleeping with her frail, elderly aunt. The idea shocked and revolted her, but she had no doubt of it—the brief conversation, her aunt's voice, could not have been more plain.

Ellen ran down the sandy, weedy incline toward the narrow beach, wanting to lose her knowledge. She didn't know how she could face her aunt, how she could stay in a house where—

She heard Danny's voice, tired, contemptuous, yet still caring: "You're so naive about sex, Ellen. You think everything's black or white. You're such a child."

Ellen started to cry, thinking of Danny, wishing she had not run away from him. What would he say to her about this? That her aunt had a right to pleasure, too, and age was just another prejudice.

But what about *him*? Ellen wondered. What about Peter—what did he get out of it? He was using her aunt in some way, she was certain of it. Perhaps he was stealing from her—she thought of all the empty rooms upstairs and wondered.

She found a piece of Kleenex in a pocket of her jeans and wiped away the tears. So much more was explained by this, she thought. Now she knew why her aunt was so desperate not to leave this rotting hulk of a house, why she didn't want her brother to come.

"Hello, Ellen Morrow."

She raised her head, startled, and found him standing directly in her path, smiling his hard smile. She briefly met, then glanced away from his dark, ungiving eyes.

"You're not very friendly," he said. "You left us so quickly. I didn't get a chance to talk to you."

She glared at him and tried to walk around him, but he fell into step with her. "You shouldn't be so unfriendly," he said. "You should try to get to know me."

She stopped walking and faced him. "Why? I don't know who you are, or what you're doing in my aunt's house."

"I think you have some idea," he said. His cool assumption nearly took her breath away. "I look after your aunt. She was all alone here before I came, with no family or friends. She was completely unprotected. *You* may find it shocking, but she's grateful to me now. She wouldn't approve of your trying to send me away."

"I'm here now," Ellen said. "I'm a part of her family. And her brother will come here too. She won't be left alone—at the mercy of some stranger."

"She doesn't want me to leave—not for your family or for anyone."

Ellen was silent for a moment. Then she said, "She's a sick, lonely old woman—she needs someone. But what do you get out of it? Do you think she's going to leave you her money when she dies?"

He smiled contemptuously. "Your aunt doesn't have any money. All she has is that wreck of a house—which she plans to leave to you. I give her what she needs, and she gives me what I need—which is something a lot more basic and important than money."

Afraid that she was blushing. Not wanting him to see, Ellen turned and began striding across the sand, back toward the house. She could feel him keeping pace with her at her side, but she did not acknowledge his presence.

Until he grabbed her arm—and she let out a gasp that embarrassed her as soon as she heard it. But Peter made no sign that he had noticed. Now that he had halted her, he was directing her attention to something on the ground.

Feeling foolish, still a little frightened, she let him draw her down into a crouching position beside him. It was a battle that had drawn his attention—a fight for survival in a small sandy arena. A spider, pale as the sand, danced warily on pipe-cleaner legs. Circling it, chitinous body gleaming darkly in the sunlight, was a deadly black dart of a wasp.

There was something eerily fascinating in the way the tiny antagonists circled each other, feinting, freezing, drawing back, and darting forward. The spider on its delicate legs seemed nervous to Ellen, while the wasp was steady and single-minded. Although she liked neither spiders nor wasps, Ellen hoped that the spider would win.

Suddenly the wasp shot forward; the spider rolled over, legs clenching and kicking like fingers from a fist, and the two seemed to wrestle for a moment.

"Ah, now she's got him," murmured Ellen's companion. Ellen saw that his face was intent, and he was absorbed by the deadly battle.

Glancing down again, she saw that the spider was lying perfectly still while the wasp circled it warily.

"He killed him," Ellen said.

"Not he, she," Peter corrected her. "And the spider isn't dead. Just paralyzed. The wasp is making sure that her sting has him completely under control before going on. She'll dig a hole and pull the spider into it, then lay her egg on his body. The spider won't be able to do a thing but lie in the home of his enemy and wait for the egg to hatch and start eating him." He smiled his unpleasant smile.

Ellen stood up.

"Of course, he can't feel a thing," Peter continued. "He's alive, but only in the most superficial sense. That paralyzing poison the wasp filled him with has effectively deadened him. A more advanced creature might torment himself with fears about the future, the inevitability of his approaching death—but this is just a spider. And what does a spider know?"

Ellen walked away, saying nothing. She expected him to follow her, but when she looked back she saw that he was still on his hands and knees, watching the wasp at her deadly work.

Once inside the house, Ellen locked the front door behind her, then went around locking the other doors and checking the windows. Although she knew it was likely that her aunt had given Peter a key to the house, she didn't want to be surprised by him again. She was locking the side door, close by her aunt's room, when the feeble voice called, "Is that you, dear?"

"It's me, Aunt May," Ellen said, wondering who that "dear" was meant for. Pity warred briefly with disgust, and then she entered the bedroom.

From the bed her aunt gave a weak smile. "I tire so easily now," she said. "I think I may just spend the rest of the day in bed. What else is there for me to do except wait?"

"Aunt May, I could rent a car and take you to a doctor —or maybe we could find a doctor who'd be willing to come out here."

May turned her gray head back and forth on the pillow. "No. No. There's nothing a doctor can do, no medicine in the world that can help me now."

"Something to make you feel better . . ."

"My dear, I feel very little. No pain at all. Don't worry about me. Please."

She looks so exhausted, Ellen thought. Almost all used up. And looking down at the small figure surrounded by bedclothes, Ellen felt her eyes fill with tears. Suddenly, she flung herself down beside the bed. "Aunt May, I don't *want* you to die!"

"Now, now," the old woman said softly, making no other movement. "Now, don't you fret. I felt the same way myself, once, but I've gotten over that. I've accepted what has happened, and so must you. So must you."

"No," Ellen whispered, her face pressed against the bed. She wanted to hold her aunt, but she didn't dare—the old woman's stillness seemed to forbid it. Ellen wished her aunt would put out her hand or turn her face to be kissed: she could not make the first move herself.

At last Ellen stopped crying and raised her head. She saw that her aunt had closed her eyes and was breathing slowly and peacefully, obviously asleep. Ellen stood up and backed out of the room. She longed for her father, for someone to share this sorrow with her.

She spent the rest of the day reading and wandering aimlessly through the house, thinking now of Danny and then of her aunt and the unpleasant stranger called Peter, feeling frustrated because she could do nothing. The wind began to blow again, and the old house creaked, setting her nerves on edge. Feeling trapped in the moldering carcass of the house, Ellen walked out onto the front porch. There she leaned against the railing and stared out at the gray and white ocean. Out here she enjoyed the bite of the wind, and the creaking of the balcony above her head did not bother her.

Idly, her attention turned to the wooden railing beneath her hands, and she picked at a projecting splinter with one of her fingernails. To her surprise, more than just a splinter came away beneath her fingers: some square inches of the badly painted wood fell away, revealing an interior as soft and full of holes as a sponge. The wood seemed to be trembling, and after a moment of blankness, Ellen suddenly realized that the wood was infested with termites. With a small cry of disgust Ellen backed away, staring at the interior world she had uncovered. Then she went back into the house, locking the door behind her.

It grew dark, and Ellen began to think longingly of food and companionship. She realized she had heard nothing from her aunt's room since she had left her sleeping there that morning. After checking the kitchen to see what sort of dinner could be made, Ellen went back to wake up her aunt.

The room was dark and much too quiet. An apprehension stopped Ellen in the doorway where, listening, straining her ears for some sound, she suddenly realized the meaning of the silence: May was not breathing.

Ellen turned on the light and hurried to her aunt's bed. "Aunt May. Aunt May," she said, already hopeless. She grabbed hold of one cool hand, hoping for a pulse, and laid her head against her aunt's chest, holding her own breath to listen for the heart.

There was nothing. May was dead. Ellen drew back, crouching on her knees beside the bed, her aunt's hand still held within her own. She stared at the empty face—the eyes were closed, but the mouth hung slightly open—and felt the sorrow building slowly inside her.

At first she took it for a drop of blood. Dark and shining, it appeared on May's lower lip and slipped slowly out of the corner of her mouth. Ellen stared, stupefied, as the droplet detached itself from May's lip and moved, without leaving a trace behind, down her chin.

Then Ellen saw what it was.

It was a small, shiny black bug, no larger than the nail on her little finger. And, as Ellen watched, a second tiny insect crawled slowly out onto the shelf of May's dead lip.

Ellen scrambled away from the bed, backward, on her hands and knees. Her skin was crawling, her stomach churning, and there seemed to be a horrible smell in her nostrils. Somehow, she managed to get to her feet and out of the room without either vomiting or fainting.

In the hallway she leaned against the wall and tried to gather her thoughts.

May was dead.

Into her mind came the vision of a stream of black insects bubbling out of the dead woman's mouth.

Ellen moaned, and clamped her teeth together, and tried to think of something else. *It hadn't happened.* She wouldn't think about it.

But May was dead, and that had to be dealt with. Ellen's eyes filled with tears—then, suddenly impatient, she blinked them away. No time for that. Tears wouldn't do any good. She had to think. Should she call a funeral home? No, a doctor first, surely, even if she was truly past saving. A doctor would tell her what had to be done, who had to be notified.

She went into the kitchen and turned on the light, noticing as she did so how the darkness outside seemed to drop like a curtain against the window. In the cabinet near the phone she found the thin local phone book and looked up the listing for physicians. There were only a few of them. Ellen chose the first number and—hoping that a town this size had an answering service for its doctors—lifted the receiver.

There was no dial tone. Puzzled, she pressed the button and released it. Still nothing. Yet she didn't think the line was dead, because it wasn't completely silent. She could hear what might have been a gentle breathing on the other end of the line, as if someone somewhere else in the house had picked up the phone and was listening to her.

Jarred by the thought, Ellen slammed the receiver back into the cradle. There could be no one else in the house. But one of the other phones might be off the hook. She tried to remember if there was another phone upstairs, because she shrank at the thought of returning to her aunt's room without a doctor, someone in charge, to go with her.

But even if there were another phone upstairs, Ellen realized, she had not seen it or used it, and it was not likely to be causing the trouble. But the phone in her aunt's room could have been left off the hook by either her aunt or herself. She would have to go and check.

He was waiting for her in the hall.

The breath backed up in her throat to choke her, and she couldn't make a sound. She stepped back.

He stepped forward, closing the space between them.

Ellen managed to find her voice and, conquering for the moment her nearly instinctive fear of this man, said, "Peter, you must go get a doctor for my aunt."

"Your aunt has said she doesn't want a doctor," he said. His voice came almost as a relief after the ominous silence.

"It's not a matter of what my aunt wants anymore," Ellen said. "She's dead."

The silence buzzed around them. In the darkness of the hall Ellen could not be sure, but she thought that he smiled.

"Will you go and get a doctor?"

"No," he said.

Ellen backed away, and again he followed her.

"Why don't you go and look at her," Ellen suggested.

"If she's dead," he said, "she doesn't need a doctor. And the morning will be soon enough to have her body disposed of."

Ellen kept backing away, afraid to turn her back on him. Once in the kitchen, she could try the phone again.

But he didn't let her. Before she could reach for the receiver, his hand shot out, and he wrenched the cord out of the wall. He had a peculiar smile on his face. Then he lifted the telephone, long cord dangling, into the air above his own head, and as Ellen pulled nervously away, he threw the whole thing, with great force, at the floor. It crashed jarringly against the linoleum, inches from Ellen's feet.

Ellen stared at him in horror, unable to move or speak, trying frantically to think how to escape him. She thought of the darkness outside, and of the long, unpaved road with no one near, and the deserted beach. Then she thought of her aunt's room, which had a heavy wooden door and a telephone which might still work.

He watched her all this time, making no move. Ellen had the odd idea that he was trying to hypnotize her, to keep her from running, or perhaps he was simply waiting for her to make the first move, watching for the telltale tension in her muscles that would signal her intentions.

Finally, Ellen knew she had to do something—she could not keep waiting for him to act forever. Because he was so close to her, she didn't dare try to run past him. Instead, she feinted to the left, as if she would run around him and toward the front door, but instead she ran to the right.

He caught her in his powerful arms before she had taken three steps. She screamed, and his mouth came down on hers, swallowing the scream.

The feel of his mouth on hers terrified her more than anything else. Somehow, she had not thought of that—for all her fear of him, it had not occurred to her until now that he meant to rape her.

She struggled frantically, feeling his arms crush her more tightly, pinning her arms to her sides and pressing the breath out of her. She tried to kick him or to bring a knee up into his crotch, but she could not raise her leg far enough, and her kicks were feeble little blows against his legs.

He pulled his mouth away from hers and dragged her back into the darkness of the hall and pressed her to the floor, immobilizing her with the weight of his body. Ellen was grateful for her jeans, which were tight-fitting. To get them off—but she wouldn't let him take them off. As soon as he released her, even for a moment, she would go for his eyes, she decided.

This thought was firmly in her mind as he rose off her, but he held her wrists in a crushing grip. She began to kick as soon as her legs were free of his weight, but her legs thrashed about his legs, her kicks doing no harm.

Abruptly, he dropped her hands. She had scarcely become aware of it and hadn't had time to do more than think of going for his eyes, when he, in one smooth, deceptively casual motion, punched her hard in the stomach.

She couldn't breathe. Quite involuntarily, she half doubled over, knowing nothing but the agonizing pain. He, meanwhile, skinned her jeans and underpants down to her knees, flipped her unresisting body over as if it were some piece of furniture, and set her down on her knees.

While she trembled, dry-retched, and tried to draw a full breath of air, she was aware of his fumbling at her genitals as scarcely more than a minor distraction. Shortly thereafter she felt a new pain, dry and tearing, as he penetrated her.

It was the thing she felt. One moment of pain and helplessness, and then the numbness began. She felt—or rather, she ceased to feel—a numbing tide, like intense cold, flowing from her groin into her stomach and hips and down into her legs. Her ribs were numbed, and the blow he had given her no longer pained her. There was nothing—no pain, no messages of any kind from her abused body. She could still feel her lips, and she could open and close her eyes, but from below the chin she might as well have been dead.

And besides the loss of feeling, there was loss of control. All at once she fell like a rag doll to the floor, cracking her chin painfully.

She suspected she was still being raped, but she could not even raise her head and turn to see.

Above her own labored breathing, Ellen became aware of another sound, a low, buzzing hum. From time to time her body rocked and flopped gently, presumably in response to whatever he was still doing to it.

Ellen closed her eyes and prayed to wake. Behind her shut lids, vivid images appeared. Again she saw the insect on her aunt's dead lip, a bug as black, hard, and shiny as Peter's eyes. The wasp in the sand dune, circling the paralyzed spider. Aunt May's corpse covered with a glistening tide of insects, crawling over her, feasting on her.

And when they had finished with her aunt, would they come and find her here on the floor, paralyzed and ready for them?

She cried out at the thought, and her eyes flew open. She saw Peter's feet in front of her. So he had finished. She began to cry.

"Don't leave me like this," she mumbled, her mind still swarming with fears.

She heard his dry chuckle. "Leave? But this is my home."

And then she understood. Of course he would not leave. He would stay here with her as he had stayed with her aunt, looking after her as she grew weaker, until finally she died and spilled out the living cargo he had planted in her.

"You won't feel a thing," he said.

HAND IN GLOVE

ROBERT AICKMAN

Until his death several years ago, England's Robert Aickman was interested and active in many areas, including architecture, opera, wildlife, waterways, and psychic research. He was a film and dramatic critic, lecturer and broadcaster, but we know him best as author of numerous and superb strange tales, including "Ringing the Changes," "Pages from a Young Girl's Journal" (winner of the First World Fantasy Award for best short work), and the story you are about to read, a modern Gothic tale with a number of subtle twists. It is the story of a young woman who has had a bad love affair and asks: "What is the way to mend a broken heart?" And receives the answer: "To kill the man who has broken it . . ."

. . . *that subtle gauzy haze which one only finds in Essex.*
—SIR HENRY CHANNON

When Millicent finally broke it off with Nigel and felt that the last tiny bit of meaning had ebbed from her life (apart, of course, from her job), it was natural that Winifred should suggest a picnic, combined with a visit, "not too serious," as Winifred put it, to a Great House. Millicent realized that there was no alternative to clutching at the idea and vouchsafed quite effectively the expected blend of pallor and gratitude. She was likely to see much more of Winifred in the future, provided always that Winifred did not somehow choose this precise moment to dart off in some new direction.

Everyone knew about Millicent and Nigel and took it for granted, so that now she was peacefully alotted an odd day or two off, despite the importance of what she did. After all, she had been linked with Nigel, in one way or another, for a long time; and the deceptively small gradations between the different ways were the business only of the two parties. Winifred, on the other hand, had quite a struggle to escape, but she persisted because she realized how much it must matter to Millicent. There are too many people about to make it sensible to assess most kinds of employment objectively. In one important respect, Winifred's life was simpler than Millicent's: "I have never been in love," she would say. "I really don't understand about it." Indeed, the matter arose but rarely, and less often now than ten or twelve years ago.

"What about Baddeley End?" suggested Winifred, attempting a black joke, inducing the ghost of a smile. Winifred had seldom supposed that the Nigel business would end other than as it had.

"Perfect," said Millicent, entering into the spirit, extending phantom hands in gratitude.

"I'll look on the map for a picnic spot," said Winifred. Winifred had found picnic spots for them in the Cevennes, the Apennines, the Dolomites, the Sierra de Guadarrama, even the Carpathians. Incidentally, it was exactly the kind of thing at which Nigel was rather hopeless. Encountering Nigel, one seldom forgot the bull and the gate.

"We'd better use my car," continued Winifred. "Then you'll only have to do what you want to do."

And at first, upon the face of it, things had all gone charmingly as always. Millicent could be in no doubt of that. It is difficult at these times to know which to prefer: friends who understand (up to a point) or those who do not understand at all and thus offer their own kind of momentary escape.

Winifred brought the car to a stand at the end of a long lane, perhaps even bridle path, imperfectly surfaced, at least for modern traffic, even though they were no farther from their respective flats than somewhere in Essex. She had been carrying a great part of their route in her head. Now she was envisaging the picnic site.

"It's a rather pretty spot," she said with confidence. "There's a right of way, or at least a footpath, through the churchyard and down to the river."

"What river is it?" enquired Millicent idly.

"It's only a stream. Well, perhaps a *little* more than that. It's called the Waste."

"Is it really?"

"Yes, it is. Can you please hand me out the rucksack?"

In hours of freedom, Winifred always packed things into a rucksack, where earlier generations would have prepared a luncheon basket or a cabin trunk.

"I'm sorry I've made no contribution," said Millicent, not for the first time.

"Don't be foolish," said Winifred.

"At least let me carry something?"

"All right, the half bottle and the glasses. I couldn't get them in."

"How sweet of you," said Millicent. Potation was normally eschewed in the middle of the day.

"I imagine we go through the kissing gate."

From even that accepted locution Millicent slightly shrank.

The iron kissing gate stood beside the wooden lich gate, opened only on specific occasions.

With the ancient church on their right, little, low, and li-
chened, they descended the track between the graves. The path
had at one time been paved with bricks, but many of the bricks
were now missing, and weeds grew between the others.

"It's very slippery," said Millicent. "I shouldn't like to
have to hurry back up." It was appropriate that she should
make a remark of some kind, should show that she was still
alive.

"It can't really be slippery. It hasn't rained for weeks."

Millicent had to admit the truth of that.

"Perhaps it would be better if I were to go first?" continued
Winifred. "Then you could take your time with the glasses.
Sorry they're so fragile."

"*You* know where we're going," responded Millicent,
falling into second place.

"We'll look inside the church before we leave."

Though ivy had begun to entangle the mossy little church
like a steathily encroaching octopus, Millicent had to admit
that the considerable number of apparently new graves suggested the continuing usefulness of the building. On the
other hand, the plastered rectory or vicarage to their left,
behind the dangerous-looking hedge, was stained and grimed,
and with no visible open window on this almost ideal day.

Whatever Winifred might say, the churchyard seemed
very moist. But then, much of Essex is heavy clay. Everyone
in the world knows that.

At the far end was another kissing gate, very creaky and
arbitrary, and, beyond, a big green sloping field. There were
cows drawn together in the far upper corner: "a mixed lot
of animals," as Millicent's stepfather would have put it in
the old days—the very old days they seemed at that moment.

Down the emerald field ran no visible track, but Winifred, with the dotted map in the forefront of her mind,
pursued a steady course. Millicent knew from experience
that at the bottom of Winifred's rucksack was a spacious
groundsheet. It seemed just as well.

Winifred led the way through an almost nonexistent gate

to the left and along a curious muddy passage between rank hedges down to the brink of the river.

Here there were small islands of banked mud with tall plants growing on them that looked almost tropical, and, to the right, a crumbling stone bridge, with an ornament of some kind upon the central panel. Rich, heavy foliage shaded the scene, but early dragonflies glinted across vague streaks of sunlight.

"The right of way goes over the bridge," remarked Winifred, "but we might do better on this side."

Sedgy and umbrous, the picnic spot was romantic in the extreme; most unlikely of discovery even at so short a distance from the human hive, from their own north side of the park. After the repast, one might well seek the brittle bones of once-loitering knights; or one might aforetime have done that, when one had the energy and the faith. Besides, Millicent had noticed that the bridge was obstructed from end to end by rusty barbed wire, with long spikes, mostly bent.

In repose on the groundsheet, they were a handsome pair: trim, effective, still, despite everything, expectant. They wore sweaters in plain colors and stained, familiar trousers. In the symphony of Millicent's abundant hair were themes of pale gray. Winifred's stout tow was at all times sturdily neutral. A poet lingering upon the bridge might have felt sad that life had offered them no more. Few people can pick out, merely from the lines on a map, so ideal a region for a friend's grief. Few people can look so sensuous in sadness as Millicent, away from the office, momentarily oblivious to its ambiguous, paranoid satisfactions.

It had indeed been resourceful of Winifred to buy and bring the half bottle, but Millicent found that the noontide wine made no difference. How could it? How could anything? Almost anything?

But then—

"Winifred! Where have all these mushrooms come from?"

"I expect they were there when we arrived."

"I'm quite certain they were not."

"Of course they were," said Winifred. "Mushrooms grow fast but not *that* fast."

"They were not. I shouldn't have sat down if they had been. I don't like sitting among a lot of giant mushrooms."

"They're quite the normal size," said Winifred, smiling and drawing up her legs. "Would you like to go?"

"Well, we *have* finished the picnic," said Millicent. "Thanks very much, Winifred, it was lovely."

They rose: two exiled dryads, the poet on the bridge might have said. On their side on the shallow, marshy, wandering river were mushrooms as far as the eye could see, downstream and up, though it was true that in neither direction could the eye see very far along the bank, being impeded one way by the bridge and the other by the near-jungle.

"It's the damp," said Millicent. "Everything is so terribly damp."

"If it is," said Winifred, "it must be always like it, because there's been very little rain. I said that before."

Millicent felt ashamed of herself, as happened the whole time now. "It was very clever of you to find such a perfect place," she said immediately. "But you always do. Everything was absolutely for the best until the mushrooms came."

"I'm not really sure that they *are* mushrooms," said Winifred. "Perhaps merely fungi."

"Let's not put it to the test," said Millicent. "Let's go. Oh, I'm so sorry. You haven't finished repacking."

Duly, the ascent was far more laborious. "Tacky" was the word that Millicent's stepfather would have applied to the going.

"Why do all the cows stay clustered in one corner?" asked Millicent. "They haven't moved one leg since we arrived."

"It's to do with the flies," said Winifred knowledgeably.

"They're not waving their tails about. They're not tossing their heads. They're not lowing. In fact, they might be stuffed or modeled."

"I expect they're chewing the cud, Millicent."

"I don't think they are." Millicent, of course, really knew more of country matters than Winifred.

"I'm not sure they're there at all," said Millicent.

"Oh, hang on, Millicent," said Winifred, without, however, ceasing to plod and without even looking back at Millicent over her shoulder, let alone at the distant cows.

Millicent knew that people were being kind to her and that it was an unsuitable moment for her to make even the smallest fuss, except perhaps a fun fuss, flattering to the other party.

They reached the willful kissing gate at the bottom of the churchyard. It made its noise as soon as it was even touched and clanged back spitefully at Millicent when Winifred had passed safely through it.

Millicent had not remembered the gate's behavior on their outward trip. Probably one tackled things differently according to whether one was descending or ascending.

But—

"Winifred, look!"

Millicent, so carefully self-contained the entire day, had all but screamed.

"None of that was there just now."

She could not raise her arm to point. Ahead of them, to the left of the ascending craggy path through the churchyard, was a pile of wreaths and sprays, harps wrought from lilies, red roses twisted into hearts, irises concocted into archangel trumpets. Commerce and the commemorative instinct could hardly collaborate further.

"You didn't notice it," replied Winifred upon the instant. She even added, as at another time that day she certainly would not have done, "Your mind was on other things." She then looked over her shoulder at Millicent and smiled.

"They weren't there," said Millicent, more sure of her facts than of herself. "There's been a funeral while we were by the river."

"I think we'd have heard something," replied Winifred,

still smiling. "Besides, you don't bury people in the lunch hour."

"Well, something's happened."

"Last time you just didn't notice," replied Winifred, turning away and looking ahead of her at the weedy path. "That's all."

The challenge was too much for Millicent's resolutions of mousiness. "Well, did *you*?" she inquired.

But Winifred had prepared herself. "I'm not sure whether I did or didn't, Millicent. Does it matter?"

Winifred took several steps forward and then asked, "Would you rather give the church a miss?"

"Not at all," replied Millicent. "Inside there might be an explanation of some kind."

Millicent was glad she was in the rear, because at first she had difficulty in passing the banked-up tributes. They all looked so terribly new. The oblong mound beneath them was concealed, but one could scarcely doubt that it was there. At first, the flowers seemed to smell as if they were unforced and freshly picked, not like proper funerary flowers at all, which either smell not, or smell merely of accepted mortality. But then, on second thought, or at a second intake of Millicent's breath, the smell was not exactly as of garden or even of hedgerow flowers either. After a few seconds, the smell seemed as unaccountable as the sudden apparition of the flowers themselves. Certainly it was not in the least a smell that Millicent would have expected or could ever much care for.

She noticed that Winifred was stumping along, still looking at the battered bricks beneath her feet.

Millicent hesitated. "Perhaps we ought to inspect some of the cards?" she suggested.

That must have been a mischievous idea because this time Winifred just walked on in silence. And, as a matter of fact, Millicent had to admit to herself that she could in any case see no cards attached to the flowers, and whatever else might be attached to them.

Winifred walked silently ahead of Millicent right up to the church porch. As she entered it, a sudden bird flopped out just above her head and straight into Millicent's face.

"That's an owl," said Millicent. "We've woken him up."

She almost expected Winifred to say that for owls it was the wrong time of day, or the wrong weather, or the close season; but Winifred was, in fact, simply staring at the wooden church door.

"Won't it open?" inquired Millicent.

"I don't really know. I can see no handle."

The awakened owl had begun to hoot mournfully, which Millicent fancied really was a little odd of it in the early afternoon.

Millicent in turn stared at the door.

"There's nothing at all."

"Not even a keyhole that we can look through," said Winifred.

"I suppose the church has simply been closed and boarded up."

"I'm not sure," said Winifred. "It looks like the original door to me. Old as old, wouldn't you say? Built like that. With no proper admittance offered."

Gazing at the door, Millicent could certainly see what Winifred meant. There were no church notices either, no local address of the Samaritans, no lists of ladies to do things.

"Let's see if we can peep in through a window," proposed Winifred.

"I shouldn't think we could. It's usually pretty difficult."

"That's because there are usually lookers-on to cramp one's style. We may find it easier here."

When they emerged from the porch, Millicent surmised that there were now two owls hooting, two at least. However, the once-bright day was losing its luster, becoming middle-aged and overcast.

"God, it's muggy," said Millicent.

"I expect there's rain on the way. You know we could do with it."

"Yes, but not here, not now."

Winifred was squeezing the tips of her shoes and her feet into places where the mortar had fallen out of the church wall, and sometimes even whole flints. She was adhering to ledges and small projections. She was forcing herself upward in the attempt to look first through one window and then, upon failing and falling, through another. "I simply can't imagine what it can look like inside," she said.

They always did things thoroughly and properly, whatever the things were, but it was not a day in her life when Millicent felt like any kind of emulation. Moreover, she did not see how she could even give assistance to Winifred. They were no longer two schoolgirls, one able to hoist up the other as easily as Santa Claus's sack.

Unavailingly, Winifred had essayed two windows on the south side of the nave and one on the south side of the chancel, which three offered clear glass, however smudgy. In the two remaining windows on that side of the church, the glass was painted, and so it was with the east window. Winifred went round to the north side, with Millicent following. Here the sun did not fall, and it seemed to Millicent that the moping owls had eased off. En route the churchyard grasses had been rank and razory.

But here the masonry was further gone in decomposition, and Winifred could jump up quite readily at the first attempt.

For a surprisingly long time, or so it seemed, Winifred stared in through the eastermost window on the northern side of the nave, but speaking no word. Here many of the small panes were missing. Indeed, one pane fell into the church from somewhere with a small, sharp clatter even while Winifred was still gazing and Millicent still standing. The whole structure was in a state of molder.

At her own rather long last, Winifred descended stiffly.

She began trying to remove the aged, clinging rubble from the knees of her trousers, but the dust was damp, too, on this side of the church particularly damp.

"Want to have a look?" Winifred asked.

"What is there to see?"

"Nothing in particular." Winifred was rubbing away, though almost certainly making matters worse. "Really, nothing. I shouldn't bother."

"Then I won't," said Millicent. "You look like a pilgrim: more on her knees than on her back, or whatever it is."

"Most of the things have been taken away," continued Winifred informatively.

"In that case, where did the funeral happen? Where did they hold the service?"

Winifred went on fiddling with her trousers for a moment before attempting a reply. "Somewhere else, I suppose. That's quite common nowadays."

"There's something wrong," said Millicent. "There's something very wrong with almost everything."

They plowed back through the coarse grass to the brick path up to the porch. The owls seemed indeed to have retired once more to their carnivorous bothies.

"We must get on with things or we shall miss Baddeley," said Winifred. "Not that it hasn't all been well worthwhile, as I hope you will agree."

But—

On the path, straight before them, between the church porch and the other by now almost familiar path which ran across the descending graveyard, right in the center of things, lay a glove.

"That wasn't there either," said Millicent immediately.

Winifred picked up the glove and they inspected it together. It was a left-hand glove in black leather or kid, seemingly new or almost so, and really rather elegant. It would have been a remarkably small left hand that fitted it, Millicent thought. People occasionally remarked upon the smallness of her own hands, which was always something that pleased her. The tiny but expensive-looking body of the glove terminated in a wider, gauntletlike frill or extension of rougher design.

"We'd better hand it in," said Winifred.

"Where?"

"At the rectory, I suppose, if that is what the place is."

"Do you think we must?"

"Well, what else? We can't go off with it. It looks costly."

"There's someone else around the place," said Millicent. "Perhaps more than one of them." She could not quite have said why she thought there might be such a crowd.

But Winifred again remained silent and did not ask why.

"I'll carry the glove," said Millicent. Winifred was still bearing the rucksack and its remaining contents, including the empty half bottle, for which the graveyard offered no litter basket.

The carriage gate, which had once been painted in some kind of blue and was now falling apart, crossbar from socket, and spikework from woodwork, offered no clue as to whether the abode was, or had been, rectory or vicarage. The short drive was weedy and littered. Either the trees predated the mid-Victorian building, or they were prematurely senile.

The front-door bell rang quite sharply when Winifred pushed it, but nothing followed. After a longish, silent pause, with Millicent holding the glove to the fore, Winifred rang again. Again, nothing followed.

Millicent spoke: "I believe it's open."

She pushed and together they entered, merely a few steps. The hall within, which had originally been designed more or less in the Gothic manner, was furnished, though not abundantly, and seemed to be "lived in." Coming toward them, moreover, was a bent figure, female, hirsute, and wearing a discolored apron, depending vaguely.

"We found this in the churchyard," said Winifred in her clear voice, pointing to the glove.

"I can't hear the bell," said the figure. "That's why the door's left open. I lost my hearing. You know how."

Millicent knew that Winifred was no good with the deaf: so often a matter not of decibels, but presumably of psychology.

"We found this glove," she said, holding it up and speaking quite naturally.

"I can't hear anything," said the figure disappointingly. "You know why."

"We don't," said Millicent. "Why?"

But of course that could not be heard either. It was no good trying further.

The retainer, if such she was, saved the situation. "I'll go for madam," she said, and withdrew without inviting them to seat themselves on one of the haphazard sofas or uncertain-looking chairs.

"I suppose we shut the door," said Winifred, and did so.

They stood about for a little. There was nothing to look at apart from a single colored print of lambs in the Holy Land. At each corner of the frame, the fretwork made a cross, though one of the crosses had been partly broken off.

"Nonetheless, I don't think it's still the rectory," said Winifred. "*Or* the vicarage."

"You're right." A middle-aged woman had appeared, wearing a loose dress. The color of the dress lay between oatmeal and cream, and round the oblong neck and the ends of the elbow-length sleeves ran wide strips of a cherry hue. The woman's shoes were faded, and she had taken little trouble with her bird's-nest hair. "You're perfectly right," said the woman. "Hasn't been a clergyman here for years. There are some funny old rectories in this county, as you may have heard."

"Boreley, you mean," said Millicent, who had always been quite interested in such things.

"That place and a number of other places," said the woman. "Each little community has its specialty."

"This was a *rectory*," Winifred inquired in the way she often did, politely elevating her eyebrows, "not a vicarage?"

"They would have found it even more difficult to keep a vicar," said the woman in the most matter-of-fact way. Millicent could see there was no wedding ring on her hand. Indeed, there was no ring of any kind on either of her rather massive, rather unshaped hands. For that matter, there were no gems in her ears, no geegaws round her neck, no Castilian combs in her wild hair.

"Sit down," said the woman. "What can I do for you? My name's Stock. Pansy Stock. Ridiculous, isn't it? But it's a perfectly common name in Essex."

Winifred often went on in that very same way about "Essex," had indeed already done so more than once during the journey down, but Millicent had always supposed it to be one of Winifred's mild fancies, which it was up to her friends to indulge. She had never supposed it to have any objective metaphysic. Nor had she ever brought herself to address anyone as Pansy and was glad that the need was unlikely to arise now.

They sat, and because it seemed to be called for, Winifred introduced herself and then Millicent. Miss Stock sat upon the other sofa. She was wearing woolly midgreen stockings.

"It's simply about this glove," went on Winifred. "We explained to your servant, but we couldn't quite make her understand."

"Lettice has heard nothing since it happened. That was the effect it had on her."

"Since *what* happened?" asked Winifred. "If we may ask, that is."

"Since she was jilted, of course," answered Miss Stock.

"That sounds very sad," said Winifred in her affable and emolient way. Millicent, after all, had not exactly been jilted, not exactly. Technically, it was she who was the jilt. Socially, it still made a difference.

"It's the usual thing in this place. I've said that each community has its specialty. This is ours."

"How extraordinary!" said Winifred.

"It happens to all the females, and not only when they're still girls."

"I wonder they remain," responded Winifred smilingly.

"They don't remain. They come back."

"In what way?" asked Winifred.

"In what is known as spirit form," said Miss Stock.

Winifred considered. She was perfectly accustomed to claims of that kind, to the many sorts it takes to make a world.

"Like the willis in *Giselle*?" she inquired helpfully.

"I believe so," said Miss Stock. "I've never been inside a theater. I was brought up not to go, and I've never seen any good reason for breaking the rule."

"It's become so expensive too," said Winifred, if only because it was what she would have said in other, doubtless more conventional circumstances.

"This glove," interrupted Millicent, actually dropping it on the floor because she had no wish to hold it any longer. "We saw it lying by itself on the churchyard path."

"I daresay you did," said Miss Stock. "It's not the only thing that's been seen lying in and around the churchyard."

Winifred politely picked up the glove, rose, and placed it on Miss Stock's sofa. "We thought we should hand it in locally."

"That's good of you," said Miss Stock. "Though no one will claim it. There's a room half full of things like it. Trinkets, knicknacks, great gold hearts the size of oysters, souvenirs of all kinds, even a pair of riding boots. Things seem to appear and disappear just as they please. No one ever inquires again for them. That's not why the females come back. Of course it was a kind action on your part. Sometimes people benefit, I suppose. They say that if one finds something, or sees something, one will come back anyway." Miss Stock paused for half a second. Then she asked casually, "Which of you was it?"

At once Millicent replied, "It was I who saw the glove first, and several other things too."

"Then you'd better take the greatest possible care," said Miss Stock, still quite lightly. "Avoid all entanglements of the heart, or you may end like Lettice."

Winifred, who was still on her feet, said, "Millicent, we really must go, or we shall *never* get to Baddeley End."

Miss Stock said at once, "Baddeley End is closed all day on Thursdays. So wherever else you go, there's no point in going *there*."

"You're right about Thursdays, Miss Stock," said Winifred, "because I looked it up most carefully in the book before we left. But this is Wednesday."

"It's not," said Millicent. "It's Thursday."

"Whatever else it may be," confirmed Miss Stock, "it indubitably is Thursday."

There was an embarrassing blank in time, while an angel flitted through the room, or perhaps a demon.

"I now realize that it is Thursday," said Winifred. She turned pale. "Millicent, I *am* sorry. I must be going mad."

"Of course there are many, many other places you can visit," said Miss Stock. "Endless places. Almost every little hamlet has something of its own to offer."

"Yes," said Winifred. "We must have a look round."

"What, then, *do* they come back for," asked Millicent, interrupting again, "if it's not for their property?"

"I didn't say it wasn't for their property. It depends *what* property. Not for their gloves or their rings or their little false thises and thats, but for their property, nonetheless. For what they *regard* as their property, anyway. One's broken heart, if it can be mended at all, can be mended only in one way."

"And yet at times," said Millicent, "the whole thing seems so trivial, so unreal. So absurd, even. Never really there at all. Utterly not worth the melodrama."

"Indubitably," said Miss Stock. "And the same is true of religious faith, or poetry, of a walk round a lake, of existence itself."

"I suppose so," said Millicent. "But personal feeling is quite particularly—" She could not find the word.

"Millicent," said Winifred. "Let's go." She seemed past conventions with their hostess. She looked white and upset. "We've got rid of the glove. Let's go."

"Tell me," said Millicent. "What *is* the one way to mend a broken heart? If we are to take the matter so seriously, we need to be told."

"Millicent," said Winifred, "I'll wait for you in the car. At the end of the drive, you remember."

"I'm flattered that you call it a drive," said Miss Stock.

Winifred opened the front door and walked out. The door flopped slowly back behind her.

"Tell me," said Millicent. "What is the one way to mend a broken heart?" She spoke as if in capital letters.

"You know what it is," said Miss Stock. "It is to kill the man who has broken it. Or at least to see to it that he dies."

"Yes, I imagined it was that," said Millicent. Her eyes were on the Palestinian lamblets.

"It is the sole possible test of whether the feeling is real," explained Miss Stock as if she were a senior demonstrator.

"Or *was* real?"

"There can be no *was*, if the feeling's real."

Millicent withdrew her gaze from the gamboling livestock. "And have you yourself taken the necessary steps? If you don't mind my asking, of course?"

"No. The matter has never arisen in my case. I live here and I look on."

"It doesn't seem a very jolly place to live."

"It's a very instructive place to live. Very cautionary. I profit greatly."

Millicent again paused for a moment, staring across the sparsely endowed room at Miss Stock in her alarming clothes.

"What, Miss Stock, would be your final words of guidance?"

"The matter is probably out of your hands by now, let alone of mine."

Millicent could not bring herself to leave it at that.

"Do girls—women—come here from outside the village? If there really is a village? My friend and I haven't seen one and the church appears to be disused. It seems to have been disused for a very long time."

"Of course there's a village," said Miss Stock quite fiercely. "And the church is not *entirely* disused, I assure you. And there are cows and a place where they are kept; and a river and a bridge. All the normal things, in fact, though, in each case, with a local emphasis, as is only right and proper. And, yes, females frequently come from outside the village. They find themselves here, often before they know it. Or so I take it to be."

Millicent rose.

"Thank you, Miss Stock, for bearing with us and for taking in our glove."

"Perhaps something of your own will be brought to me one day," remarked Miss Stock.

"Who knows?" replied Millicent, entering into the spirit, as she regularly tried to do.

Millicent detected a yellow collecting box on a broken table to the right of the front door. In large black letters a label proclaimed JOSEPHINE BUTLER AID FOR UNFORTUNATES. From her trousers pocket Millicent extracted a contribution. She was glad she did not have to grope ridiculously through a handbag while Miss Stock smiled and waited.

Miss Stock had risen to her feet but had not advanced to see Millicent out. She merely stood there, a little dimly.

"Good-bye, Miss Stock."

In the front door, as with many rectories and vicarages, there were two large panes of glass, frosted overall but patterned *en clair* round the edge, so that in places one could narrowly see through to the outer world. About to pull the door open, which Winifred had left unlatched, Millicent apprehended the shape of a substantial entity standing noiselessly without. It was simply one thing too many. For a second time that day, Millicent found it difficult not to scream. But Miss Stock was in the mistiness behind her, and Millicent drew the door open.

"Nigel, my God!"

Millicent managed to pull fast the door behind her. Then his arms enveloped her, as ivy was enveloping the little church.

"I'm having nothing more to do with you. How did you know I was here?"

"Winifred told me, of course."

"I don't believe you. She's sitting in her car anyway, just by the gate. I'll ask her."

"She's not," said Nigel. "She's left."

"She can't have left. She was waiting for me. Please let me go, Nigel."

"I'll let you go, and then you can see for yourself."

They walked side by side in silence down the depressing, weedy drive. Millicent wondered whether Miss Stock was watching them through the narrow, distorting streaks of machine-cut glass.

There was no Winifred and no car. Thick brown leaves were strewn over the place where the car had stood. It seemed to Millicent for a moment as if the car had been buried there.

"Never mind, my dear. If you behave yourself, I'll drive you home."

"I can't see your car either." It was a notably inadequate rejoinder, but at least spontaneous.

"Naturally not. It's hidden."

"Why is it hidden?"

"Because I don't want you careering off in it and leaving me behind. You've tried to ditch me once, and once is enough for any human being."

"I didn't *try* to ditch you, Nigel. I completed the job. You were smashing up my entire life."

"Not your life, sweet. Only your idiot career, so-called."

"*Not* only."

"Albeit, I shan't leave you to walk home."

"Not home. Only to the station. I know precisely where

it is. Winifred pointed it out. She saw it on the map. She said there are still trains."

"You really can't rely on Winifred."

Millicent knew that this was a lie. Whatever had happened to Winifred, Nigel was lying. Almost everything he said was a lie, more or less. Years ago it had been among the criteria by which she had realized how deeply and truly she loved him.

"You can't always rely on maps either," said Nigel.

"What's happened to Winifred?" How absurd and school-girlish she always seemed in her own eyes when trying to reach anything like equal terms with Nigel! The silly words leapt to her lips without her choosing or willing them.

"She's gone. Let's do a little sightseeing before we drive home. You can tell me about the crockets and finials. It will help to calm us down."

Again he put his arm tightly round her and, despite her half-simulated resistance, pushed and pulled her through the kissing gate into the churchyard. Her resistance was half-simulated because she knew from experience how useless with Nigel was anything more. He knew all the tricks by which at school big boys pinion and compel small ones, and he had never hesitated to use them against Millicent, normally, of course, upon a more or less agreed basis of high spirits, good fun, and knowing better than she what it would be sensible for them to do next. His frequent use of real and serious physical force had been another thing that had attracted her.

He dragged her down the uneven path. "Beautiful place. Peaceful. Silent as the grave."

And, indeed, it *was* quiet now, singularly different in small ways from when Millicent had been there with Winifred. Not only the owls but all the hedgerow birds had ceased to utter. One could not even detect an approaching aircraft. The breeze had dropped, and all the long grass looked dead or painted.

"Tell me about the architecture," said Nigel. "Tell me what to look at."

"The church is shut," said Millicent. "It's been closed for years."

"Then it shouldn't be," said Nigel. "Churches aren't meant to be shut. We'll have to see."

He propelled her up the path where earlier she had first seen the glove. The hand that belonged to it must be very nearly the hand of a child: Millicent realized that now.

In the porch, Nigel sat her down upon the single battered wooden bench, perhaps at one time borrowed from the local school, when there had been a local school. "Don't move, or I'll catch you one. I'm not having you leave me again, yet a while."

Nigel set about examining the church door, but really there was little to examine. The situation could be taken in very nearly at a glance and a push.

Nigel took a couple of steps back and massed himself sideways. Wasting no time, he had decided to charge the door, to break it down. Quite possibly it was already rickety, despite appearances.

But that time Millicent really did scream.

"No!"

The noise she had made seemed all the shriller when bursting upon the remarkable quietness that surrounded them. She could almost certainly have been heard in the erstwhile rectory, even though not by poor Lettice. Millicent had quite surprised herself. She was an unpracticed screamer.

She had even deflected Nigel for a moment.

She expostulated further. "Don't! Please don't!"

"Why not, chicken?" Almost beyond doubt, his surprise was largely real.

"If you want to, climb up outside and look in through the window, first." The volume and quality of her scream had given her a momentary ascendancy over him. "The other side of the church is easier."

He was staring at her. "All right. If you say so."

They went outside without his even holding on to her.

"No need to go round to the back," said Nigel. "I can manage perfectly well here. So can you, for that matter. Let's jump up together."

"No," said Millicent.

"Please yourself," said Nigel. "I suppose you've seen the bogey already. Or is it the black mass?" He was up in a single spring and adhering to nothing visible, like an ape. His head was sunk between his shoulders as he peered, so that his red curls made him resemble a larger Quasimodo, who, Millicent recollected, was always clinging to Gothic walls and descrying.

Nigel flopped down in silence. "I see what you mean," he said upon landing. "Not in the least a sight for sore eyes. Not a sight for little girls at all. Or even for big ones." He paused for a moment, while Millicent omitted to look at him. "All right. What else is there? Show me. Where do we go next?"

He propelled her back to the path across the churchyard and they began to descend toward the river.

It was, therefore, only another moment or two before Millicent realized that the pile of wreaths was no longer there: no sprays, no harps, no hearts, no angelic trumpets; only a handful of field flowers bound with common string. For a moment Millicent merely doubted her eyes yet again, though not only her eyes.

"Don't think they use this place any longer," said Nigel. "Seems full up to me. That would explain whatever it is that's been going on in the church. What happens if we go through that gate?"

"There's a big meadow with cows in it and then a sort of passage down to the river."

"*What* sort of passage?"

"It runs between briars, and it's muddy."

"We don't mind a little mud, do we, rooster? What's the river called, anyway?"

"Winifred says it's called the Waste."

"Appropriate," said Nigel. "Though not anymore, I hasten to add, not anymore."

It was exactly as he said it that Millicent noticed the headstone. "Nigel Alsopp Ormathwaite Ticknor. Strong, Patient, and True. Called to Higher Service." And a date. No date of birth: only the one date. That day's date.

The day that she had known to be a Thursday when Winifred had not.

The stone was in gray granite, or perhaps near granite. The section of it bearing the inscription had been planed and polished. When she had been here last, Millicent had been noticing little, and on the return from the picnic the inscription would not have confronted her in any case, as was shown by its confronting her now.

"Not anymore," said Nigel a third time. "Let's make it up yet again, henny."

At least, Millicent stopped. She was staring at the inscription. Nigel's hands and arms were in no way upon or around her or particularly near her.

"I love you, chickpeas," said Nigel. "That's the trouble, isn't it? We got on better when I didn't."

Seldom had Nigel been so clear-sighted. It was eerie. Still, the time of which he spoke was another thing that had been long, long ago.

"I don't know what to say," said Millicent. What other words were possible? No longer were they children, or young people, or anything at all like that.

They went forward a few paces so that the headstone now stood behind Millicent. She did not turn to see whether there were words upon the back of it.

Nigel went through the second kissing gate ahead of her. "Don't you bother," he said. "I expect you've been down to the river with Winifred. I know you won't run away now. I'll just take a quick peek at the fishing."

However, there seemed by now no point in not following him, and Millicent pushed back the gate in her turn.

"Please yourself," said Nigel.

But Millicent had become aware of a development. The animals formerly in the far and upper corner were now racing across the open space toward Nigel and her, and so silently that Nigel had not so much as noticed them: "cows," she had described them, when speaking of them to Winifred; "stock," as her stepfather might have termed them. There is always an element of the absurd about British domestic animals behaving as if they were in the Wild West. Still, this time it was an element that might be overlooked.

"Nigel!" exclaimed Millicent, and drew back through the gate, which clanged away from her.

"Nigel!!"

He went sturdily on. We really should not be frightened of domestic animals in fields. Moreover, so quiet were these particular fields that Nigel still seemed unaware of anything moving other than himself.

"Nigel!!!"

The animals were upon him and leaving little doubt of their intentions, insofar as the last word was applicable. In no time, on the grass and on the hides, there was blood, and worse than blood. Before long, there was completely silent but visibly most rampageous trampling. Tails were raised now, and eyes untypically stark. But the mob of beasts, by its mere mass, probably concealed the worst from Millicent.

Seek help. That is what one is called upon to do in these cases. At the least, call for help. Millicent, recently so vocal, found that she could make no noise. The grand quietness had taken her in as well.

"Oh, Nigel, love."

But soon the animals were merely nuzzling around interestedly. It was as if they had played no part in the consummation toward which they were sniffing and over which they were slobbering.

Millicent clung to the iron gate. Never before that day had she screamed. Never yet in her life had she fainted.

Then she became aware that the churchyard had somehow filled with women, or, at least, that women were dotted

here and there among the mounds and memorials, sometimes in twos, threes, and fours, though more commonly
as single spies.

These women were not like the willis in Winifred's favorite ballet. They were bleak and commonplace and often
not young at all. Millicent could not feel herself drawn to
them. But she realized that they were not merely in the
churchyard but in the meadow, too, from which the tem-
pestuous cattle seemed to have withdrawn while for a second
her back had been turned. In fact, at that moment the
women were just about everywhere.

Absurd, absurd. Even now Millicent could not overlook
that element. The whole business simply could not be worth
all this, and, in the world around her, everyone knew that
it was not. Sometimes one suffered acutely, yes, but not
even the suffering was ever quite real, let alone the events
and experience supposedly suffered over. Life was not entirely, or even mainly, a matter of walking round a lake, if
one might adopt Miss Stock's persuasive analogy.

Nonetheless, it must have been more or less at this point
that Millicent somehow lost consciousness.

Winifred was looking from above into her face. Winifred
was no longer pale, but nearly her usual color, and renewed
in confidence.

"My dear Millicent, I should have put you to bed instead
of taking you out into the country! How on earth did you
come to fall asleep?"

"Where are the cows?"

Winifred looked through the ironwork of the gate into
the field behind her. "Not there, as far as I can see. I expect
they've gone to be milked."

"They're not really cows at all, Winifred. Not ordinary
cows."

"My dear girl!" Winifred looked at her hard, then seemed
more seriously concerned. "Have you been attacked? Or
frightened?"

"Not *me*," said Millicent.

"Then who?"

Millicent gulped and drew herself together.

"It was a dream. Merely a dream. I'd rather not talk about it."

"Poor sweet, you must be worn out. But how did you get down here? Have you been sleepwalking?"

"I was taken. That was part of the dream."

"It was shocking, that Stock woman going on as she did. You should have closed your ears."

"And eyes," said Millicent.

"I expect so," said Winifred, smiling. "It was a hideous place. If you're fully awake now, I expect you'd like to go? I've made a mess of the whole day."

"I couldn't see the car. I was looking for it."

"I moved it. I wanted to be out of sight. You couldn't have supposed I'd driven it through the churchyard."

"Anything seems possible," said Millicent as they walked up the slope. "Anything. For example, you saw all those flowers. You saw them with your own eyes. Where are they?"

"They've been taken off to some hospital. It's what people do after funerals nowadays."

"And the mushrooms down by the river?"

"They were there from the first, as I told you."

"And Miss Stock's stories?"

"She just needs a man. Oh, I'm sorry, Millicent."

"And the inside of the church?"

"That was really rather nasty. I'm not going to talk about it, I'm not even going to think about it, and I'm certainly not going to let you look at it."

"Oughtn't whatever it is to be reported somewhere?"

"Not by me," said Winifred with finality.

As they had passed for the last time through the gate leading out of the churchyard, Winifred had said, "We're going home as quickly as possible. I'm taking you to my place, and I'm putting you to bed with a sedative. I don't really know about this kind of trouble, but I've seen what I've seen, and what you need in the first place is a good, long sleep, I'm sure of it."

Millicent herself knew that grief, especially repressed grief, was said to induce second sight, let alone second thoughts.

Nonetheless, Millicent woke up at just before half past eleven. Long ago, in the early days with Nigel, one of them had each night telephoned the other at that time, and often they had conversed until midnight, when it had been agreed that the closure be applied. Such simplicities had come to an end years and years before, but on no evening since she had given up Nigel had Millicent gone to bed before that particular hour.

There was little chance of Nigel even remembering the old, sentimental arrangement and less chance of his now having anything easeful to say to her. Still, Millicent, having looked at her watch, lay there sedated and addled, but awake; and duly the telephone rang.

An extension led to the bedside in Winifred's cozy spare room. Winifred herself could not relax in a room without a telephone.

Millicent had the receiver in her hand at the first half ping of the delicate little bell.

"Hello," said Millicent softly to the darkness. Winifred had drawn all the curtains quite tight, since that was the way Winifred liked her own room at night.

"Hello," said Millicent softly, a second time. At least it could hardly now be a call for Winifred. It was all the more important not to waken her.

On the line, or at the other end of it, something seemed to stir. There could be little doubt of it. It was not a mere reflex of the mechanism.

"Hello," repeated Millicent softly.

Third time lucky, because at last there was a reply.

"Hello, feathers," said Nigel.

In all the circumstances, Millicent could not possibly just

ring off, as rationally she should have done. "Are you all right?" she asked.

"What a sight you look in Winifred's nightwear. Not your style at all, crop."

Every inch of Millicent's flesh started simultaneously to fall inward. "Nigel! Where are you?"

"I'm right outside your door, gizzard. Better come at once. But do wear your own pajamas. The scarlet ones. The proper ones."

"I'm not coming, Nigel. I've told you that. I mean it."

"I'm sure you mean it since you left me to be trodden upon by a lot of bloody heifers without doing one thing except grin. It makes no difference. Less difference than ever, in fact. I want you and I'm waiting outside your door now."

She simply couldn't speak. What could she possibly say?

"You come to me, three toes," said Nigel, "*and* wearing your own clothes. Or, make no mistake, I'm coming to you."

The receiver fell from Millicent's hand. It crashed to the bedroom floor, but the carpet in Winifred's guest bedroom was substantial, and Winifred heard nothing. In any case, Winifred herself had just passed a trying day also and needed her rest before the demands of life on the morrow, the renewed call of the wild.

A group of concerned friends, male and female, clustered round Winifred after the inquest, for which a surprising number had taken time off.

"I have never been in love," said Winifred. "I really don't understand about it."

People had to accept that and get on with things, routine and otherwise. What else could they do?

STILLBORN

MIKE CONNER

Mike Conner lives in California with his wife and four children and says he is probably the only writer of science fiction and fantasy to emerge from Hopkins, Minnesota, the raspberry capital of the world. Mr. Conner's excellent stories for *F & SF* have all examined the shadowy, hidden sides of what appear, at first glance, to be benign, although perhaps uncomfortable, situations; what emerges from those shadows, however, is malignant. "Stillborn" tells the story of Claudia Fenster, a newcomer to a southern Missouri mining town, and of her exposure to the glitter of its social life and the darkness of its caverns . . . and secrets.

"I'm afraid that dress won't do, my dear," said Mrs. Phillip Ash. "Have you an extra shawl in your carriage?"

Claudia Fenster groaned inwardly at the sharp-faced older woman's critical appraisal. It was a typically hot and oppressive August day in southern Missouri, and she had worn a dress of light poplin, never dreaming it might not be appropriate.

"No," she said. "I came in the trolley." Why hadn't her husband, who had inspected Claudia the way a captain inspected his troops before he allowed her to leave the house, warned her that the dress wasn't right? It wasn't dark and heavy as the stuff Mrs. Ash and the other three ladies of the Wednesday Afternoon Club wore. Claudia felt the color rising to her cheeks, but another of the ladies, Mrs. Elly Corporan, smiled sympathetically.

"Don't worry, my dear, I have one for you. Olivia is concerned about your catching a chill when we go down to the caverns."

"Caverns?"

"The Crystal Caverns," Mrs. Phillip Ash snapped. "We generally have our cards there all summer, unless it is raining and not too hot here. You don't fear close quarters, do you, Mrs. Fenster?"

Claudia relaxed some. "I have entered my husband's tunnels on occasion without ill effect."

"Good. Because you would be surprised at how many women whose husbands derive their wealth from the earth swoon at the notion of being swallowed up anywhere near a hole in the ground. Ah! There's Jimbo with the carriage. Ladies."

Mrs. Ash took the front seat with the wife of the Baptist minister, Mrs. Burgess, while Claudia sat behind, between Mrs. Corporan and Mrs. Titus Blakely, for the short trip along East Street to the mouth of the Crystal Caverns. Jimbo drove them slowly, so that the common citizens could see the ladies who held the prosperity of Corinth in their grasp.

The husbands of Mmes. Ash and Corporan and Blakely had many years ago formed the companies which mined zinc and sulfur and galenite and white lead from the limestone strata beneath the town. In the first days they had employed oxen; now they used steam and even electricity to sustain this town. Thirty years before, Corinth had been little more than a wagon stop on a two-rut road west toward the Oklahoma Indian country.

The sun beat through the haze fearsomely, however, and even Mrs. Ash quickly grew tired of showing herself to the few people out on the street. Jimbo snapped the reins; a few moments later he pulled them up underneath the merciful shade of some hickory trees.

"You'll want this, I promise you." Mrs. Corporan smiled, pressing a crocheted wrap into Claudia's hand as they came from the carriage. While the ladies waited to one side, Jimbo opened a circuit box on a pole and threw a switch.

"Electric lights," Mrs. Blakely said proudly. Her husband had formed the Southern Missouri Mazda Lamp Company six years before. Except for St. Louis and Springfield, Corinth led the whole of the state in numbers of electric lights and machines. All the streetcar lines were being converted from horse to electric power too.

"The path is smooth, my dear, but keep one hand on the wall of the cave. We don't descend very far—else Reverend Burgess would not allow his wife to join us!" The other ladies laughed as though Mrs. Ash had said the funniest thing in the world. Then they all proceeded on the path through the opening in the limestone bank.

At first, the way seemed to lead to absolute darkness in spite of the bright bulbs strung above the way. But then Claudia's eyes began to adjust and she could detect a faint sparkling on the opposite wall of the cave, and the dagger tips of long stalactites which hung from the roof. They had not gone very far before it became hard for Claudia to believe there was a hot Missouri town above them. This was a silent world, cool and peaceful, with a breeze of its own running through the passages like the sigh of the earth herself.

Finally they reached a place with more lights, where a table for cards had been erected and there was even a sideboard with glasses and silver for the sweets and lemonade Jimbo had brought down in a hamper. Claudia looked at it all with wonder.

"Don't you fear thieves, Mrs. Ash?"

"The sort of people who resort to thievery usually are afraid of spooks and such and won't come into a place like this even with the lights on. I had to beat Jimbo to get him to come the first time. Didn't I, Jimbo?"

"Yes'um."

"You come back the usual time. And mind you, don't go wearing down the horses!"

Mrs. Ash sat down. The other ladies took it as their signal to do likewise. Claudia could not help looking around at the wonderful formations of rock which lay half hidden in the stark shadows thrown off by the Mazda lamps. What a wonderful place this was! She could easily imagine rubies or whole diamonds the size of her fist that could be scooped from the walls with a spoon. Who had first found this place, she wondered. Some lone traveling Indian, perhaps, seeking shelter from a storm?

"I asked, dear, what sort of game you prefer?"

"I'm sorry, Mrs. Ash." Claudia felt the others were not at all interested in where they were, and thus it would be impolite to remark on the natural wonder of this parlor in the earth. "I do like hearts."

"Unfortunately, we are five. Do you know canasta?"

"A little."

"Then that is what we shall deal." As she ruffled the cards, Claudia noticed that Mrs. Ash's voice—and those of the other ladies as well—seemed louder here, ringing harshly from the walls of the cave. And in the electric light, their complexions and features seemed like line drawings—though

Claudia was certain hers must look equally pallorous as well. Mrs. Ash finished dealing the hand, and the game began.

"You are from Michigan, I believe?" Mrs. Burgess asked.

"Until I was married, I lived in Saginaw. Then Mr. Fenster and I took a residence near his business in Uniontown, Pennsylvania." She smiled. "Until he made his decision to purchase the tripoli enterprise here."

"Your husband makes water filters." Mrs. Ash said. It was not a question.

"And grinds tripoli into all manner of rouge and rottenstone for use in the glass and metal polishing trade. It really is an amazing material.

"In the olden days we called it chat. There's piles of it alongside any road you take leaving town."

"Your husband is to be commended for finding a use for it," Mrs. Corporan said kindly. Claudia, meanwhile, had trouble following which cards had been played and could do nothing to organize her hand, and soon the round was won by Mrs. Burgess. She took the deal and play resumed.

"Dear Mrs. Fenster, I should warn you that we try to leave convention a little behind when we come to play here. So I hope you won't be shocked if I should try to satisfy my curiosity. It's one I have cultivated ever since Phillip made your husband's acquaintance last fall. How is it he has married a girl so young as you?"

In spite of the warning, Claudia was a little shocked. Perhaps it was the strange way voices sounded in these caverns, but in Mrs. Ash's voice there seemed a distinct accusatory tone.

"Perhaps she craves tripoli," Mrs. Blakely said, and the others laughed. Claudia waited for it to subside.

"My husband was a widower, of long acquaintance with my father. They were comrades in a Pennsylvania regiment during the Great War. Both my father and my husband learned the transport trade during their service."

"Abolitionists, were they?" Mrs. Ash asked sharply.

Claudia very carefully answered, "They worked as expediters and semaphore operators."

"Then your husband was a clerk! Mercy me, ladies, it is a comfort to know we shall all be safe in our beds. Mrs. Fenster excepted, of course!" She poured herself a tumbler of lemonade and drank. "But you still did not explain how love blossomed between you. Where were all the eager boys of Saginaw?"

Claudia felt her heart pounding. They were all looking at her, waiting for her answer. A cold draft swept through the cavern with a faint whining sound which came through a small opening in a passage that was walled off with boards.

"Mrs. Ash, my marriage was an arrangement between my father and my husband to which I gave my full consent—for both their sakes. Being long without a wife and childless, my husband naturally wished for a wife who could bear him an heir—" She halted, wishing she could take back the words. Was that glee in Mrs. Phillip Ash's face?

"Of course we were aware of your difficulty in the spring. It must be very difficult to lose a child, difficult indeed." The cave wind rose, so that the sound became like a cry. Suddenly, Claudia felt chilled to her very bones. Mrs. Ash put a cold hand upon her wrist.

"Ah, but you have youth on your side. Youth conquers all afflictions. I dare say you'll soon have an entire regiment of powder grinders running underfoot."

She knows! The thought that Mrs. Ash was being deliberately cruel sickened her, and she suddenly stood. "Ladies, I beg your pardon, but the chill is really too much. Next time I shall have to dress for this place; thank you for asking me along, Mrs. Ash." Claudia turned away from the surprised women and took the path back up to the surface. The heat met her at the mouth of the cave with the force of a blow, but, somehow, Claudia found it a blessed relief.

"And so you ran away, like some silly schoolgirl? It's beyond belief, by God!" Ulysses Fenster poured himself a bourbon and adjusted his considerable girth in the direction of his wife, who had been weeping in a chair.

"I don't like them! The only woman there with any sympathy at all was Elly Corporan, but all of them are cowed by Mrs. Ash, and I will not be."

Fenster's cheeks grew red, as they invariably did when he became angry. "I have explained to you, Claudia, that our acceptance into the so-called society of this miserable town rests entirely with that woman! I'm not asking you to embrace her, but surely you can be amusing for an hour or two and demonstrate to her that you do have some modicum of breeding and poise!"

"She mocked you, Ulysses! She practically accused you of robbing the cradle, and me of seducing a foolish old man for my own gain. Was I to smile sweetly and say, 'Of course, Mrs. Ash, how amusing you are to outline such a comedy'? She'd think me weak if I didn't rise to your defense!"

"I do not require defending!" Fenster roared. "I have thus far survived the barbs of my fellow man without your assistance, and I dare say I'll continue. By God, Claudia, if you cannot give me a child, at least help me secure a place in society!"

Claudia looked up defiantly, tears filling her eyes. "I would spare you," she said, "but Mrs. Ash knows I can have no more children and she made light of it to her friends. None of them opposed her! None . . ." She collapsed into tears. Ulysses Fenster put down his glass and, looking crestfallen, knelt beside the chair.

"Claudia . . . child, I am sorry if it's true. Even her husband will agree that his wife is difficult. But don't you see she is trying to test you, to gauge your character?"

"I will not be judged by her!"

"And you shall not be, in the end. But consider how much easier life will be once we are finally accepted here.

My business will prosper—and then we shall have a fine house in Carthage with a proper staff and electric lights, perhaps even a motorcar!"

"Can Mrs. Ash bring me a child?" She saw her husband's stricken expression and immediately regretted what she had said. No one had been more considerate and kind to her than Ulysses during her convalescence following her fateful and tragically unsuccessful pregnancy. Claudia touched his face.

"I promise you I shall try again. I am worth a dozen of Mrs. Phillip Ash!"

"That's the girl!" Ulysses checked his watch. "Well, I must be off to the Eagle's Club. Shall I tell Ash his wife may expect you next week?"

"If she wants me, yes!" She kissed him, and he was gone. Claudia could not help wishing that Mrs. Ash would not want her again, ever.

But she did. This time Claudia dressed in dark blue satin, with bloomers and a camisole underneath against the chill of the caverns. She rode the trolley to her destination, with the window thrown wide open, fanning herself and resisting a comic urge to pant like a dog in the back of a wagon. By the time she reached her stop on East Street, she was very grateful for the opportunity to escape the heat, if only for an hour or two. There would be heat of a different sort waiting for her in the person of Mrs. Ash, but the intervening week since she had last played cards had given Claudia time to prepare herself. She had long since accepted the death of her child, though it pained her because of the waste of that or any life. Why then should she be bothered by Mrs. Ash's cruelty in mentioning it, as though the death were Claudia's fault? God had a reason for taking the baby's life, and it was not for Claudia or Mrs. Ash to question His wisdom. Firm in her faith, Claudia entered the Crystal Caverns confidently.

The lights had been turned on, but the caverns were

empty. Claudia mopped her forehead with a handkerchief and breathed deeply of the cool, refreshing air. The cave sighed in return.

Suddenly, as she had the week before, Claudia felt a strong draft stir the folds of her skirt, and a sound like a cry that seemed to come from beyond the boarded-up passageway. Claudia listened closely, unsure of what she heard. It could have just been the natural vibration of wind passing through spaces between the boards. Yet, there was something about the pitch that gave the sound an eerie, almost human character. Fascinated, Claudia made her way carefully to the spot, putting her hands on the boards and discovering that several of them were loose. She could feel air blowing through them against her fingertips, but now she was convinced that the sound, whatever it was, originated well beyond the barrier. At the same time, she realized it was not exactly like a whistle of wind either. There was a hitch in it, as though the cavern must take its next breath.

Like the caverns are crying, she thought, pulling at one of the loose boards. Then, all at once, something was pulling on her, and she let out a scream.

Jimbo, Mrs. Ash's driver, stared at her.

"You got no business with that, Mis' Fenster."

"I'm sorry!" She laughed quickly to mask her shock. "I suppose I'm a bit early and—well, I suppose it's the child in me that insists on exploring places like this." Claudia touched the boards again. "Can you tell me why this barrier's here?"

"The pit's in there."

"The pit?"

"Some of the folks call it Indian Hell. It's a place where there ain't no bottom. You toss a rock off the ledge and you never hear it drop. Too many children lost here. Mis' Ash lost her little girl here, crawled in and fell, folks say."

"That's awful!"

"It put a change on her. Always does, something like

that. When the earth swallows somethin' up, folks gotta suffer. You hear what I'm saying."

"Of course," Claudia said, wanting him to go away. She did not really think he was dangerous, but deep in this cave she felt anything could happen.

"You was right to run outa here last week, mis'."

"I don't believe that's any of your concern!" she snapped, face suddenly hot in spite of the cool draft from the passage. Jimbo hardly blinked; he might have been made of stone himself.

"You'll leave these caves again. Mind you take the right way." He turned away as Claudia was about to ask what he had meant. Just then the other ladies—with the exception of Mrs. Burgess, who had the croup and could not come—came down the path. Claudia took a place next to Elly Corporan and steeled herself against some new assault by Mrs. Ash, but that lady now seemed very cordial and even allowed Claudia to deal a game of hearts. After several hands Mrs. Ash produced a cut-glass bottle from the hamper Jimbo had brought down and poured glasses for all.

"This is brandy flavored with verbena and lemon—a concoction my husband swears is a poison! But I believe it has a beneficial effect upon the respiration. Ladies!"

Claudia sipped as the others drank. Apparently it was the habit of the Wednesday Afternoon Club to indulge when Mrs. Burgess was not present, and Claudia perceived the impression that the preacher's wife had withdrawn today out of consideration for that custom. Soon laughter echoed through the caverns, and the play grew sloppier. The discussion turned to various ladies of the town and the grand Miners' Ball to be held within the fortnight at the new Connor Hotel. Claudia did her best to maintain her interest in the proceedings, though the wine had made her dizzy. Occasionally, above the sound of laughter and the slap of cards, she heard the crying noise. Each time it sounded

more and more lifelike, and she could not help but think
of Mrs. Ash's child and her terrible fate. To fall, tumbling,
into the blackness without hope . . .

At last Mrs. Ash declared the session adjourned for the
day. Claudia walked unsteadily back to the surface with a
pang of regret, for today she had felt safe and comfortable
—and, yes, invulnerable too. Perhaps Mrs. Ash sensed it
and was wise enough to renew her challenge at another
time and place, for in spite of that lady's seeming
friendliness—or perhaps because of it—Claudia in no way
felt she had been accepted or approved the way her husband
wished.

What do they want from me, she thought, boarding the
trolley. Perhaps if she could suddenly become old and dried-
up and barren as they were. Surely she qualified for the last
point; the other two she could do nothing about.

The heat and the sound of trolley car wheels began to
make her drowsy. Almost against her will she was pulled
into fitful sleep, where she saw the look of terror on Ulysses's
face when her labor had begun with a gush of waters during
dinner. He thought she had damaged herself somehow and
had practically beaten the housemaid to death urging her
to go fetch the young physician, Dr. Vincent, and then
Claudia's labor had begun in earnest, hours of back spasms
that no amount of pillows underneath her could relieve.
Claudia had closed her eyes and tried to regulate the pressure
by thinking of the baby this effort—for it was more work
than pain until the end—would bring her. Ulysses, whey-
faced and gasping, had valiantly held her hand until at last
the handsome Dr. Vincent had arrived to take control of
the delivery, telling her she had not long to go, urging her
to conserve her energy, ordering the maid to bring com-
presses for her head and chipped ice to relieve her burning
throat.

And then he said, "We're ready now, Claudia—" She
remembered quite clearly, remembered smiling and how
her heart soared for the final effort of pushing her child

free. She watched his face as he probed with his fingers to guide the infant's head through the birth passage and give its shoulders the half twist that would free it from Claudia's body. He was intent, concentrating, a look of power and confidence on his features, until, suddenly, his mastery faltered, and Vincent became as frightened as her obese old husband.

Claudia gave a final push and felt the euphoria and relief of birth, saw, for an instant, the baby in Vincent's hands and a glimpse of dark, wet hair. "Oh, let me hold him, let me—" But Vincent gave a tight-lipped shake of his head and covered the child in a blanket after severing the cord, gave the bundle to the maid with a terse instruction that Claudia could not quite hear.

"Why can't I see the baby!" she'd screamed.

"You've got to rest. I'm giving you a powder now, to help you sleep. Afterward, I'll be back to speak with you."

Claudia struggled, kicking and screaming until at last Vincent poured ether into a handerchief and held it over her mouth, a sensation she would never forget, one of drowning, of falling utterly away from her baby, the little hands stretching toward her, trying to hold her but failing with a cry that was like the sound of wind, the last sigh of a summer storm, cold and trembling and moist.

She had never seen her child. Claudia slept for a day and a night, and when she awoke it was to Dr. Vincent again, agonized with the responsibility of telling her the babe had been stillborn and that she must not risk having children again because of some incompatibility between her blood and that of the child that had eventually killed the babe while it was still in the womb. The tiny casket at the funeral was sealed. Claudia had not been allowed to see the body, and yet when she tried to lift the casket top, the whole box had tilted, and it seemed so light, as though it were empty.

What had they done with her baby?

The sound of the Crystal Caverns came to her, and

she realized with a shiver that she had heard that same cry the moment the doctor had put ether on her face. . . .

"*Ma'am?*"

She sat upright, bumping her head against the trolley window. The conductor smiled at her. "End of the line, ma'am."

"End of the line . . ." She rubbed her eyes with her fingertips. "Oh, dear, I've missed my stop. Where are we?"

"Electric Park, ma'am. Northern terminus. I'll be turning around in eight minutes if you want to ride back."

"No . . . no, thank you. I think I'll walk for a while."

"We'll be running until the park closes at ten-thirty."

Claudia thanked him again and stepped down from the car. Though it was barely past suppertime, the park was crowded with children and people looking for a few hours' recreation after a long day in the mines or factories. For, although Electric Park was regularly the subject of fiery sermons from all the church pulpits of Corinth, it was in truth more popular than the churches, with its amusement arcades that featured a ride called the Washtub—"the most terrifying attraction in all Missouri!"—its beautiful Rose Grotto, and, most famous of all, the Electric Tower, a tribute to the zinc and sulfur and lead mining that made the storage of electricity in batteries possible. The tower was two hundred feet tall and carried over 80,000 Mazda lamps which, when kindled at dusk, threw off a beacon of light that could be seen for fifty miles. Even in daylight the tower was an impressive structure. This was the first time Claudia had ever seen it, for her husband had declared Electric Park to be patronized by the lowest orders of Corinth and had refused to take her there.

At any rate, the crowds made her feel better somehow. The people seemed happy, and there was joyful music from the big steam carrousel and the smell of popcorn and frankfurter sausages. Claudia watched a young couple pushing their baby carriage, and though it pained her, her heart went out to them.

She saw the entrance to the Rose Grotto and hurried toward it, for the baby had begun to cry and it had reminded her of her awful dream and the sounds she had heard in the caverns. *I wish I were stronger*, she thought a little desperately, shaken that the recovery which seemed certain a month ago seemed to be disintegrating rapidly.

"Mrs. Fenster! Is that you?"

Claudia turned, and to her dismay recognized Dr. Vincent. He smiled affably, looking handsome in an off-white suit and straw boater. She smiled as bravely as she could.

"You're looking very well! Are you here alone?" He gazed over her shoulder, searching for her husband. There had been an ugly scene between them on that awful night, and Vincent did not relish the prospect of seeing Ulysses Fenster once more. However, she put his mind at ease.

"I'm afraid I fell asleep on the trolley and came here by accident."

"Seeing you strikes my conscience hard, Mrs. Fenster. I had intended looking in on you, but your husband . . . objected to my seeing you again professionally."

Her face clouded as she was reminded of her vivid dream. She could almost smell the ether. "Perhaps he needed to fix responsibility for what happened, Doctor. So it would make some sense to him."

Vincent nodded. They began to stroll and entered the grotto. The blooms were not as numerous as earlier in the season, but there was color enough, and lovely fragrance.

"And you, Mrs. Fenster. Did you fix blame?"

"I took it myself. It seemed the easiest thing to do."

"Mrs. Fenster, I want you to know that if I had not been removed as your physician, I would have advised you to try to have another baby. I believe chances for a successful pregnancy would be good."

"Do you rely on intuition?"

"Statistics, ma'am. Diseases of the blood sometimes show a mathematical pattern in families. We don't know why, but you and your husband may have simply been unlucky."

"Yes. But please, don't speak of it. Really, I have quite forgotten about my affliction."

"Of course. Forgive me."

She turned to him suddenly. "Dr. Vincent, was the baby well formed? I know it had dark hair, but were the eyes like mine? Did Monica—" it was the first time Claudia had ever used the child's baptismal name—"did she resemble either of her parents?"

"Mrs. Fenster, please—"

"No!" She struggled to keep her voice steady. "No, you see, Doctor, when you saw fit to . . . help me to sleep, I thought for a moment I might have heard something, a squeak, a cry from the other room where you'd taken her, and I wanted to go there!"

"It was best that you didn't see. You had suffered enough already!"

"But for what! Doctor, I had a right to see that baby! I believe that I wouldn't be so plagued now if I had been able to rest my mind, to see her face, to see her lying peacefully—"

Vincent tilted his head. "Plagued, Mrs. Fenster? How are you plagued."

The words came from the depth unbidden, with a life and force of their own that shocked Claudia as much as they surprised the doctor. "I hear my baby calling for me! Oh, God, that I should believe such a thing, but late at night I hear the voice of a child on the wind, and I know it belongs to Monica. And she wants me so badly, needs to know that I still think of her and still care, and I begin to think that she is somewhere near, just beyond a veil that I must tear down with my own hands if I am to survive. I wake up knowing that Monica is still alive!" Tears prevented her from saying more; Vincent mumbled assurances and took her shoulders to steady and comfort her. She dabbed her eyes, trying to laugh.

"Oh, you must think I'm mad!"

"Not at all," he said with absolute calm. "Let's go a little farther." They rounded a turn in the path marked by clusters of white peony. "There is a reason for what has happened to you, and it is perfectly natural; you have suffered a grievous emotional injury. Your mind, in attempting to isolate that hurt and prevent it from occurring again, conjures the illusion that the baby exists somewhere. It gives you hope and prevents you from succumbing to an otherwise devastating depression of spirit."

"But surely hallucinations are a sign of some defect working its way through me."

"Perhaps." Vincent smiled. "I am no expert, of course, but I have read the case histories of a man in Vienna, a Dr. Freud, who has traced the emotional maladies of his patients to their roots deep inside life memories which seemingly were forgotten long ago. He calls this secret inner life the 'subconscious,' and finds it to be a powerful force working in all of us. How may I explain it to you? If you'd cut your finger, say, the bleeding soon stops by itself, even if you do nothing to staunch the wound. I believe that the mind is capable of the same protective action. Now you experience the bleeding—hallucination in this case. But in a little while it will stop. All you must do is recognize what you experience for what it really is and accept the phenomena. Soon they will pass."

She thought of the sounds she heard in the caverns. How could the cries not be real? It frightened her to think that her mind could no longer discriminate between the actual world and the fancies it generated—in secret!—for itself.

"Oh, look!" Vincent said as they emerged from the grotto along the eastern border of the amusement arcade. "They're going to light the tower soon." Together they watched as a brilliant red ball slowly ascended toward the pinnacle of the

structure. For the moment, activity in the park ceased as
everyone waited for the thousands of electric lamps to come
to life. Higher and higher the globe climbed, and Claudia
felt herself being caught up in the rising excitement. Here
was light, made by men to replace the fading beams of the
sun.

"We have banished darkness," she heard the doctor say.
Without thinking she held his arm more tightly, pulling
herself close to him, then leaning her head against his
shoulder. For a moment she could sense power in him,
rising from the ground beneath their feet, the same power
that in a few moments would cause a mere frame of lumber
to blaze with an almost celestial glory. Her fears shriveled.
Dr. Vincent was right; she had been foolish, and now she
knew it, now the cries would vanish and she could get on
with the business of living with the people of Corinth,
helping her husband to gain the position in society he wanted
so desperately.

And then came the sound of a voice that, if loud enough,
would have shaken the tower to bits. "Mrs. Fenster!" At
first Claudia did not realize who the pinch-faced woman
in the gray temperance uniform was—until she remembered that Mrs. Phillip Ash sometimes did temperance work
at this very park. She gazed at Claudia coolly. There was
hatred in her eyes, and triumph too.

"And Dr. Vincent. I had believed you possessed better
sense than this."

"This is a chance meeting, Mrs. Ash, nothing more."

"I wonder if her husband would think the same thing. I'm
sorry to have seen this, Claudia Fenster. I was beginning to
think you were a nice young woman after all." Claudia's heart
sank as Mrs. Ash turned abruptly and disappeared into the
crowd. Vincent took a step as if to intercept her, but people
closed in, craning for a better look and blocking his path.

A moment later they were lost in the sudden, terrifying glare
of 80,000 Mazda lamps. And above the excited cheering of

the crowd, Claudia thought she heard Dr. Vincent say, "And now must darkness be appeased." Then he was gone.

Two days later and near the same time of evening, Claudia and her husband drove toward the Connor Hotel in the cabriolet Ulysses had hired for the occasion of the Miners' Ball. He was very angry, his arms trembling so much he had difficulty controlling the reins.

"You've ruined me!" he shouted, not caring that his voice carried far along Main Street. "It is bad enough she saw you with a man not your husband in that park, but then to go to her house, to burst in uninvited to scream at her like a disgruntled scullery maid!"

"The woman hates us! Ulysses, how in the name of heaven can you wish to earn favor she will never grant? As God is my witness, I would have torn the hair from her head if her driver hadn't come to her rescue! In a day and a half she's poisoned my good name and made you a fool, and yet you still take her side—"

"Silence!" He roared. "You have broken your promise to me, Claudia, you've failed miserably to help me gain what I want most. Do you know what Ash said to me this afternoon? 'Sorry, old man, if it was up to me, you'd be in in a minute. Only Olivia believes your wife is absolutely unsuitable for the auxiliary, and, well, one goes with the other. Maybe next year,' he says. Next year! Your cracked brain has cost me at least ten thousand dollars in new business and possibly much more."

"I'm not cracked! I'm not!"

"I've half a mind to send you home to your father, if the shame wouldn't kill him! You deserve to be a spinster—"

"Ulysses— "

"Let go of my arm, damn you!"

"Turn the coach back, please. We don't have to endure this, don't you understand, it's not me, or you, *it's they* who don't know how to behave! This is Mrs. Ash's circle, the rules are hers. Let's go home. Ulysses, I can please you if you'll just give me the chance. It was father's wish, and I have always tried—"

Without warning he slapped her with the back of his hand. "You have never tried! You made a sick man of your father with your willful behavior, and now you try to do the same with me. But I won't be so easy for you, I swear! You are coming with me down that stairway, and you will smile as they all look at you. You'll smile for the whole world!"

Furiously, he lashed at the horse until they arrived in the front of the hotel. Claudia wiped her eyes and tried desperately to compose herself. She had been foolish to go see Mrs. Ash yesterday, but she had gone only to explain how she had met Dr. Vincent at Electric Park, and then to try, somehow, to reach an understanding with the older woman. But Olivia Ash had fended off any explanation or compromise; instead, viciously, she had berated Claudia for feeling sorry for herself, for thinking herself better than everyone in Corinth simply because she had lost her baby.

"I've lost one; so had Elly Corporan, and Mrs. Blakely. All of us have made the required sacrifice, but you with your whining and moaning are interested only in showing us up. How great a tragedy you suffered, my poor, poor dear—"

It was then that the glee in her eyes had set Claudia off. Something in her, strained to the breaking point, finally snapped, and she'd flown at the other woman fully intent on throttling her. Only Jimbo's quick intervention had prevented a scratching, kicking battle between them.

"You don't know what real sorrow is, dearie," Mrs. Ash had screeched. "But you will! Soon enough you will!"

Now Ulysses, jaw set, stood outside the carriage with his arm out, ready to escort her into the ballroom. She made a final, silent plea, but he was cold and adamant; Claudia was certain he would carry her inside if she didn't come of her own free will. Together they entered the carpeted lobby, followed a stairway to a mezzanine, then passed through double doors opening onto the grand carved-rosewood stairs down to the grand ballroom. The floor was crowded with the ladies and the men of Corinth, swirling about to the latest Austrian waltzes. The orchestra had been imported from St. Louis; guests had come from that city, too, and from Columbia and Springfield, and even the cow town up north, Kansas City. Claudia's heartbeat quickened. The light was dim, and there were people enough that perhaps she could pass unnoticed onto the floor. Then she gasped, as there would be no such luck for her. Mrs. Olivia Ash headed a reception line directly at the foot of the stairs. Ulysses pulled her closer.

"You'll greet her civilly, by God!"

Claudia gathered her skirts, and they descended. Mrs. Ash's eyes were the color and sheen of raven's feathers, but the woman smiled!

"Claudia, my dear! You look lovely." Mrs. Ash took Claudia's shoulders in her cold hands and kissed her on the mouth. Her lips were very dry. "You must be proud of her, Ulysses."

Ulysses was clearly startled. "Eh? Yes. Why, yes, by God! The handsomest woman in the room, present company excluded!" Mrs. Ash laughed in a precise burst.

"Go in, go in! We'll see you both later."

"There!" Ulysses whispered as they walked across the room. "She's a perfectly reasonable woman, and a better Christian than you, offering friendship after your inexcusable behavior. Do you wish to dance?"

"No."

"I see Titus Blakely over there. Perhaps I can repair some of the damage you've caused. Look cheerful, by God!" Claudia watched him move off, then found herself a seat by the balcony doors. As she sat there, she began to realize that the orchestra was slightly off-key and that the guests, who seemed elegant from the vantage at the top of the grand staircase, looked a little ragged, their dresses and cutaways stale, perhaps from hanging the whole year in storage against this occasion. This wasn't Paris, after all, nor New York or even Chicago; this was a middling town hard by the borders of Arkansas, Kansas, and the Indian Territory. The people here were acting as they thought grand people ought to act. *They were performing*, almost as if the movement and music were part of a ritual whose purpose they did not understand. Perhaps they did not want to understand.

She searched the room for Ulysses, found she could not see him. She felt faint, and the music annoyed her; so she rose and went outside to the balcony for some air.

The doors closed behind her and produced a blessed silence. After a moment she could hear the faint sound of a far-off calliope, then distant screaming that puzzled and frightened her until she remembered the Washtub at Electric Park. The tower burned magnesium-bright, imposing-looking even seven miles away, and suddenly Claudia longed to be beneath it, feeling the joy of the people who'd come to lose themselves in the light and the color and the sounds of the arcade. That was so much better than the spectacle inside the ballroom. Claudia put her hand to her face, feeling the cold place where Olivia Ash had kissed her.

You don't know what real sorrow is, dearie!

And then the wind rose, and she heard the cry again. There was no mistaking it, for it was plaintive and cold and seemed to rise from the heart of the darkened city between this balcony and the tower to the north. She held her breath, praying desperately for the sound to be just another hallucination, but it came again, louder, shaking her to her soul. For an instant she almost fainted, but then anger tore through her fear.

"Why?" she yelled, gripping the balcony rail. "Why must I suffer this!" But there was no answer, only the cry of a child on the warm night wind. Claudia looked out and could see the tops of the hickory trees that sheltered the entrance to the Crystal Caverns no more than a hundred yards from where she stood. Dr. Vincent had told her confidently that her emotional wounds would staunch themselves. Now Claudia knew that something far more serious was happening, that she must take action or the child in her mind would live on and destroy what was left of her life.

Quickly she looked into the ballroom. There was no sign of Ulysses, or Mrs. Ash, or anyone else Claudia knew. Before the balcony doors was a long table with a display of polished miner's tools. Claudia took a brass coal-oil lamp, shook it to test for fuel, then ran outside and down the steps to the back of the hotel, trying to reassure herself as she hurried along toward the caves. *It is a rational thing I'm doing. . . . Proving to myself that this thing, this voice . . . this child! . . . does not, cannot exist. Monica was dead before she ever left my womb!*

She reached the grove, approached the switch box to turn on the cavern lights. Something grabbed her arm, and she cried out, dropping the lantern. The glass chimney broke with a sound that was almost like bells.

"Mis' Fenster." The impassive black face materialized from the darkness.

"J-Jimbo? What are you doing here?" The anger came back. "Let go of me!"

"You don't want to go down there, Mis' Fenster." His eyes glittered in the moonlight, but there was no hostility in his long, wrinkled face, only sadness. Claudia recovered a little.

"I—I must go down. I believe I may have lost something valuable when I was here Wednesday. A brooch. Have you found one?"

"No, mis'."

"Well, then, I must have a look for my—" She halted, because clear and very loud came the cry, not once, but three times and echoing within the walls of the caverns. There was no mistaking it now, for Jimbo was clearly startled. Gently, Claudia pried his fingers free of her arm.

"Your given name is James?"

"Yes."

"James what?"

"I'm James Woods, Mis' Fenster, and I'm askin' you not to go down. Your child's lost once, leave it be."

"I am going down." Her voice was terribly calm. "Wait for me here, please."

James Woods shrugged finally and threw the light switch. Claudia descended the path that led into the earth, slowing to listen when she reached the card tables. There was a murmuring—maybe only the stirring of the cave wind—but then she saw that the boards had been removed from the passageway over Indian Hell. Silently cursing her trailing gown and wishing she had not broken her lantern, Claudia stepped over the pulled-away planks into a passage dark enough to swallow her whole.

At the moment she heard the cry for the third time that night, a light sputtered on ahead of her. Claudia gathered her skirts and ran, heedless of where the ledge was, or that she might fall into the abyss. A draft rose from below, humid and smelling of the earth, and she was conscious of descending slightly into a larger space and the sound of water trickling as she skirted an outcropping of dark rock and saw them waiting for her.

Men and women held torches whose light failed in the deep crevasse beyond the ledge: men and women Claudia knew. There was Dr. Vincent, wearing traces of a smile on his face, and Elly Corporan and Mrs. Burgess. In the shadows just beyond this circle she saw Phillip Ash and Ulysses, who colored and looked away.

In the center, Olivia Ash, who held in her arms a most remarkable child that was perhaps a year old. Her skin was the color of bone china, her hair silk-fine and white as sugar or salt, while grave eyes, huge like the eyes of a deer, focused on Claudia. There was a spark of recognition, then: "*Maaa-maaa!*"

"Come in, my dear," Mrs. Ash said, her reedy voice echoing in the darkness. "She wants you, and it's time."

Claudia rushed forward, pushing through the circle and snatching the baby away, to Mrs. Ash's laughter.

"She has been well cared for, though she's never seen the sun and never shall. Jimbo's been her mother and kept her well for this."

"Monica?" The child pressed close, and Claudia felt the beating of her tiny heart. Her mouth formed the word: *Why?*

"We live by what we take from the earth and in return she demands something of us. I've given, so has Elly; all of us who live from the earth must offer and give in return. You must give the child now. When you do, you'll be fertile again. You'll have as many more as you want."

"No! Ulysses!" But she could not see him because of the torches. "I won't give her up! Not again."

"You will, or you'll fall too. It won't be the first time. Present the child!"

"No!"

"Doctor, perhaps you can make the decision easier." Claudia saw Vincent step from the circle with a cloth pad in hand; she caught the sharp odor of ether. *"Not again! Lord God, not again!"* Her baby clutched at her dress as the circle closed around her, pushing her toward the brink, Vincent smiling at her, Olivia Ash laughing louder and louder—

She held Monica tightly under both her tiny arms, then suddenly, with a burst of desperate energy, swung the child around as though she were nothing but a sack of grain. The little feet caught Olivia Ash squarely in the breast, sending her gasping back into Dr. Vincent. Monica howled with fright.

"You fool!" Mrs. Ash screamed. "You'll ruin us all! Grab her, somebody!"

"No! This is my baby, understand me, mine, mine! If you want her again, you'll have to take her. How about it?" She held Monica out at arm's length toward Mrs. Ash and moved forward, shaking the baby like a doll. "Take her from me!" Mrs. Ash opened her arms. "Take her. *Take her!"* With a sudden thrust, she used the wailing child as a weapon for the second time, holding on to her clothing with her fists as she pushed Monica forward into Mrs. Ash and lunged, pushing with her legs as hard as she could before pulling back suddenly at the brink of the pit. Mrs. Ash screamed as she went over. The scream continued for a long, long time, and while it lasted, Claudia turned and ran before the others could recover from their shock and pursue her. She ran until her lungs felt as though they'd burst, and then she saw stars and heard the wind stirring the hickory trees.

James Woods blocked her path.

"I can't let you go, Mis' Fenster. That girl don't belong to you no more."

"You raised her. You fed her, damn you! Can't you see she wants to live? Can't you? Can't you? Let me take the wagon, please!"

"Mis' Ash—"

"Is dead! Do you understand, I've killed her for what she's done to us. God Almighty, they're coming!"

James Woods shifted his weight. Shouts of rage and confusion came from the mouth of the caverns. Monica whimpered, blinking painfully as though even starlight was too much for her. And then, suddenly, James turned and yanked open the switch for the cavern lights. Both of them listened to the screams.

"They took what they wanted out of her. Now she'll take back what she wants." As he said this, he helped mother and child onto the buckboard.

BALGRUMMO'S HELL

RUSSELL KIRK

When we hear the term "horror story" we usually
think Gothic effects: the crumbling, shadowy estate
set in a remote locale; the supernatural influence
oozing down the passageway; the denial of the rational and the triumph of intuition and
superstition—the dark secrets hidden in a world we
thought we knew. Russell Kirk, perhaps more than
any other modern writer, captures and adapts traditional gothic elements in his fantasies to create,
in his own words, "tales more of the outer darkness
than of the twilight zone." Balgrummo's Lodging is
truly a dark and evil place. When "Balgrummo's
Hell" was first published in *F & SF*, Russell Kirk
noted that "it has more than a grain of true nar-
ration at the core of it, and the setting is genuine."
Russell Kirk has walked in some haunted places
indeed.

The moment that Horgan had slipped through the pend, Jock Jamieson had glanced up, grunted, and run for his shotgun at the gate cottage. But Horgan, having long legs, had contrived to cosh Jock right on the threshold. Now Horgan had most of the night to lift the pictures out of Balgrummo Lodging.

Before Jock could close those rusty iron gates, Nan Stennis—in her improbable role of new night nurse to Lord Balgrummo—had stalled her car in the pend. In the rain, Jock couldn't possibly have made out Nan's face, and now Horgan pulled off the silk stocking of Nan's that he had worn over his own head. With Nan's help, he trussed and gagged Jock, the tough old nut breathing convulsively, and dragged him into a kitchen cupboard of the gate cottage, and turned the key on him. Jock's morning mate, and the morning nurse, wouldn't come to relieve him until seven o'clock. That left no one between Horgan and those paintings except Alexander Fillan Inchburn, tenth Baron Balgrummo, incredibly old, incredibly depraved, and incredibly decayed in Balgrummo Lodging, which he had not left for half a century.

In that nocturnal February drizzle, Nan shivered; perhaps she shuddered. Though there could have been no one within a quarter of a mile to hear them, she was whispering. "Rafe, can you really get through it without me? I hate to think of you going into that place all alone, darling."

Competent Rafe Horgan kissed her competently. She had left her husband for him, and she had been quite useful. He honestly meant to meet her at the Mayfair by the end of the month, and take her to the Canaries; by that time he should have disposed of the Romney portrait for a fat sum, to an assured Swiss collector with a Leeds agent, enabling Horgan to take his time in disposing of the other Balgrummo pictures. Nan could have lent him a hand inside Balgrummo Lodging, but it was important for her to establish an alibi; she would change automobiles with him now, drive into Edinburgh and show herself at a restaurant, and then take the midnight train to King's Cross. The principal trouble with operations like this was simply that too many people became involved, and some of them were given to bragging. But Nan was a close one, and Horgan had spent months planning.

The only real risk was that someone might discover his name wasn't Horgan. For that, however, a thorough investigation would be required. And who would think of investigating the past of Rafe Horgan, Esq., a South African gentleman of private means who now lived in a pleasant flat near Charlotte Square? Not Dr. Euphemia Inchburn, gray spinster who liked his smile and his talk; not T. M. Gillespie, Writer to the Signet, chairman of the trustees of Lord Balgrummo's Trust. With them he had been patient and prudent, asking questions about Balgrummo Lodging only casually, in an antiquarian way. Besides, did he look as if he would carry the cosh? No, the police would be after every gang in Fossie housing estate, which sprawled almost to the policies of Balgrummo Lodging. Horgan's expenditure of charm, and even of money, would be repaid five thousand times over. The big obstacle had been Jock's shotgun, and that was overcome now.

"His high and mighty lordship's bedridden," Horgan told Nan, kissing her again, "and blind, too, they say. I'll finish here by three o'clock, girl. Ring me about teatime tomorrow, if you feel you must; but simply talk about the weather, Nan, when you do. You'll love Las Palmas."

He stood at the forgotten gate, watching Nan get into the car in which he had come and had parked in the shadow of the derelict linoleum works that ran cheek by jowl with the north dyke of Balgrummo Lodging. When she had gone, he started up Nan's own inconspicuous black Ford, moving it far enough for him to shut the gates. He locked those gates with the big brass padlock that Jock had removed to admit "Nurse" Nan. Then, slowly and with only his dims

showing, he drove up the avenue—rhododendron jungle
pressing in from either side—that led to the seventeenth-
century facade of Balgrummo Lodging.

"Uncle Alec and his house have everything," Dr. Effie
Ichburn had said once: "Dry rot, wet rot, woodworm, death-
watch beetle." Also, among those few who remembered
Lord Balgrummo and Balgrummo Lodging, the twain had
a most nasty repute. It was a positive duty to take the pictures
out of that foul house and convey them into the possession
of collectors who, if they would keep them no less private,
certainly would care for them better.

Sliding out of the car with his dispatch case of tools, Rafe
Horgan stood at the dark door of Balgrummo Lodging. The
front was the work of Sir William Bruce, they said, although
part of the house was older. It all looked solid enough by
night, however rotten the timbers and the man within.
Horgan had taken Jamieson's big ring of keys from the gate
cottage, but the heavy main door stood slightly ajar, anyway.
No light showed anywhere. Before entering, Horgan took
a brief complacent survey of the tall ashlar face of what T.
M. Gillespie, that mordant stick of a solicitor, called "Balgrummo's Hell."

Living well enough by his wits, Horgan had come upon
Balgrummo Lodging by good fortune, less than a month
after he had found it convenient to roost in Edinburgh. In
a car with false license plates, he had driven out to Fossie
housing estate in search of a certain rough customer who
might do a job for him. Fossie, only seven years old but
already slum, was the usual complex of crescents and ter-
races of drab council houses. Horgan had taken a wrong
turn and had found himself driving down a neglected and
uninhabited old lane; behind the nasty brick wall on his
right had been a derelict marshaling yard for goods wagons,
declared redundant by Dr. Beeching of British Railways.
On his left, he had passed the immense hulk of a disused

linoleum works, empty for several years, its every window-pane smashed by the lively bairns of Fossie.

Beyond the linoleum factory he had come upon a remarkably high old stone dyke, unpleasant shards of broken glass set thick in cement all along its top. Behind the wall he had made out the limbs and trunks of limes and beeches, a forest amidst suburbia. Abruptly, a formal ancient pend or vaulted gateway had loomed up. On either side, a seventeenth-century stone beast effigy kept guard, life-size almost: a lion and a griffin, but so hacked and battered by young vandals as to be almost unrecognizable. The griffin's whole head was lacking.

So much Horgan had seen at a glance, taking it that these were the vacant policies of some demolished or ruined mansion house. He had driven on to the end of the street, hoping to circle back to the housing estate, but had found himself in a cul-de-sac, the Fettinch burn flowing through bogs beyond the brick wall at the end. This triangle of wooded policies, hemmed in by goods yards, wrecked factory, and polluted streams, must be the last scrap of some laird's estate of yesteryear, swallowed but not yet digested by the city's fringe. Probably the squalor and unhealthiness of the low site had deterred Edinburgh or Midlothian—he wasn't sure within which boundary it lay—from building on it another clutch of council houses for the Fossie scheme.

Swinging round at the lane's terminal wall, Horgan had gone slowly back past the massive pend, where the harling was dropping from the rubble. To his surprise, he had noticed a gate lodge, apparently habitable, just within the iron grill of the gates; and a little wood smoke had been spiraling up from the chimney. Could there be anything worth liberating beyond those gates? He had stopped, and had found an iron bell pull that functioned. When he had rung, a tall fellow, with the look of a retired constable, had emerged from the gate cottage and had conversed with him, taciturnly, in broad Scots, through the locked grill.

Horgan had asked for directions to a certain crescent in the housing scheme, and had got them. Then he had inquired the name of this place. "Balgrummo Lodgin', sir" —with a half defensive frown. On impulse, Horgan had suggested that he would like to see the house (which, he gathered, must be standing, for he could make out beyond the trees some high dormers and roofs).

"Na, na; Himself's no receivin', ye ken." This had been uttered with a kind of incredulity at the question being put.

Growing interested, Horgan had professed himself to be something of a connoisseur of seventeenth-century domestic architecture. Where might he apply for permission to view the exterior, at any rate? He had been given to understand, surlily, that it would do no good: but everything was in the hands of Lord Balgrummo's Trust. The trust's solicitor and chairman was a Mr. T. M. Gillespie, of Reid, Gillespie, and MacIlwraith, Hanover Street.

Thus Balgrummo Lodging had been added to Rafe Horgan's list of diverse projects. A few days later, he had scraped acquaintance with Gillespie, a dehydrated bachelor. Initially, he had not mentioned Balgrummo Lodging, but had talked in Gillespie's chambers about a hypothetical Miss Horgan in Glasgow, allegedly an aunt of his, a spinster of large means, who was thinking of a family trust. Mr. Gillespie, he had heard it said, was experienced in the devising and management of such trusts. As venture capital, a check from Horgan had even been made out to Mr. Gillespie, in payment for general advice upon getting up a conceivable Janet Horgan Estates, Ltd.

Gillespie, he had discovered, was a lonely solicitor who could be cultivated, and who had a dry relish for dry sherry. After a bottle, Gillespie might talk more freely than a solicitor ought to talk. They came to dine together fairly frequently—after Horgan had learnt, from a chance remark which he affected to receive casually, that some good pictures remained at the lodging. As the weeks elapsed, they were joined for a meal, once and again, by Gillespie's old friend Dr. Euphemia Inchburn, Lord Balgrummo's niece, a superannuated gynecologist. Horgan had turned on all his charm, and Dr. Inchburn had slipped into garrulity.

Perceiving that he really might be on to a good thing, Horgan had poked into old gazeteers which might mention Balgrummo Lodging; and, as he obtained from his new friends some hint of the iniquities of the tenth Baron Balgrummo, he looked into old newspaper files. He knew a little about pictures, as he did about a number of things; and by consulting the right books and catalogues, he ascertained that on the rotting walls of Balgrummo Lodging there still must hang some highly valuable family portraits—though not family portraits only—none of them exhibited anywhere since 1913. Gillespie was interested only in Scottish portrait painters, and not passionately in them; Horgan judged it imprudent to question Dr. Effie Inchburn overmuch on the subject, lest his inquisitiveness be fixed in her memory. But he became reasonably well satisfied that Lord Balgrummo, senescent monster, must possess an Opie, a Raeburn, a Ramsay or two, perhaps even three Wilkies, a good Reynolds, possibly, and a Constable, a very good Romney, a Gainsborough, it appeared, and (happy prospect) a Hogarth, two small canvasses by William Etty, a whole row of reputed Knellers, once, and just conceivably still, a Cranach and a Holbein were to be seen at the lodging. The tenth baron's especial acquisition, about 1911, had been an enormous Fuseli, perhaps unknown to compilers of catalogues, and (judging from one of Dr. Inchburn's grimaces) probably obscene. There were more pictures—the devil knew what.

Perhaps some rare books might be found in the library, but Horgan was too little of a bibliophile to pick them out in a hurry. The silver and that sort of thing presumably were in a bank—it would have been risky to inquire. Anyone but a glutton would be content with those pictures, for one night's work.

Lethargy, and the consequences of permanent confinement to his house, naturally had made Lord Balgrummo neglect his inheritance. As the decades had slipped by, he had permitted his trustees to sell nearly everything he owned, except Balgrummo Lodging—once a residence of convenience, near Edinburgh, for the Inchburns, later a dower house—and those pictures. "After all, never going out, Alec has to look at *something*," Dr. Inchburn had murmured.

Sufficient intelligence obtained, still Horgan faced the difficulty of entering the house without the peril and expense of a gang raid, and of getting out undetected with those pictures. An attempt had been made several years before. On that occasion, Jock Jamieson, the night porter—"warden" would have been a better style—had shot to death one burglar and wounded another while they were on a ladder. Jamieson and his day mates (one of them the constable type with whom Horgan had talked at the gate) were hard, vigilant men—and, like Lord Balgrummo's nurses, excellently paid. Time had been when it seemed at least as important to keep Lord Balgrummo in (though he had given his word never to leave the policies) as to keep predators out. Gillespie had implied that the police indulged in the peculiar porters of Balgrummo Lodging a certain readiness in the use of firearms. So Horgan's expedition had been most painstakingly plotted, and it had been necessary to wait months for the coincidence of favorable circumstances, all things being held in readiness.

The presence of a nurse in the house all round the clock was a further vexation; Horgan had not relished the prospect of pursuing a frantic nurse through that crumbling warren of a place. Should she escape through some back door . . . So when, only yesterday, Gillespie had mentioned that the night nurse had quit ("Nerves, as usual, in that house— and his lordship a disagreeable patient"), and that they had not yet found a replacement, Horgan knew his moment had arrived.

For one night, Jamieson had been required to do double duty, watching the policies and looking in on Lord Balgrummo every hour. Jock Jamieson, for all his toughness, probably liked being inside the place at night no more than did the nurses. So doubtless Jock had rejoiced when a la-di-dah feminine voice (Nan Stennis's, of course) had informed him late that evening that she was calling on behalf of Mr. Gillespie, and that a new night nurse would make her appearance, in an hour or so, in her own car.

It had gone smoothly enough. Jock had opened the gate at Nan's honk, and then it had been up to Horgan, in the shadows. Had Jock been ten years younger, and less given to beer, he might have gotten his hands on the shotgun before Horgan could have reached him. But though disliking unnecessary roughness, Horgan had coshed men before, and he coshed Jock swiftly and well. No one came down that obscure lane after dark—few, indeed, in daylight. Therefore the investment in drinks and dinners for Gillespie and the Inchburn old maid, and the expenditure of Horgan's hours now would be compensated for at an hourly rate of return beyond the dreams of avarice. Swinging his handsome dispatch case, Horgan entered Balgrummo Lodging.

Within the chilly entrance hall, the first thing Horgan noticed was the pervasive odor of dry rot. With this stench of doom, what wonder they had to pay triple wages to any nurse! Condemned to solitude, neglectful of business, and latterly penurious, Lord Balgrummo had postponed repairs until the cost of restoring the lodging would have been gigantic. Even could he have found the money without selling some of his pictures, old Balgrummo probably would not have saved the house; he had no heirs of his body, the entail had been broken long before, and his heir presumptive—Dr. Effie—never would choose to live in this desolation screened by the tumbledown linoleum works. There remained only the question as to which would first tumble into atoms—Lord Balgrummo or his prison mansion.

Horgan sent the beam of his big electric torch round the

hall. It flashed across the surface of what appeared to be a vast Canaletto—a prospect of Ravenna, perhaps. Was it the real article, or only from Canaletto's school? Horgan wished he knew whether it was worth the difficulty of taking and concealing, its size considered. Well, he would leave it to the last, securing the certified goods first.

He had known there was no electric light in Balgrummo Lodging: nothing had been improved there—or much repaired—since 1913. He found, however, elaborate bronze gas brackets. After fumbling, he found also that he did not know how to light them; or perhaps the gas was turned off, here in the hall. No matter: the torch would suffice, even if the black caverns beyond its ray were distressing.

Before he went to work, he must have a glance at old Balgrummo, to be quite sure that the crazy old creature couldn't totter out to do some feeble mischief. (In this house, more than fifty years before, he had done great mischief indeed.) Where would his bedroom be? On the second story, at the front, just above the library, likely enough, judging from the plan of the lodging, at which Horgan had once managed a hasty glance in Gillespie's chambers. Hanging the torch about his neck, Horgan made his way up the broad oak staircase, at first leaning on the balustrade—but presently touching that rail only gingerly, since here and there, even though he wore gloves, it felt spongy to the touch, and trembled in its rottenness when he put too much weight upon it.

At the first floor turning of the stair, Horgan paused. Had anything scraped or shuffled down there below, down in the black well of the ground floor? Of course it couldn't have, unless it was a rat. (Balgrummo kept no dogs: "The brutes don't live long at the lodging," Gillespie had murmured in an obscure aside.) How had those night nurses endured this situation, at whatever wages? One reason that Balgrummo Lodging hadn't been pillaged before this, Horgan ruminated, was the ghastly reputation of the place, lingering over five decades. Few enterprising lads, even from

Fossie housing estate, would be inclined to venture into the auld bogle nobleman's precincts. Well, that ghostly wind had blown him good. No one could be more effectively rational than Rafe Horgan, who wouldn't fret about blood spilt before the First World War. Still, indubitably this was an oppressive house—stagnant, stagnant.

"Haunted?" Dr. Effie Inchburn had replied hesitantly to Horgan's jocular inquiry. "If you mean haunted by dead ancestors, Major Horgan—why, no more than most old houses here in Scotland, I suppose. Who would be troubled, after so many generations, by old General Sir Angus Inchburn in his Covenanting jackboots? Ghostly phenomena, or so I've read, seldom linger long after a man's or a woman's death and burial. But if you ask whether there's something fey at work in the house—oh, I certainly suppose so."

Having paused to polish her spectacles, Dr. Effie continued calmly enough: "That's Uncle Alec's fault. He's not present merely in one room, you know; he fills the house, every room, every hour. Presumably I seem silly to you, Major Horgan, but my impulses won't let me visit Balgrummo more than I must, even if Alec does mean to leave everything to me. Balgrummo Lodging is like a saturated sponge, dripping with the shame and the longing of Alexander Fillan Inchburn. Can you understand that my uncle loathes what he did, and yet might do it again—even the worst of it—if there were opportunity? The horror of Balgrummo Lodging isn't Lord Balgrummo nine-tenths dead; it's Balgrummo one-tenth alive, but in torment."

The tedious old girl-doctor was nearly as cracked as her noble uncle, Horgan thought. Actually he had learned from some interesting research the general character of Lord Balgrummo's offenses so long ago—acts which would have produced the hanging of anyone but a peer, in those days. Horgan nevertheless had amused himself by endeavoring, slyly and politely, to force Dr. Effie to tell him just why Balgrummo had been given the choice of standing trial for his life (by the Lords, of course, as a peer, which might have damaged the repute of that body) or of being kept in a kind of perpetual house arrest, without sentence being passed by anyone. The latter choice would not have been offered—and accepted—even so, but for the general belief that he must be a maniac.

As he had anticipated, Dr. Euphemia had turned prude. "Poor Alec was very naughty when he was young. There were others as bad as himself, but he took the whole blame on his shoulders. He was told that if he would swear never to go out, all his life, and to receive no visitors except members of his family or his solicitors, no formal charges would be pressed against him. They required him to put everything he owned into trust; and the trustees were to engage the men to watch the policies of Balgrummo Lodging, and the servants. All the original set of trustees are dead and buried; Mr. Gillespie and I weren't much more than babies when Uncle Alec had his 'trouble.' "

From Gillespie, later, Rafe Horgan had learned more about that trouble. But what was he doing, pausing in the darkness of the second-floor corridor to reminisce? A hasty inspection by the torch showed him that the Knellers, all great noses, velvets, and bosoms, were hung on this floor. And there was the Gainsborough, a good one, though it badly needed cleaning: Margaret, Lady Ross, second daughter of the fifth Lord Balgrummo. The worm had got into the picture frame, but the canvas seemed to be in decent condition, he made out on closer examination. Well, Horgan meant to cut his pictures out of their frames, to save time and space. First, though, he must look in upon Himself.

The corridor was all dust and mildew. A single charwoman, Gillespie had mentioned, came a few hours daily, Monday through Friday, to keep Balgrummo's bedroom and small parlor neat, to clean the stairs and to wash dishes in the kitchen. Otherwise, the many rooms and passages of the lodging were unceasingly shuttered against sun and moon, and the damask might fall in tatters from the walls, the ceilings drip with cobwebs, for all old Balgrummo cared. Nearly every room was left locked, though the keys, all but a few, were in the bunch (each with its metal tag) that Horgan had taken from unconscious Jock. Even Gillespie, who waited on his client four or five times a year, never had contrived to see the chapel. Balgrummo kept the chapel key in his own pocket, Gillespie fancied—and, over coffee and brandy, had mentioned this, together with other trivia, to Horgan. "It was in the chapel, you see, Rafe, that the worst of the trouble happened."

Acquiring that chapel key was an additional reason that Horgan must pay his respects to Lord Balgrummo—though he relished that necessity less, somehow, with every minute that elapsed. Henry Fuseli's most indecorous painting might be in that chapel; for the tenth baron's liturgy and ritual, fifty years before, had been a synthesis of Benin witch rites with memories of Scots diabolism, and whatever might excite the frantic fancy had been employed—all gross images. So, at least, Horgan had surmised from what he had garnered from the old newspaper files, and what Gillespie had let drop.

Uncertain of quite where he was in the house, Horgan tried the knobs of three doors in that corridor. The first two were locked; and it was improbable that the trustees ever had gone so far, even when Balgrummo was stronger, as to have him locked into his rooms at night. But the third door opened creakingly. Flashing round his light, Horgan entered an old-fashioned parlor, with what appeared to be two bonafide Wilkie landscapes on opposite walls. Across the parlor, which was scarcely bigger than a dressing room, a mahogany door stood half open. How silent! Yet something scraped or ticked faintly—a morose death-watch beetle in the paneling, probably. Despite irrational misgivings, Horgan compelled himself to pass through the inner doorway.

The beam of his torch swept to a Queen Anne bed. In it lay, motionless and with eyes shut, an extremely old man, skin and bone under a single sheet and a single blanket. A coal fire smoldered in the grate, so the room was not altogether dark. Horgan's flesh crept perceptibly—but that would be the old rumors, and the old truths, about this enfeebled thing in the bed. "In his prime, we called him Ozymandias," Gillespie had put it. But Lord Balgrummo was past obscenities and atrocities now.

"Hello, Alec!" Horgan was loud and jocular. His right hand rested on the cosh in his coat pocket. "Alec, you old toad, I've come for your pictures." But Alexander Fillan Inchburn, the last of a line that went back to a bastard of William the Lion, did not stir or speak.

T. M. Gillespie was proud of Lord Balgrummo, as the most remarkable person whose business ever had come his way. "Our Scots Giles de Rais," Gillespie had chuckled aridly while enjoying a Jamaican cigar from Horgan's case, "probably would not be found insane by a board of medical examiners—not even after fifty years of restriction to his own private hell. I don't think it was from malice that the procurator-fiscal of that day recommended Balgrummo Lodging—where the capital offenses had been committed —as the place of isolated residence: it merely happened that this particular house of Lord Balgrummo's was secluded enough to keep his lordship out of the public eye (for he might have been stoned), and yet near enough to the city for police surveillance, during the earlier decades. I take it that the police have forgotten his existence, or almost forgotten, by this time: for the past three or four years, he wouldn't have been able to walk unaided so far as the gate cottage."

It was something of a relief to Horgan, finding that Lord Balgrummo was past giving coherent evidence in a court of law—and therefore need not be given the quietus. Even though they no longer hanged anybody for anything, and even though Balgrummo could have been eliminated in thirty seconds by a pillow over his face, the police pursued a homicide much more energetically than they did a picture fancier.

But was this penny-dreadful monster of fifty years ago, with his white beard now making him sham-venerable in this four-poster, still among the living? Horgan almost could see the bones through his skin; Balgrummo might have come to his end during the hour or so since Jamieson had made his rounds. To be sure, Horgan took a mirror from the dressing table and held it close to the pallid sunken face. Setting his torch on its base, he inspected the mirror's surface; yes, there was a faint moist film, so the tenth baron still breathed.

Balgrummo must be stone deaf, or in a coma. Dr. Effie had said he had gone almost blind recently. Was it true? Horgan nearly yielded to a loathsome impulse to roll back those withered eyelids, but he reminded himself that somehow he wouldn't be able to endure seeing his own image in this dying man's malign pupils.

The coshing of Jock, the nervous partial exploration of this dismal house, the sight of loathsome old Balgrummo on the edge of dissolution—these trials had told on Horgan, old hand though he was at predatory ventures. With all the hours left to him, it would do no harm to sit for a few minutes in this easy chair, almost as if he were Balgrummo's nurse—keeping watch on the bed, surely, to make certain that Balgrummo wasn't (in reason's spite) shamming in some way—and to review in his brain the pictures he ought to secure first, and the rooms in which he was likely to find them.

But it would be heartening to have more light than his torch. Never turning his back on the bed, Horgan contrived to light a gas bracket near the door; either these gas fittings were simpler than those below stairs, or he had gotten the trick of the operation. The interior shutters of this bedroom being closed, there wasn't the faintest danger of a glimmer of light being perceived by chance passersby—not that anybody conceivably could pass by Balgrummo Lodging on a rainy midnight.

Lord Balgrummo seemed no less grisly in the flood of gaslight. However much exhausted by strain, you couldn't think of going to sleep, for the briefest nap, in a chair only six feet distant from this unspeaking and unspeakable thing in the bed; not when you knew just how "very naughty," in Dr. Euphemia's phrase, Balgrummo had been. The trouble for which he had paid had been only the culmination of a series of arcane episodes, progressing from hocus-pocus to the ultimate horror.

"No, not lunatic, in any ordinary definition of the term," Gillespie had declared. "Balgrummo recognized the moral character of his acts—aye, more fully than does the average sensual man. Also he was, and is, quite rational, in the sense that he can transact some ordinary business of life when pressed. He fell into a devil of a temper when we proposed to sell some of his pictures to pay for putting the house and the policies in order; he knows his rights, and that the trustees can't dispose of his plenishings against his explicit disapproval. He's civil enough, in his mocking way, to his niece, Effie, when she calls—and to me, when I have to see him. He still reads a good deal—or did, until his sight began to fail—though only books in his own library; half the ceiling has fallen in the library, but he shuffles through the broken plaster on the shaky floor."

On the right of the bed-head there hung an indubitable Constable; on the left, a probable Etty. The two were fairly small, and Horgan could take them whenever he wished. But his throat was dry, this house being so damned dusty. A decanter stood on the dressing table, a silver brandy label round its neck, and by it two cut-glass tumblers. "Not a drop for you, Alec?" inquired Horgan, grinning defiantly at the silent man on the bed. He seated himself in the velvet-upholstered armchair again and drank the brandy neat.

"No, one can't say," Gillespie had continued (in that last conversation which now seemed so far away and long ago) "that his lordship is wholly incompetent to take a hand in the management of his affairs. It's rather that he's *distant* —preoccupied, in more senses than one. He has to exert his will to bring his consciousness back from wherever it drifts—and one can see that the effort isn't easy for him."

"He's in a brown study, you mean, Tom?" Horgan had inquired, not much interested at that time.

"It's not the phrase I would choose, Rafe. Dr. Effie talks about the 'astral body' and such rubbish, as if she half believed in it—you've heard her. That silliness was a principal subject of Balgrummo's 'researches' for two years before the trouble, you understand; his trouble was the culmination of those experiments. But of course . . ."

"Of course he's only living in the past," Horgan had put in.

"*Living?* Who really knows what that word means?" T. M. Gillespie, W.S., devoted to the memory of David Hume, professed a contempt for rationalism as profound as his contempt for superstition. "And why say *past?* Did you never think that a man might be ossified in time? What you call Balgrummo's past, Rafe, may be Balgrummo's own present, as much as this table talk of ours is the present for you and me. The trouble is his lordship's obsessive reality. Attaining to genuine evil requires strict application to the discipline, eh? Balgrummo is not merely remembering the events of what you and I call 1913, or even 'reliving' those events. No, I suspect it's this: he's embedded in those events, like a beetle in amber. For Balgrummo, one certain night in Balgrummo Lodging continues forever.

"When Dr. Effie and I distract him by raising the trivia of current business, he has to depart from *his* reality, and gropes briefly through a vexatious little dream world in which his niece and his solicitor are insubstantial shadows. In Alexander Inchburn's consciousness, I mean, there is no remembrance and no anticipation. He's not 'living in the past,' not engaging in an exercise of retrospection; for him, time is restricted to one certain night, and space is restricted to one certain house, or perhaps one certain room. Passionate experience has chained him to a fixed point in time, so to speak. But time, as so many have said, is a human convention, not an objective reality. Can you prove that your time is more substantial than his?"

Horgan hadn't quite followed Gillespie, and said so.

"I put it this way, Rafe," Gillespie had gone on didactically. "What's the time of day in hell? Why, hell is timeless—or so my grandfather told me, and he was minister at the Tron. Hell knows no future and no past, but only the everlasting moment of damnation. Also hell is spaceless; or, conceivably, it's a locked box, damnably confining. Here we have Lord Balgrummo shut up perpetually in his box called Balgrummo Lodging, where the fire is not quenched and the worm never dieth. One bloody and atrocious act, committed in that very box, literally is his enduring *reality*. He's not recollecting; he's experiencing, here and (for him) now. All the frightful excitement of that trouble, the very act of profanation and terror, lifts him out of what we call time. Between Dr. Effie and me on the one side, and distant Balgrummo on the other, a great gulf is fixed.

"If you like, you can call that gulf time. For that gulf, I praise whatever gods there be. For if any man's or woman's consciousness should penetrate to Balgrummo's consciousness, to his time scheme, to his world beyond the world— or if, through some vortex of mind and soul, anyone were sucked into that narrow place of torment—then the intruder would end like *this*." Gillespie, tapping his cigar upon an ashtray, knocked into powder a long projection of gray ash. "Consumed, Rafe."

Scratch the canny Scot, Horgan had thought then, even the pedant of the law, and you find the bogle-dreading Pict. "I suppose you mean, really, Tom, that he's out of his head," Horgan had commented, bored with tipsy and unprofitable speculation.

"I mean precisely the contrary, Rafe. I mean that anyone who encounters Lord Balgrummo ought to be on his guard against being drawn into Balgrummo's head. In what you and I designate as 1913 (though, as I said, dates have no significance for Balgrummo), his lordship was a being of immense moral power, magnetic and seductive. I'm not being facetious. Moral power is a catalyst, and can work for good or for evil. Even now I'm acutely uneasy when I sit with Balgrummo, aware that this old man might absorb me. I shouldn't wish to stir those sleeping fires by touching his passions. That's why Balgrummo had to be confined, five decades of ours ago—but not simply because he might be *physically* dangerous. Yet I can't explain to you; you've not watched Balgrummo in what you call his 'brown study,' and you never will, happy man." Their conversation then had shifted to Miss Janet Horgan's hypothetical trust.

Yet Gillespie had been a bad prophet. Here he was, clever Rafe Horgan, man of supple talents and slippery fingers, leisurely watching Lord Balgrummo in his brown study— or in his coma, more precisely—and finishing his lordship's decanter of praiseworthy brandy. You had to remember to keep watching that cadaverous face above the sheet, though; if you let your eyes close even for a second, *his* might open, for all you could tell. After all, you were only a guest in Balgrummo's very own little hell. The host mustn't be permitted to forget his manners.

Now, where would the expiring monster keep his privy effects—the key to that chapel on the floor above, for instance? Steady, Rafe boy: keep your eyes on his face as you open his bedside drawer. Right you are, Rafe; you always were lucky; the nurse had put old Alec's three keys on a chain, along with watch and pocket comb and such effects, into this very drawer. One of these keys should let you into the chapel, Rafe. Get on with you; you've drunk all the brandy a reasonable man needs.

"Don't you mean to give me a guided tour, Alec? Stately homes of Scotia, and all that? Won't you show me your chapel, where you and your young chums played your dirty little games, and got your fingers burned? Cheerio, then; don't blame me if you can't be bothered to keep an eye on your goods and chattels."

Back away from him, toward the door, Rafe. Let him lie. How had Dr. Effie put it? "He fills the house, every room, every hour." Cheerless thought, that, fit for a scrawny old maid. The talkative Euphemia must have nearly as many screws loose as had her uncle; probably she envied him his revels.

"I really believe the others led Uncle Alec into the whole business gradually," Dr. Effie had droned on the last time he had seen her. "But once in, he took command, as natural to him. He was out in Nigeria before people called it Nigeria, you know, and in Guinea, and all up and down that coast. He began collecting materials for a monograph on African magic—raising the dead, and summoning devils, and more. Presently he was dabbling in the spells, not merely collecting them—so my father told me, forty years ago. After Uncle Alec came home, he didn't stop dabbling. Some very reputable people dabbled when I was a girl. But the ones around Uncle Alec weren't in the least reputable.

"Charlatans? Not quite; I wish they had been. They fed Balgrummo's appetite. Yet he was after knowledge, at least in the beginning; and though he may have boggled, more than once, at the steps he had to descend toward the source of that knowledge, he grew more eager as he pressed down into the dark. Or so Father guessed; Father became one of Uncle Alec's original trustees, and felt it his duty to collect some evidence of what had happened—though it sickened Father, the more he uncovered of his brother's queerness.

"Toward the end, Balgrummo may have forgotten about knowledge and have leapt into passion and power. One didn't *learn* what one had sought to apprehend; one *became* the mystery, possessing it and possessed by it.

"No, not charlatans—not altogether. They took a fortune out of Uncle Alec, one way or another; and he had to pay even more to keep people quiet in those years. They had told Balgrummo, in effect, that they could raise the devil —though they didn't put it in quite that crude way. Yet they must have been astounded by their success, when it came at last. Balgrummo had paid before, and he has paid ever since. Those others paid, too—especially the man and the woman who died. They had thought they were raising the devil *for* Lord Balgrummo. But as it turned out, they raised the devil *through* Balgrummo and *in* Balgrummo. After that, everything fell to pieces."

But to hell with recollections of Euphemia Inchburn, Rafe. Dry rot, wet rot, woodworm, death-watch beetle: the devil take them all, and Balgrummo Lodging besides. One thing the devil shouldn't have—these pictures. Get on to the chapel, Rafe, and then give Nan the glad news. Thanks for the brandy, Alec: I mightn't have got through the business without it.

Yet one dram too many, possibly? Horgan was aware of a certain giddiness, but not fully aware of how he had got up those Stygian stairs, or of what he had done with his torch. Had he turned the key in the lock of the chapel door? He couldn't recall having done so. Still, here he was in the chapel.

No need for the torch; the room, a long gallery, was lit by all those candle flames in the many-branched candle-sticks. Who kept Lord Balgrummo's candles alight? The stench of decay was even stronger here than it had been down below. Under foot, the floorboards were almost ooz-ing, and mushroom rot squashed beneath his shoes. Some of the paneling had fallen away altogether. High up in the shifting shadows, the molded plaster ceiling sagged and bulged as if the lightest touch would bring it all down in slimy little particles.

Back of the altar—the altar of the catastrophic act of Balgrummo's trouble—hung the unknown Fuseli. It was no painting, but an immense cartoon, and the most un-inhibited museum director never would dare show it to the most broadminded critics of art. Those naked and contorted forms, the instruments of torment fixed upon their flesh, were the inversion of the Agony. Even Horgan could not bear to look at them long.

Look at them? All those candles were guttering. Two winked out simultaneously; others failed. As the little flames sank toward extinction, Rafe Horgan became aware that he was not alone.

It was as if presences skulked in corners or behind the broken furniture. And there could be no retreat toward the door; for something approached from that end of the gallery. As if Horgan's extremity of terror fed it, the shape took on increasing clarity of outline, substance, strength.

Tall, arrogant, implacable, mindless, it drifted toward him. The face was Balgrummo's, or what Balgrummo's must have been fifty years before, but possessed: eager, eager; eager; all appetite, passion, yearning after the abyss. In one hand glittered a long knife.

Horgan bleated and ran. He fell against the cobwebby altar. And in the final act of destruction, something strode across the great gulf of time.

THE OLD DARKNESS

PAMELA SARGENT

Pamela Sargent began publishing science fiction and fantasy with her "Landed Minority" in *F & SF* in 1970 and has developed into one of the most distinctive, if underrated, voices in sf. Her most recent novel is *The Shore of Women* (1986). Her writings are typified by strong characters and by her unflinching ability to examine human relationships. As an editor, her anthologies (such as the 1975 *Women of Wonder*) include stories that boast female protagonists as well as the aforementioned qualities. "The Old Darkness" examines a small group caught in a power failure and their reactions; if you thought there was something romantic about a blackout, this story may quickly change your mind.

The kitchen window was white with light; a thousand invisible hands clapped in unison. Nina tensed. The kitchen was suddenly dark; outside, the wind howled as rain drummed against the window.

"What was that?" Andrew shouted from the living room.

"I don't know. It sounded like something hit the house."

"It had to happen now—bottom of the ninth, with a tie." She heard her husband shuffle through the hallway toward the kitchen. It was growing darker outside; evening's dim gray light was fading.

"I don't know what I'm going to do about supper," Nina said, staring at her now-useless food processor. "I was just going to chop the onions."

Andrew leaned against the refrigerator. "You used to chop them without that thing."

"I know, but it's made me lazy. I can't do anything without it." She crossed the room, crept into the hall, and opened the door, peering into the dark corridor. "Everything's out."

"Nina?"

She recognized her neighbor's voice. "Rosalie?"

"Yeah, it's me. I looked outside a second ago. I can't see a light on the whole street."

"Dammit," Nina said. "I was fixing supper."

"Well, the gas is still on. Just be glad you don't have an electric stove."

Nina cleared her throat. The darkness was making her uneasy; the air in the hallway seemed heavy and thick. She backed into her apartment, closing the door.

Andrew was still in the kitchen, dialing a number. "Who are you calling?" she asked.

"Power company. Hello? Yeah, I wanted to ask—okay, I'll wait." He leaned against the wall. Thunder rolled overhead as Nina went to the window; the wind shrieked. The rain was a silver sheet nearly parallel to the ground, a curtain buffeted by the wind.

"Hello? Yeah, I just wanted to know—uh-huh. We're

on the north side. Yeah." Andrew paused. "How soon? Uh-huh. Okay. Well, thanks." He hung up. "One of the main lines is down. They said they should have it fixed in an hour or two."

"I guess we can eat late. I can't make this dish without the Cuisinart."

"Oh, come on. You can get along without electricity."

"I can't even see what I'm doing."

"We've got candles. I'll set some up for you. We've got a flashlight." He rummaged in one drawer, pulling out a box of matches. "We can rough it for one evening."

Nina finished preparing dinner by the flickering yellow light of the candles. Andrew had set one on the stove, another on the countertop, and two more on the table, with a mirror behind them to catch the light.

She shivered. The air seemed unusually cold in spite of the oven's heat. She felt oddly vulnerable without the familiar presence of electricity, unable to prepare food without it, unable to read—she couldn't even dry her long, thick hair without a hair dryer. The artifacts of technology had made her only more incompetent; she thought of the past, imagining families going about their tasks as the sun set, reading to one another by the light of a fire, drawing close against the night.

Her grandparents, believers in progress, had always told her things were better now. Human minds had been darker when people couldn't read late at night, their prejudices greater when they had lacked television's images of other places, their work harder without the appliances many took for granted. Nina was not so sure; technical civilization had isolated people from the basics of life, and had fooled them into believing that they controlled the world.

Andrew set the table, then put a portable radio and cassette player near the candles. "This isn't so bad. Kind of romantic, actually. We should do this more often."

"They still haven't repaired the line."

"They will."

"Everything in the freezer's going to get ruined."

"Forget about the freezer. It'll keep. Just don't open the door." He uncorked a bottle of wine while she served the stuffed peppers.

As she carried the plates to the table, the thunder rumbled again. Storms had always frightened her, and the darkness beyond the lighted room was filled with threatening shadows. She sat down, facing the mirror. The smell of melting wax mingled with the odor of tomato sauce and spices.

"We've got food. We've even got music." Andrew's voice sounded hollow and distant. A dark shadow loomed behind Nina, about to cloak her in black; she stared at the mirror, afraid to move. Andrew popped a cassette into the player, and the sound of Bach filled the room.

The music was soothing. Andrew began to conduct with his fork. "Magnificat," he bellowed along with the chorus.

A fist pounded on the door. Nina started. "Who is it?"

"Rosalie."

That surprised her; Rosalie usually had a gentle, tentative knock. As Nina left the light of the kitchen, the air pressed in around her; she was once again afraid. She opened the door. "Come on in."

The words were hardly out of her mouth before her neighbor was inside. Rosalie panted, then leaned against the wall, hands over her belly. Nina took her arm and led Rosalie into the kitchen, seating her across from Andrew.

"I'm all right now," Rosalie said. "It's the dark. I guess it got to me. I really got scared."

"It's okay. Do you want a pepper?"

Rosalie shook her head but accepted a glass of wine from Andrew. "I wouldn't have come over, but I couldn't stay there alone. I was going to go over to Jeff's, but the radio said people should stay off the roads—the wind's knocking down trees."

"Where's Lisanne?"

"At her father's for the weekend." Rosalie lifted her glass;

her hand was shaking. She sipped some wine. "All I've got is a flashlight, so I wasn't very prepared."

Andrew turned down the music; a shadow in the corner seemed to darken. "I felt it too," Nina said. "I got the creeps when I went to answer the door."

"You're too suggestible," Andrew said in a loud voice.

"It was cold," Rosalie said in a flat tone as the candlelight flickered on her face, adding a golden glow to her coppery hair. "I was in the living room, and I felt a cold spot, right in the center of the room. Then the O'Haras started screaming at each other—I could hear them through the floor."

"The O'Haras were fighting?" Nina said, surprised.

"You bet. I didn't know she knew that kind of language. The living room got colder. Something was breathing down my neck, and I thought I heard a sigh. Then I thought, if I don't get out of here, I'll be trapped—I won't be able to—"

"A draft." Andrew gestured with his knife. "There's always a draft in this building."

"It wasn't a draft. The air was just sitting there."

Nina tried to smile. "It's a good thing my grandparents aren't here. They'd be telling old stories by now. You know, there's a legend that the first people who settled in this valley disappeared—just vanished into the woods. And once—" Andrew was warning her with his eyes. "It's just a story. No one believed it."

"You grew up here, didn't you?" Rosalie asked.

Nina nodded. "Lived here all my life, except for college." The rest of her family had left, moving to places of warmth and light, while she had remained behind, afraid to live among strangers unilluminated by familiarity.

The Bach cantata came to an end; Andrew clicked off the cassette player.

"They *still* haven't repaired the line," Nina said.

"The storm's probably worse than they expected." Rosalie's voice echoed in the kitchen. The room was darker; the candle on the stove had gone out. The shadow in the corner was now a misshapen birdlike figure; its wingtips fluttered. "I hope," Rosalie went on, "that you've got more candles. These won't last much longer."

"There's a scented one in the living room." Andrew stood up. "I'd better go get it."

"Take the flashlight," Nina said.

"I can find my way."

Nina turned toward her neighbor as Andrew left the kitchen. She was about to speak, when she saw Rosalie's lips draw back over her teeth; the woman was a predator, her jaws ready to bite, her hands claws. "That bastard," Rosalie said softly. "Ever since our divorce, he's been making Lisanne think he's the good guy. I'll bet he's telling her right now that it was all my fault."

Nina drew back. Rosalie had always been on good terms with her ex-husband; their divorce had been notable for its lack of rancor. "He was the one who wanted it," Rosalie continued. "He manipulated me into court, and I didn't even see it. I thought he was being nice, and so I got screwed on the settlement—he knew I wouldn't fight it."

Nina felt trapped. The kitchen seemed small, the walls too close. Then she heard a thud in the front of the apartment, and a cry.

She jumped up, grabbed the flashlight from the counter, and hurried into the living room. "Andy?"

He was lying on the floor, his face pale in the flashlight's beam. "Something hit me." He picked up a thick book and put it on the coffee table.

"Are you all right?" She knelt beside him. He nodded, rubbing his head. "You'd better put up another shelf."

"I haven't had time."

"Then get rid of some of that junk." Nina's voice was sharp. "It's taking over the place. Pretty soon we'll have to get an apartment just for the books." She was shouting, longing to sweep the rows of hardcover mysteries from the shelves and hurl them into the rain. "And you never do your share of the dusting either." She took a breath, feeling light-headed; the feeling of oppression had lifted.

A candle danced in the darkness, illuminating Rosalie's face. "Anything wrong?"

Nina sighed as Andrew climbed to his feet. "Book hit me in the head, that's all."

Andrew cleared the table and put the dirty dishes into the sink, then moved their remaining candles into the living room, along with the cassette player. He lighted only the scented candle, saving the others.

"We've got about three or four hours' worth of candles," he said. "They have to have the line repaired by then." Nina, listening to the whine of the wind, was not so sure.

Andrew turned on the cassette player. Voices singing God's praises wavered, missing a few notes. He hit the machine, then turned it off.

"Haven't you got anything else?" Rosalie asked.

"I've got Vivaldi, and Handel, and some—"

"I should have brought my tapes," Rosalie interrupted. "Unfortunately, I left them in my car." She glanced at the window. "And I'm not going out in that."

Andrew said, "I can't say I'm sorry."

Rosalie lifted her head. "What's that supposed to mean?"

"I can't stand that music you're always playing—if you can even call it music."

"And just what's wrong with it?"

"It's all screaming and percussion—a perfect example of human primitivism and banality."

"Really! I suppose you think that Tinker Toy music is better."

"Don't call it Tinker Toy music."

"It's boring," Rosalie said. "It's all the same."

"How can you say that?"

"Stop it!" Nina shouted. Rosalie sank back on the couch; Andrew, seated on the floor, draped one arm over the coffee

table. "We don't have to argue about it." Nina's stomach
was tight with tension; she wondered if the stuffed peppers
were giving her indigestion. "It's a matter of taste."

Lightning brightened the room for an instant; Andrew's
mustache was black against his face. "It's a matter of taste,
all right," he said. "Good taste and bad."

Before Rosalie could respond, he had turned on the music
again. Andrew shook his head. "I'm sorry, Rosalie."

"It's okay. I'm sorry too."

Nina heard footsteps on the stairs, then a knock on the
door; a child squealed. "I'll get it," Andrew said.

As he made his way out of the room, Nina leaned toward
Rosalie. "He didn't mean it."

"I know. I feel all right now. I just wanted to lash out at
someone all of a sudden."

Andrew was speaking to their callers; Nina recognized
the voices of Jill and Tony Levitas. Their daughter Melanie
preceded them into the room, sat down at one end of the
sofa, and began to suck her thumb. The music sounded
sluggish; Nina turned off the cassette player.

"Sorry," Jill said as she sat in a chair. "We didn't want
to come upstairs, but—I don't know how to put it."

"You were getting the creeps," Rosalie said. "That's why
I came over."

Jill lowered her voice. "Our dining room table started to
move—honest to God. Then Melanie got hysterical. She
said there was something in her room, and she refused to
go to bed. She's never been afraid of the dark before."

Rosalie said, "The O'Haras were fighting. Can you believe it?"

"I heard them. It sounded pretty grim."

"I brought a libation," Tony said, setting a jug of wine
on the table. Andrew came in with more glasses and poured
the wine, then retreated to a corner with Tony.

"We were going to go out tonight," Jill said. "Then the
baby-sitter called and said she couldn't make it—a tree fell

in her driveway. Not that it matters—the theater's probably blacked out too. So we're stuck."

"Steinbrenner should just leave them alone and let them play ball," Andrew was saying.

"He's paying them." Tony wrapped his arms around his long, thin legs.

"Of course, we have to have this storm on practically the first night in months we were going out," Jill said bitterly. "And it'll probably be ages before we go out again. Let that be a lesson to you, Nina." Two reflected flames fluttered on Jill's glasses. "Don't have a kid until you've done everything you want to do, because you don't get a chance later on. And don't expect your husband to help."

"I heard that," Tony said.

"It's true."

"Look, I have to work. I do my share on the weekends."

"You were the one who talked me into quitting my job."

"Because it would have cost us more for you to work."

"So what? Doesn't my peace of mind mean anything to you?"

"Jill! You *hated* that job."

"At least I was with adults. I'm regressing. The biggest intellectual effort I make now is comparing the merits of *General Hospital* with *The Young and the Restless.*"

"You wanted the kid, Jill."

"*You* wanted her!"

"You know what your trouble is?" Tony's voice was unusually high. "You never bothered to look for a job you liked, because you thought some man would take care of you. Now you're bitching because you don't like housework. Well, make up your mind."

Melanie curled up, covering her head with her hands. Nina rubbed her arms; the room felt cold. Something rustled; she heard a crack. Several books flew off the shelves, crashing to the floor; one struck her in the back.

She jumped up. Inside her a snake uncoiled, creeping

up to her throat. "Dammit, Andy! Do you have to get so many books?" She was shouting again. She rarely shouted, and she had done so twice in a few minutes. She strode to the window, peering out at the storm. Lights twinkled on a distant hill, reminding her of stars; at least the South Side still had power.

Five men, barely visible, were on the sidewalk below. They were drinking, ignoring the rain that drenched them. Water streamed from their jackets and hair, making them look as though they were melting. One man held his beer bottle by its top, then pitched it over the fence into the front yard.

"Shit," Nina muttered. "Somebody just threw a bottle into the yard."

Andrew was at her side. He pushed up the window, then opened the storm window behind it. Rain sprayed Nina's face.

"Hey!" Andrew shouted above the wind as he shone his flashlight on the litterers. "Pick up your bottle!" The men were still. "Don't throw your crap in our yard."

Another man drew his arm back; a bottle flew, smashing against the side of the building. A second bottle followed it, landing in the branches of the pine tree.

Nina closed the storm window hastily. "Call the police."

"You can't," Tony responded. "The phones are out now. I tried to call you before we came upstairs."

Andrew turned off the flashlight. "I've seen those guys before. They never acted like that."

Melanie whimpered and began to cry. "Hush," Jill said. Melanie wailed. "Be quiet!"

Rosalie reached for the child, trying to soothe her. "Leave her alone."

"There's something to be said for divorce," Jill said. "At least you get to unload Lisanne once in a while. How's that sound, Tony? I'll even give you custody."

"Shut up, Jill."

"I'll even pay child support."

Tony lumbered across the room. "Shut up, dammit."

"I don't know what you're complaining about," Rosalie cried. "I wish I had more time with my kid. That goddamned Elliott made sure he had someone else lined up before he told me he wanted a divorce."

Nina leaned against the windowsill. The bitter voices seemed far away, the harsh words dim. The room was warmer, as if her friends' anger had driven away the cold. She gazed at the fluttering shadows near the couch, surprised that the placid Jill and the cheerful Rosalie had such strong feelings.

Andrew gulped down his wine, reached for the jug, and poured another glass. A breath of air tickled Nina's ear. "He's had enough to drink." The voice was so low she could barely hear it; she looked around quickly. "He can't handle it. He never could hold his liquor." Before she could see where the voice was coming from, rage had taken hold of her; she clenched her fists.

Andrew knelt, hitting the cassette player. "Damn battery's dead. Go get some more."

Nina said, "There aren't any more."

"You mean you didn't pick any up?"

"I was going to get some tomorrow." She screamed the words. "You expect me to remember everything."

Andrew poured himself more wine. Nina reached for the bottle; he pulled it away.

"You've had enough, Andy."

"Get off my case." He gulped the wine defiantly.

"Andy, stop it. You know you can't drink that much."

"I'll do what I please. I don't need your permission."

"He'll be a drunk, just like his father," the voice sighed.

"You'll be like your father," Nina said. "You'll drink yourself right into the hospital."

"It's only wine, for Christ's sake." Andrew stood up. "I can't tell you how many times I've wanted to tie one on, and how many times I resisted. You and your nagging. Leave me alone. You'd like to see me drunk, wouldn't you, just to prove your point."

Nina heard a slap. "You son of a bitch!" Jill shouted. "Now you're turning into a wife beater. Go ahead, hit me again."

Tony said, "I'll give you more than a slap next time."

Nina wanted to scream. The voice was whispering again. "Jill always has her television set on too loud. And Tony forgets to mow the lawn. And Melanie leaves her toys on the stairs." She covered her ears, but could still hear the voice. "Admit it," the voice said. "You hate them."

"No!" Nina cried. Melanie had stopped weeping; the racking sobs she heard now were Rosalie's. "We've got to stop this." She felt a sharp pain in her chest, and gasped for air. The room was darker; the walls creaked as the wind outside gusted. "We've never had arguments before—what's the matter with us?" The pain was worse; she sat down, clutching her abdomen. She hated everyone in the room, and the only way she could get rid of the hate was to let it out.

"She's right," Tony said; his voice sounded hoarse. The coffee table rattled; the candle danced. Another book flew across the room, hitting the wall with a thud. The whispers were now so pronounced that Nina could barely hear anything else.

"You know what it is?" Tony said, crackling. "I didn't bless the wine. My parents always told me to bless my food or it would do bad things to me." His voice cracked as he sang a prayer in Hebrew.

Nina's pain was fading. She sniffed; the air, so heavy before, now smelled clean. "What's going on?"

"I don't know," Tony replied.

"Keep praying," Andrew said. Tony sang another prayer. "That's it. If we only had some batteries—we could play more Bach."

"What's that got to do with it?" Rosalie asked.

"It's sacred music. Didn't you notice? When the cassette was on, we were okay. Now Tony's praying, and I can't hear those voices anymore."

"You heard them too?"

"I think we all did."

Nina reached for Andrew's hand. Tony paused for breath; Rosalie began to sing "Rock of Ages." "It's the power failure," Andrew went on. "It's as if electricity is some sort of white magic, keeping things in check. Now we have to use older magic."

Nina trembled. An unseen hand pressed against her head, waiting to crush her when the songs failed. She had always dismissed her grandparents' lore, and even they had not taken it all that seriously. Now she recalled their tales of objects flying across rooms, of occasional murders which usually happened at night, of people barring their doors against the darkness.

"I can't believe it," Tony said. "This is the twentieth century, for God's sake." Rosalie was now singing "Amazing Grace"; her voice faltered on the high notes.

Out in the kitchen a dish smashed to the floor. The candle on the coffee table went out.

Nina felt as though she were at the center of a vortex; unseen beings whirled around her. Rosalie continued to sing as Andrew lit the candle. The walls, Nina felt, would cave in on her; whatever was with them would not be held off by a few simple songs and prayers.

"We have to get out of here," Andrew said. "The South Side still has power. We ought to be safe there."

"We can't," Jill replied. "It's too risky. They told people to stay off the roads unless it's an emergency."

"This is an emergency. I think we should get into our cars and go."

"No," Rosalie said as Tony began to sing. "We're safer here."

"As long as you keep singing." Books hopped on the shelves. "And maybe not even then."

"Andy's right," Nina said. A cushion of cold air seemed

to swallow her words. "Please come with us." She glanced at the sofa. "At least let us take Melanie."

"No," Jill said, moving toward the child and shielding her with one arm.

Nina retreated to the door with Andrew. At the end of the hall the refrigerator rattled; more dishes fell. She reached for her purse, pulling it off a hook. "I'd better drive. You can't with all that wine in you." The words sounded harsher than she had intended; the pain was returning.

Andrew opened the door. Nina looked back at her neighbors, who were huddled around the candle; a misty barrier now separated her from them. She crept into the hall and down the darkened stairway, clinging to the railing. There was an ominous silence behind the O'Haras' door.

As she opened the front door, the wind nearly tore it from her grasp; she hung on. Andrew took her purse, fumbling for the car keys. She pushed the door shut.

He threw her the purse and sprinted toward the car, which was parked across the street. A large puddle had formed on the lawn, reaching to the sidewalk. Rain poured over her, plastering her clothes against her body. Next door, a man stood outside his house, screaming at the porch. Nina could not see the rest of the street; the sky, dark as it was, seemed lighter than the black earth below it.

Lightning lit her way. A shape was crouching near the building; it barked. "Oscar," she murmured, recognizing the O'Haras' dachshund, and wondering what it was doing outside. "Poor thing."

The dog leapt at her, biting at her leg. Claws and teeth tore at her jeans. She swung her purse, hitting the animal in the head and knocking it against the door.

"Come on, Nina!" She ran for the car, climbing in next to Andrew, and started the engine. Windshield wipers fanned back and forth, but the rain was so heavy she could see nothing else.

She turned on the headlights. The car crawled down the road. A tree had fallen, blocking the left side of the street;

a group of people were in the right lane. Some were grinning; the headlights caught the white of their teeth and made their eyes gleam.

Nina honked her horn. The crowd rushed the car. She braked. Fists beat against the windows; the car rocked.

"Get going!" Andrew shouted.

She gunned the motor. The car shot forward; the people dropped away. She made a right turn, toward the south. "We'll make it," Andrew said. "Not much farther to go."

The car stalled. Nina turned the key, pumping the pedal. "Damn." The motor turned over and died. "What's wrong with it?"

"I don't know."

"You forgot to take it to the garage. I told you, and you forgot."

"I didn't have time."

"Dammit, Andy!" She struck at him; he grabbed her fists, holding her back. She tried to kick.

"Nina!" He shook her. "We'll have to walk, that's all."

"Out there?"

"You're already soaked. Come on."

They got out of the car. As they ran to the sidewalk, the wind howled, nearly knocking Nina to the ground. She heard a sharp crack. A tree toppled over, smashing the abandoned car.

Andrew grabbed her arm, leading her down the darkened street.

A dark mass milled in front of the shopping center; Nina heard the sound of shattering glass. Two men brushed past her, carrying a case of bourbon; a boy hurried by with a portable television set.

A crowd had gathered in front of the blacked-out stores. Several people were inside, hurling clothes, small appliances, and bottles through the broken windows to those in the parking lot.

Andrew stopped. Nina tugged at his arm. "We'd better

get going!" she shouted. "The police will be here pretty soon." Alarms powered by batteries whined and clanged; the crowd cheered as a microwave oven hurtled through one window. She looked around hastily, wondering where the police were.

Another mob was running toward them; Nina and Andrew were suddenly in the midst of the crowd, being pushed toward the stores. She reached for her husband and clutched air.

"Andy!" She struggled to stay on her feet, afraid she would be trampled if she fell. "Andy!"

A toaster flew past her, hitting another woman, who dropped out of sight. A few people were carrying flashlights, holding them as if they were torches. A young girl raced past, her arms filled with jeans. Nina reached out for a post and held on as the crowd surged toward the liquor store.

Several people were lying on the walkway; she heard groans. Lightning lit up the scene; Nina imagined that she saw a black pool of blood near one man's head. "Andy!"

"Nina."

Andrew was near her, sprawled on the ground. She leaned over, pulling at him. He moaned. "My leg—it's hurt."

She pulled him up; he leaned against her heavily. More people ran past them, joining the crowd looting the nearby hardware store. "I don't think I can make it. You'd better leave me."

"Save yourself," the voice whispered.

"I won't!" Nina shouted. She said a prayer as she hauled Andrew through the parking lot and toward the road.

The wind had died down; the rain was falling more slowly. Trees threatened Nina with their branches as she passed, swatting at her as she struggled along with the limping Andrew. She was muttering prayers almost automatically, surprised that she, who had not said them in years, could remember so many.

They passed a lawn littered with furniture, and heard a

distant scream. A beam blinded her for a moment; pebbles struck her as children laughed. Nina flailed at the air with her free arm. The flashlight fled from her as the children retreated.

She peered through the rain, seeing a hazy golden glow. "Light," she said. "We're almost there." She could now make out streetlights and tried to move faster; Andrew was slowing her down. She said, "You won't get me." A lighted road wound up a hill; an electric company truck was blocking it. She moved toward the truck.

A police car was parked under a streetlight, near the truck. Leading Andrew toward it, she approached the boundary between darkness and light, then stopped.

She tried to step forward and could not; something was holding her back. She pushed; her knees locked.

"No!" she screamed.

A door opened on one side of the police car; a man in a slicker hurried toward her. "What are you doing out here?" he shouted.

"Help us," she said, stretching out an arm. She couldn't reach him. He grabbed at her, then fell back.

"We can't get in," the policeman said. "We've tried. We're still trying."

"And you can't get out," the voice whispered.

She tried to step forward again, and felt herself stumble back; Andrew slipped to the ground.

"I can't help you, lady." The policeman waved his arms helplessly. "I wish I could."

She sank to the ground, cradling Andrew in her arms. The night was suddenly brighter; she was having delusions, seeing the light she longed for. The wind howled its rage. Arms seized her; she held on to Andrew.

"Come on, lady!" The policeman was holding her; he had reached her somehow. He let go and pulled Andrew up. She stumbled to her feet and followed the two men to the car, where the policeman's partner was waiting.

"Look!" the partner shouted.

Nina turned. Her side of town was now starry with light.
A solid blackness lifted from the ground, then began to roll
back toward the hills in the north. "We're safe," she said
to Andrew. "We're safe." The policeman was shaking his
head as he gazed at the ebony fog.

Sparks danced along a power line overhead; the line
snapped, writhing down at them like a snake. They dragged
Andrew to the car. The North Side was once again dark,
and growing darker; soon the impenetrable darkness was so
thick that Nina, safe in the light, could not see through the
blackness at all.

She had dozed off. Nina awoke with a start, shook herself,
and got out of the police car.

The rain had stopped. In the dim light she could see a
medic wrapping a bandage around Andrew's leg. A crowd
stood in the street, staring at the black veil before them.

"It's on!" a man's voice shouted. "Power's back!"

As the sun peeped over the hills to Nina's right, the black
wall rolled away, defeated by the light. Someone cried out.
Only blackened earth lay where the darkness had been; the
gloom had taken everything away, leaving only a vast, scarred
plain. Only the power lines, the town's humming sentries,
remained on the ravaged North Side.

Nina thought of her friends, trapped forever in the dark.
Where, she wondered, would the darkness go? She knew
It would retreat to the edge of the world, and into the people
she knew, and into her; she could feel it lurking there even
now, hiding in her mind's shadows with her fears. It would
wait for the white magic to fail.

THE NIGHT
OF WHITE
BHAIRAB

LUCIUS SHEPARD

Lucius Shepard is probably the best new short-fiction writer of the 1980s. His novella "R & R" received a Nebula award in 1987, and his stories were recently collected in a book titled *Jaguar Hunter*. The most noticeable feature of his tales is the exotic settings, which are gleaned from his own travels. "The Night of White Bhairab" first appeared in *F & SF* in October 1984 and is set in Nepal. It is the story of a young American in Katmandu searching for enlightenment, only to fall in love and into a supernatural adventure. In the tale, Lucius Shepard utilizes not only the landscape of Nepal but also its myths and legends to create an eerie entanglement in and with the "mysterious" East.

Whenever Mr. Chatterji went to Delhi on business, twice yearly, he would leave Eliot Blackford in charge of his Katmandu home, and prior to each trip, the transfer of keys and instructions would be made at the Hotel Anapurna. Eliot—an angular, sharp-featured man in his mid-thirties, with thinning blond hair and a perpetually ardent expression—knew Mr. Chatterji for a subtle soul, and he suspected that this subtlety had dictated the choice of meeting place. The Anapurna was the Nepalese equivalent of a Hilton, its bar equipped in vinyl and plastic, with a choirlike arrangement of bottles fronting the mirror. Lights were muted, napkins monogrammed. Mr. Chatterji, plump and prosperous in a business suit, would consider it an elegant refutation of Kipling's famous couplet ("East is East," etc.) that he was at home here, whereas Eliot, wearing a scruffy robe and sandals, was not; he would argue that not only the twain met, they had actually exchanged places. It was Eliot's own measure of subtlety that restrained him from pointing out what Mr. Chatterji could not perceive: that the Anapurna was a skewed version of the American Dream. The carpeting was indoor-outdoor runner; the menu was rife with ludicrous misprints (*Skotch Miss, Screwdriver*), and the lounge act—two turbaned, tuxedoed Indians on electric guitar and traps—was managing to turn "Evergreen" into a doleful raga.

"There will be one important delivery." Mr. Chatterji hailed the waiter and nudged Eliot's shot glass forward. "It should have been here days ago, but you know these customs people." He gave an effeminate shudder to express his distaste for the bureaucracy, and cast an expectant eye on Eliot, who did not disappoint.

"What is it?" he asked, certain that it would be an addition to Mr. Chatterji's collection: he enjoyed discussing the collection with Americans; it proved that he had an overview of their culture.

"Something delicious!" said Mr. Chatterji. He took the tequila bottle from the waiter and—with a fond look—

passed it to Eliot. "Are you familiar with the Carversville Terror?"

"Yeah, sure." Eliot knocked back another shot. "There was a book about it."

"Indeed," said Mr. Chatterji. "A best seller. The Cousineau mansion was once the most notorious haunted house of your New England. It was torn down several months ago, and I've succeeded in acquiring the fireplace, which"—he sipped his drink—"which was the locus of power. I'm very fortunate to have obtained it." He fitted his glass into the circle of moisture on the bar and waxed scholarly. "Aimée Cousineau was a most unusual spirit, capable of a variety of. . . ."

Eliot concentrated on his tequila. These recitals never failed to annoy him, as did—for different reasons—the sleek western disguise. When Eliot had arrived in Katmandu as a member of the Peace Corps, Mr. Chatterji had presented a far less pompous image: a scrawny kid dressed in jeans that he had wheedled from a tourist. He'd been one of the hangers-on—mostly young Tibetans—who frequented the grubby tea rooms on Freak Street, watching the American hippies giggle over their hash yogurt, lusting after their clothes, their women, their entire culture. The hippies had respected the Tibetans: they were a people of legend, symbols of the occultism then in vogue, and the fact that they like James Bond movies, fast cars, and Jimi Hendrix had increased the hippies' self-esteem. But they had found laughable the fact that Ranjeesh Chatterji—another westernized Indian—had liked these same things, and they had treated him with mean condescension. Now, thirteen years later, the roles had been reversed; it was Eliot who had become the hanger-on.

He had settled in Katmandu after his tour was up, his idea being to practice meditation, to achieve enlightenment. But it had not gone well. There was an impediment in his mind—he pictured it as a dark stone, a stone compounded of worldly attachments—that no amount of practice could wear down, and his life had fallen into a futile pattern. He would spend ten months of the year living in a small room near the temple of Swayambhunath, meditating, rubbing away at the stone; and then, during March and September, he would occupy Mr. Chatterji's house and debauch himself with liquor and sex and drugs. He was aware that Mr. Chatterji considered him a burnout, that the position of caretaker was in effect a form of revenge, a means by which his employer could exercise his own brand of condescension; but Eliot minded neither the label nor the attitude. There were worse things to be than a burnout in Nepal. It was beautiful country, it was inexpensive, it was far from Minnesota (Eliot's home). And the concept of personal failure was meaningless here. You lived, died, and were reborn over and over until at last you attained the ultimate success of nonbeing: a terrific consolation for failure.

"Yet in your country," Mr. Chatterji was saying, "evil has a sultry character. Sexy! It's as if the spirits were adopting vibrant personalities in order to contend with pop groups and movie stars."

Eliot thought of a comment, but the tequila backed up on him and he belched instead. Everything about Mr. Chatterji—teeth, eyes, hair, gold rings—seemed to be gleaming with extraordinary brilliance. He looked as unstable as a soap bubble, a fat little Hindu illusion.

Mr. Chatterji clapped a hand to his forehead. "I nearly forgot. There will be another American staying at the house. A girl. Very shapely!" He shaped an hourglass in the air. "I'm quite mad for her, but I don't know if she's trustworthy. Please see she doesn't bring in any strays."

"Right," said Eliot. "No problem."

"I believe I will gamble now," said Mr. Chatterji, standing and gazing toward the lobby. "Will you join me?"

"No, I think I'll get drunk. I guess I'll see you in October."

"You're drunk already. Eliot." Mr. Chatterji patted him on the shoulder. "Hadn't you noticed?"

·

Early the next morning, hung over, tongue cleaving to the roof of his mouth, Eliot sat himself down for a final bout of trying to visualize the Avalokitesvara Buddha. All the sounds outside—the buzzing of a motor scooter, birdsong, a girl's laughter—seemed to be repeating the mantra, and the gray stone walls of his room looked at once intensely real and yet incredibly fragile, papery, a painted backdrop he could rip with his hands. He began to feel the same fragility, as if he were being immersed in a liquid that was turning him opaque, filling him with clarity. A breath of wind could float him out the window, drift him across the fields, and he would pass through the trees and mountains, all the phantoms of the material world . . . but then a trickle of panic welled up from the bottom of his soul, from that dark stone. It was beginning to smolder, to give off poison fumes: a little briquette of anger and lust and fear. Cracks were spreading across the clear substance he had become, and if he didn't move soon, if he didn't break off the meditation, he would shatter.

He toppled out of the lotus position and lay propped on his elbows. His heart raced, his chest heaved, and he felt very much like screaming his frustration. Yeah, that was a temptation. To just say the hell with it and scream, to achieve through chaos what he could not through clarity: to empty himself into the scream. He was trembling, his emotions flowing between self-hate and self-pity. Finally, he struggled up and put on jeans and a cotton shirt. He knew he was close to a breakdown, and he realized that he usually reached this point just before taking up residence at Mr. Chatterji's. His life was a frayed thread stretched tight between those two poles of debauchery. One day it would snap.

"The hell with it," he said. He stuffed the remainder of his clothes into a duffel bag and headed into town.

•

Walking through Durbar Square—which wasn't really a square but a huge temple complex interspersed with open areas and wound through by cobbled paths—always put Eliot in mind of his brief stint as a tour guide, a career cut short when the agency received complaints about his eccentricity ("As you pick your way among the piles of human waste and fruit rinds, I caution you not to breathe too deeply of the divine afflatus; otherwise, it may forever numb you to the scent of Prairie Cove or Petitpoint Gulch or whatever citadel of gracious living it is that you call home. . . .") It had irked him to have to lecture on the carvings and history of the square, especially to the just-plain-folks who only wanted a Polaroid of Edna or Uncle Jimmy standing next to that weird monkey god on the pedestal. The square was a unique place, and, in Eliot's opinion, such unenlightened tourism demeaned it.

Pagoda-style temples of red brick and dark wood towered on all sides, their finials rising into brass lightning bolts. They were alien-looking—you half expected the sky above them to be of an otherworldly color and figured by several moons. Their eaves and window screens were ornately carved into the images of gods and demons, and behind a large window screen on the temple of White Bhairab lay the mask of that god. It was almost ten feet high, brass, with a fanciful headdress and long-lobed ears and a mouth full of white fangs; its eyebrows were enameled red, fiercely arched, but the eyes had the goofy quality common to Newari gods— no matter how wrathful they were, there was something essentially friendly about them, and they reminded Eliot of cartoon germs. Once a year—in fact, a little more than a week from now—the screens would be opened, a pipe would be inserted into the god's mouth, and rice beer would jet out into the mouths of the milling crowds; at some point a fish would be slipped into the pipe, and whoever caught it would be deemed the luckiest soul in the Katmandu Valley for the next year. It was one of Eliot's traditions to make a try for the fish, though he knew that it wasn't luck he needed.

Beyond the square, the streets were narrow, running between long brick buildings three and four stories tall, each divided into dozens of separate dwellings. The strip of sky between the roofs was bright, burning blue—a void color—and in the shade the bricks looked purplish. People hung out the windows of the upper stories, talking back and forth: an exotic tenement life. Small shrines—wooden enclosures containing statuary of stucco or brass—were tucked into wall niches and the mouths of alleys. The gods were everywhere in Katmandu, and there was hardly a corner to which their gaze did not penetrate.

On reaching Mr. Chatterji's, which occupied half a block-long building, Eliot made for the first of the interior courtyards; a stair led up from it to Mr. Chatterji's apartment, and he thought he would check on what had been left to drink. But as he entered the courtyard—a phalanx of jungly plants arranged around a lozenge of cement—he saw the girl and stopped short. She was sitting in a lawn chair, reading, and she was indeed very shapely. She wore loose cotton trousers, a T-shirt, and a long white scarf shot through with golden threads. The scarf and the trousers were the uniform of the young travelers who generally stayed in the expatriate enclave of Temal: it seemed that they all bought them immediately upon arrival in order to identify themselves to one another. Edging closer, peering between the leaves of a rubber plant, Eliot saw that the girl was doe-eyed, with honey-colored skin and shoulder-length brown hair interwoven by lighter strands. Her wide mouth had relaxed into a glum expression. Sensing him, she glanced up, startled; then she waved and set down her book.

"I'm Eliot," he said, walking over.

"I know. Ranjeesh told me." She stared at him incuriously.

"And you?" He squatted beside her.

"Michaela." She fingered the book, as if she were eager to get back to it.

"I can see you're new in town."

"How's that?"

He told her about the clothes, and she shrugged. "That's what I am," she said. "I'll probably always wear them." She folded her hands on her stomach: it was a nicely rounded stomach, and Eliot—a connoisseur of women's stomachs —felt the beginnings of arousal.

"Always?" he said. "You plan on being here that long?"

"I don't know." She ran a finger along the spine of the book. "Ranjeesh asked me to marry him, and I said maybe."

Eliot's infant plan of seduction collapsed beneath this wrecking ball of a statement, and he failed to hide his incredulity. "You're in love with Ranjeesh?"

"What's that got to do with it?" A wrinkle creased her brow: it was the perfect symptom of her mood, the line a cartoonist might have chosen to express petulant anger.

"Nothing. Not if it doesn't have anything to do with it." He tried a grin, but to no effect. "Well," he said after a pause. "How do you like Katmandu?"

"I don't get out much," she said flatly.

She obviously did not want conversation, but Eliot wasn't ready to give up. "You ought to," he said. "The festival of Indra Jatra's about to start. It's pretty wild. Especially on the night of White Bhairab. Buffalo sacrifices, torchlight. . . ."

"I don't like crowds," she said.

Strike two.

Eliot strained to think of an enticing topic, but he had the idea it was a lost cause. There was something inert about her, a veneer of listlessness redolent of Thorazine, of hospital routine. "Have you seen the Khaa?" he asked.

"The what?"

"The Khaa. It's a spirit . . . though some people will tell you it's partly animal, because over here the animal and spirit worlds overlap. But whatever it is, all the old houses

have one, and those that don't are considered unlucky.
There's one here."

"What's it look like?"

"Vaguely anthropomorphic. Black, featureless. Kind of
a living shadow. They can stand upright, but they roll instead of walk."

She laughed. "No, I haven't seen it. Have you?"

"Maybe," said Eliot. "I thought I saw it a couple of times,
but I was pretty stoned."

She sat up straighter and crossed her legs; her breasts
jiggled and Eliot fought to keep his eyes centered on her
face. "Ranjeesh tells me you're a little cracked," she said.

Good ol' Ranjeesh! He might have known that the son
of a bitch would have sandbagged him with his new lady.
"I guess I am," he said, preparing for the brush-off. "I do
a lot of meditation, and sometimes I teeter on the edge."

But she appeared more intrigued by this admission than
by anything else he had told her; a smile melted up from
her carefully composed features. "Tell me some more about
the Khaa," she said.

Eliot congratulated himself. "They're quirky sorts," he
said. "Neither good nor evil. They hide in dark corners,
though now and then they're seen in the streets or in the
fields out near Jyapu. And the oldest ones, the most powerful
ones, live in the temples in Durbar Square. There's a story
about the one here that's descriptive of how they operate
. . . if you're interested."

"Sure." Another smile.

"Before Ranjeesh bought this place, it was a guesthouse,
and one night a woman with three goiters on her neck came
to spend the night. She had two loaves of bread that she
was taking home to her family, and she stuck them under
her pillow before going to sleep. Around midnight the Khaa
rolled into her room and was struck by the sight of her
goiters rising and falling as she breathed. He thought they'd
make a beautiful necklace, so he took them and put them
on his own neck. Then he spotted the loaves sticking out

from her pillow. They looked good, so he took them as well and replaced them with two loaves of gold. When the woman woke, she was delighted. She hurried back to her village to tell her family, and on the way she met a friend, a woman who was going to market. This woman had four goiters. The first woman told her what had happened, and that night the second woman went to the guesthouse and did exactly the same things. Around midnight the Khaa rolled into her room. He'd grown bored with his necklace, and he gave it to the woman. He'd also decided that bread didn't taste very good, but he still had a loaf and he figured he'd give it another chance. So in exchange for the necklace, he took the woman's appetite for bread. When she woke, she had seven goiters, no gold, and she could never eat bread again the rest of her life."

Eliot had expected a response of mild amusement, and had hoped that the story would be the opening gambit in a game with a foregone and pleasurable conclusion; but he had not expected her to stand, to become walled off from him again.

"I've got to go," she said, and with a distracted wave she made for the front door. She walked with her head down, hands thrust into her pockets, as if counting the steps.

"Where are you going?" called Eliot, taken back.

"I don't know. Freak Street, maybe."

"Want some company?"

She turned back at the door. "It's not your fault," she said, "but I don't really enjoy your company."

Shot down!

Trailing smoke, spinning, smacking into the hillside, and blowing up into a fireball.

Eliot didn't understand why it had hit him so hard. It had happened before, and it would again. Ordinarily he would have headed for Temal and found himself another long white scarf and pair of cotton trousers, one less morbidly self-involved (that, in retrospect, was how he characterized Michaela), one who would help him refuel for another bout of trying to visualize Avalokitesvara Buddha. He did, in fact, go to Temal; but he merely sat and drank tea and smoked hashish in a restaurant, and watched the young travelers pairing up for the night. Once he caught the bus to Patan and visited a friend, an old hippie pal named Sam Chipley who ran a medical clinic; once he walked out to Swayambhunath, close enough to see the white dome of the stupa, and, atop it, the gilt structure on which the all-seeing eyes of Buddha were painted: they seemed squinty and mean-looking, as if taking unfavorable notice of his approach. But mostly over the next week he wandered through Mr. Chatterji's house, carrying a bottle, maintaining a buzz, and keeping an eye on Michaela.

The majority of the rooms were unfurnished, but many bore signs of recent habitation: broken hash pipes, ripped sleeping bags, empty packets of incense. Mr. Chatterji let travelers—those he fancied sexually, male and female— use the rooms for up to months at a time, and to walk through them was to take a historical tour of the American counterculture. The graffiti spoke of concerns as various as Vietnam, the Sex Pistols, women's lib, and the housing shortage in Great Britain, and also conveyed personal messages: "Ken Finkel please get in touch with me at Am. Ex. in Bangkok . . . love Ruth." In one of the rooms was a complicated mural depicting Farrah Fawcett sitting on the lap of a Tibetan demon, throttling his barbed phallus with her fingers. It all conjured up the image of a moldering, deranged milieu. Eliot's milieu. At first the tour amused him, but eventually it began to sour him on himself, and he took to spending more and more time on a balcony overlooking the courtyard that was shared with the connecting house, listening to the Newari women sing at their chores and reading books from Mr. Chatterji's library. One of the books was titled *The Carversville Terror*.

". . . bloodcurdling, chilling. . . ." said the *New York Times* on the front flap. ". . . the Terror is unrelenting. . . ." commented Stephen King. ". . . riveting, gut-wrenching, mind-bending horror. . . ." gushed *People* magazine. In neat letters, Eliot appended his own blurb: ". . . piece of crap. . . ." The text—written to be read by the marginally literate—was a fictionalized treatment of purportedly real events dealing with the experiences of the Whitcomb family, who had attempted to renovate the Cousineau mansion during the sixties. Following the usual buildup of apparitions, cold spots, and noisome odors, the family—Papa David, Mama Elaine, young sons Tim and Randy, and teenage Ginny—had met to discuss the situation.

Even the kids, thought David, had been aged by the house. Gathered around the dining room table, they looked like a company of the damned—haggard, shadows under their eyes, grim-faced. Even with the windows open and the light streaming in, it seemed there was a pall in the air that no light could dispel. Thank God the damned thing was dormant during the day!

"Well," he said, "I guess the floor's open for arguments."

"I wanna go home!" Tears sprang from Randy's eyes, and on cue, Tim started crying too.

"It's not that simple," said David. "This *is* home, and I don't know how we'll make it if we do leave. The savings account is just about flat."

"I suppose I could get a job," said Elaine unenthusiastically.

"I'm not leaving!" Ginny jumped to her feet, knocking over her chair. "Every time I start to make friends, we have to move!"

"But Ginny!" Elaine reached out a hand to calm her. "You were the one. . . ."

"I've changed my mind!" She backed away, as if she had just recognized them all to be mortal enemies. "You can do what you want, but I'm staying!" And she ran from the room.

"Oh, God," said Elaine wearily. "What's gotten into her?"

What had gotten into Ginny, what was in the process of getting into her and was the only interesting part of the book, was the spirit of Aimée Cousineau. Concerned with his daughter's behavior, David Whitcomb had researched the house and learned a great deal about the spirit. Aimée Cousineau, née Vuillemont, had been a native of St. Berenice, a Swiss village at the foot of the mountain known as the Eiger (its photograph, as well as one of Aimée—a coldly beautiful woman with black hair and cameo features—was included in the central section of the book). Until the age of fifteen, she had been a sweet, unexceptional child; however, in the summer of 1889, while hiking on the slopes of the Eiger, she had become lost in a cave.

The family had all but given up hope, when, to their delight—three weeks later—she had turned up on the steps of her father's store. Their delight was short-lived. This Aimée was far different from the one who had entered the cave. Violent, calculating, slatternly.

Over the next two years, she succeeded in seducing half the men of the village, including the local priest. According to his testimony, he had been admonishing her that sin was not the path to happiness, when she began to undress. "I'm wed to Happiness," she told him. "I've entwined my limbs with the God of Bliss and kissed the scaly thighs of Joy." Throughout the ensuing affair, she made cryptic comments concerning "the God below the mountain," whose soul was now forever joined to hers.

At this point the book reverted to the gruesome adventures of the Whitcomb family, and Eliot, bored, realizing it was noon and that Michaela would be sunbathing, climbed to Mr. Chatterji's apartment on the fourth floor. He tossed the book onto a shelf and went out onto the balcony. His continued interest in Michaela puzzled him. It occurred to him that he might be falling in love, and he thought that would be nice. Though it would probably lead nowhere, love would be a good kind of energy to have. But he doubted this was the case. Most likely his interest was founded on some fuming product of the dark stone inside him. Simple lust. He looked over the edge of the balcony. She was lying on a blanket—her bikini top beside her—at the bottom of a well of sunlight: thin, pure sunlight like a refinement of honey spreading down and congealing into the mold of a little gold woman. It seemed her heat that was in the air.

That night Eliot broke one of Mr. Chatterji's rules and slept in the master bedroom. It was roofed by a large skylight mounted in a ceiling painted midnight blue. The normal display of stars had not been sufficient for Mr. Chatterji, and so he'd had the skylight constructed of faceted glass that multiplied the stars, making it appear that you were at the heart of a galaxy, gazing out between the interstices of its blazing core. The walls consisted of a photomural of the Khumbu Glacier and Chomolungma; and, bathed in the starlight, the mural had acquired the illusion of depth and chill mountain silence. Lying there, Eliot could hear the faint sounds of Indra Jatra: shouts and cymbals, oboes and drums. He was drawn to the sounds; he wanted to run out into the streets, become an element of the drunken crowds, be whirled through torchlight and delirium to the feet of an idol stained with sacrificial blood. But he felt bound to the house, to Michaela. Marooned in the glow of Mr. Chatterji's starlight, floating above Chomolungma and listening to the din of the world below, he could almost believe he was a bodhisattva awaiting a call to action, that his watchfulness had some purpose.

The shipment arrived late in the afternoon of the eighth day. Five enormous crates, each requiring the combined energies of Eliot and three Newari workmen to wrangle up to the third-floor room that housed Mr. Chatterji's collection. After tipping the men, Eliot—sweaty, panting—sat down against the wall to catch his breath. The room was about twenty-five feet by fifteen, but looked smaller because of the dozens of curious objects standing around the floor and mounted one above the other on the walls. A brass doorknob, a shattered door, a straight-back chair whose arms were bound with a velvet rope to prevent anyone from sitting, a discolored sink, a mirror streaked by a brown stain, a slashed lampshade. They were all relics of some haunting or possession, some grotesque violence, and there were cards affixed to them testifying to the details and referring those who were interested to materials in Mr. Chatterji's library. Sitting surrounded by these relics, the crates looked innocuous. Bolted shut, chest-high, branded with customs stamps.

When he had recovered, Eliot strolled around the room, amused by the care that Mr. Chatterji had squandered on his hobby; the most amusing thing was that no one except Mr. Chatterji was impressed by it: it provided travelers with a footnote for their journals. Nothing more.

A wave of dizziness swept over him—he had stood too soon—and he leaned against one of the crates for support. Jesus, he was in lousy shape! And then, as he blinked away the tangles of opaque cells drifting across his field of vision, the crate shifted. Just a little shift, as if something inside had twitched in its sleep. But palpable, real. He flung himself toward the door, backing away. A chill mapped every knob and articulation of his spine, and his sweat had evaporated, leaving clammy patches on his skin. The crate was motionless. But he was afraid to take his eyes off it, certain that if he did, it would release its pent-up fury. "Hi," said Michaela from the doorway.

Her voice electrified Eliot. He let out a squawk and wheeled around, his hands outheld to ward off attack.

"I didn't mean to startle you," she said. "I'm sorry."

"Goddamn!" he said. "Don't sneak up like that!" He remembered the crate and glanced back at it. "Listen, I was just locking. . . ."

"I'm sorry," she repeated, and walked past him into the

room. "Ranjeesh is such an idiot about all this," she said, running her hand over the top of the crate. "Don't you think?"

Her familiarity with the crate eased Eliot's apprehension. Maybe he had been the one who had twitched: a spasm of overstrained muscles. "Yeah, I guess."

She walked over to the straight-back chair, slipped off the velvet rope, and sat down. She was wearing a pale brown skirt and a plaid blouse that made her look schoolgirlish. "I want to apologize about the other day," she said; she bowed her head, and the fall of her hair swung forward to obscure her face. "I've been having a bad time lately. I have trouble relating to people. To anything. But since we're living here together, I'd like to be friends." She stood and spread the folds of her skirt. "See? I even put on different clothes. I could tell the others offended you."

The innocent sexuality of the pose caused Eliot to have a rush of desire. "Looks nice," he said with forced casualness. "Why've you been having a bad time?"

She wandered to the door and gazed out. "Do you really want to hear about it?"

"Not if it's painful for you."

"It doesn't matter," she said, leaning against the doorframe. "I was in a band back in the States, and we were doing okay. Cutting an album, talking to record labels. I was living with the guitarist, in love with him. But then I had an affair. Not even an affair. It was stupid. Meaningless. I still don't know why I did it. The heat of the moment, I guess. That's what rock 'n' roll's all about, and maybe I was just acting out the myth. One of the other musicians told my boyfriend. That's the way bands are—you're friends with everyone, but never at the same time. See, I told this guy about the affair. We'd always confided. But one day he got mad at me over something. Something else stupid and meaningless." Her chin was struggling to stay firm; the breeze from the courtyard drifted fine strands of hair across her face. "My boyfriend went crazy and beat up my. . . ."

She gave a dismal laugh. "I don't know what to call him. My lover. Whatever. My boyfriend killed him. It was an accident, but he tried to run, and the police shot him."

Eliot wanted to stop her; she was obviously seeing it all again, seeing blood and police flashers and cold white morgue lights. But she was riding a wave of memory, borne along by its energy, and he knew that she had to crest with it, crash with it.

"I was out of it for a while. Dreamy. Nothing touched me. Not the funerals, the angry parents. I went away for months, to the mountains, and I started to feel better. But when I came home, I found that the musician who'd told my boyfriend had written a song about it. The affair, the killings. He'd cut a record. People were buying it, singing the hook when they walked down the street or took a shower. Dancing to it! They were dancing on blood and bones, humming grief, shelling out $5.98 for a jingle about suffering. Looking back, I realize I was crazy, but at the time everything I did seemed normal. More than normal. Directed, inspired. I bought a gun. A ladies' model, the salesman said. I remember thinking how strange it was that there were male and female guns, just like with electric razors. I felt enormous carrying it. I had to be meek and polite or else I was sure people would notice how large and purposeful I was. It wasn't hard to track down Ronnie—that's the guy who wrote the song. He was in Germany, cutting a second album. I couldn't believe it, I wasn't going to be able to kill him! I was so frustrated that one night I went down to a park and started shooting. I missed everything. Out of all the bums and joggers and squirrels, I hit leaves and air. They locked me up after that. A hospital. I think it helped, but. . . ." She blinked, waking from a trance. "But I still feel so disconnected, you now?"

Eliot carefully lifted away the strands of hair that had blown across her face and laid them back in place. Her smile flickered. "I know," he said. "I feel that way sometimes."

She nodded thoughtfully, as if to verify that she had recognized this quality in him.

They ate dinner in a Tibetan place in Temal; it had no name and was a dump with flyspecked tables and rickety chairs, specializing in water buffalo and barley soup. But it was away from the city center, which meant they could avoid the worst of the festival crowds. The waiter was a young Tibetan wearing jeans and a T-shirt that bore the legend MAGIC IS THE ANSWER; the earphones of personal stereo dangled about his neck. The walls—visible through a haze of smoke—were covered with snapshots, most featuring the waiter in the company of various tourists, but a few showing an older Tibetan in blue robes and turquoise jewelry, carrying an automatic rifle; this was the owner, one of the Khampa tribesmen who had fought a guerrilla war against the Chinese. He rarely put in an appearance at the restaurant, and when he did, his glowering presence tended to dampen conversation.

Over dinner, Eliot tried to steer clear of topics that might unsettle Michaela. He told her about Sam Chipley's clinic, the time the Dalai Lama had come to Katmandu, the musicians at Swayambhunath. Cheerful, exotic topics. Her listlessness was such an inessential part of her that Eliot was led to chip away at it, curious to learn what lay beneath; and the more he chipped away, the more animated her gestures, the more luminous her smile became. This was a different sort of smile than she had displayed on their first meeting. It came so suddenly over her face, it seemed an autonomic reaction, like the opening of a sunflower, as if she were facing not you but the principle of light upon which you were grounded. It was aware of you, of course, but it chose to see past the imperfections of the flesh and know the perfected thing you truly were. It boosted your sense of worth to realize that you were its target, and Eliot—whose sense of worth was at low ebb—would have done pratfalls to sustain it. Even when he told his own story, he told it as a joke, a metaphor for American misconceptions of Oriental pursuits.

"Why don't you quit it?" she asked. "The meditation, I mean. If it's not working out, why keep on with it?"

"My life's in perfect suspension," he said. "I'm afraid that if I quit practicing, if I change anything, I'll either sink to the bottom or fly off." He tapped his spoon against his cup, signaling for more tea. "You're not really going to marry Ranjeesh, are you?" he asked, and was surprised at the concern he felt that she actually might.

"Probably not." The waiter poured their tea, whispery drumbeats issuing from his earphones. "I was just feeling lost. You see, my parents sued Ronnie over the song, and I ended up with a lot of money—which made me feel even worse. . . ."

"Let's not talk about it," he said.

"It's all right." She touched his wrist, reassuring, and the skin remained warm after her fingers had withdrawn. "Anyway," she went on, "I decided to travel, and all the strangeness . . . I don't know. I was starting to slip away. Ranjeesh was a kind of sanctuary."

Eliot was vastly relieved.

Outside, the streets were thronged with festivalgoers, and Michaela took Eliot's arm and let him guide her through the crowds. Newar wearing Nehru hats and white trousers that bagged at the hips and wrapped tightly around the calves; groups of tourists, shouting and waving bottles of rice beer; Indians in white robes and saris. The air was spiced with incense, and the strip of empurpled sky above was so regularly patterned with stars that it looked like a banner draped between the roofs. Near the house, a wild-eyed man in a blue satin robe rushed past, bumping into them, and he was followed by two boys dragging a goat, its forehead smeared with crimson powder: a sacrifice.

"This is crazy!" Michaela laughed.

"It's nothing. Wait'll tomorrow night."

"What happens then?"

"The night of White Bhairab." Eliot put on a grimace.
"You'll have to watch yourself. Bhairab's a lusty, wrathful
sort."

She laughed again and gave his arm an affectionate squeeze.

Inside the house, the moon—past full, blank, and
golden—floated dead center of the square of night sky admitted by the roof. They stood close together in the courtyard, silent, suddenly awkward.

"I enjoyed tonight," said Michaela; she leaned forward
and brushed his cheek with her lips. "Thank you," she
whispered.

Eliot caught her as she drew back, tipped her chin, and
kissed her mouth. Her lips parted, her tongue darted out.
Then she pushed him away. "I'm tired," she said, her face
tightened with anxiety. She walked off a few steps, but
stopped and turned back. "If you want to . . . to be with
me, maybe it'll be all right. We could try."

Eliot went to her and took her hands. "I want to make
love with you," he said, no longer trying to hide his urgency.
And that *was* what he wanted: to make love. Not to ball or
bang or screw or any other inelegant version of the act.

But it was not love they made.

Under the starlit blaze of Mr. Chatterji's ceiling, she was
very beautiful, and at first she was very loving, moving with
a genuine involvement; then abruptly, she quit moving
altogether and turned her face to the pillow.

Her eyes were glistening. Left alone atop her, listening
to the animal sound of his breathing, the impact of his flesh
against hers, Eliot knew he should stop and comfort her.
But the months of abstinence, the eight days of wanting
her, all this fused into a bright flare in the small of his back,
a reactor core of lust that irradiated his conscience, and he
continued to plunge into her, hurrying to completion. She
let out a gasp when he withdrew, and curled up, facing
away from him.

"God, I'm so sorry," she said, her voice cracked.

Eliot shut his eyes. He felt sickened, reduced to the bestial. It had been like two mental patients doing nasty on the sly, two fragments of people who together didn't form a whole. He understood now why Mr. Chatterji wanted to marry her: he planned to add her to his collection, to enshrine her with the other splinters of violence. And each night he would complete his revenge, substantiate his cultural overview, by making something less than love with this sad, inert girl, this American ghost. Her shoulders shook with muffled sobs. She needed someone to console her, to help her find her own strength and capacity for love. Eliot reached out to her, willing to do his best. But he knew it shouldn't be him.

Several hours later, after she had fallen asleep, unconsolable, Eliot sat in the courtyard, thoughtless, dejected, staring at a rubber plant. It was mired in shadow, its leaves hanging limp. He had been staring for a couple of minutes, when he noticed that a shadow in back of the plant was swaying ever so slightly; he tried to make it out, and the swaying subsided. He stood. The chair scraped on the concrete, sounding unnaturally loud. His neck prickled, and he glanced behind him. Nothing. Ye Olde Mental Fatigue, he thought. Ye Olde Emotional Strain. He laughed, and the clarity of the laugh—echoing up through the empty well—alarmed him; it seemed to stir little flickers of motion everywhere in the darkness. What he needed was a drink! The problem was how to get into the bedroom without waking Michaela. Hell, maybe he should wake her. Maybe they should talk more before what had happened hardened into a set of unbreakable attitudes.

He turned toward the stairs . . . and then, yelling out in panic, entangling his feet with the lawn chairs as he leapt backward midstep, he fell onto his side. A shadow—roughly man-shaped and man-sized—was standing a yard away; it was undulating the way a strand of kelp undulates in a gentle tide. The patch of air around it was rippling, as if the entire image had been badly edited into reality. Eliot scrambled away, coming to his knees. The shadow melted downward,

puddling on the cement; it bunched in the middle like a
caterpillar, folded over itself, and flowed after him: a rolling
sort of motion. Then it reared up, again assuming its man-
like shape, looming over him.

Eliot got to his feet, still frightened, but less so. If he had
previously been asked to testify as to the existence of the
Khaa, he would have rejected the evidence of his bleared
senses and come down on the side of hallucination, folktale.
But now, though he was tempted to draw that same conclusion, there was too much evidence to the contrary. Staring at the featureless black cowl of the Khaa's head, he had
a sense of something staring back. More than a sense. A
distinct impression of personality. It was as if the Khaa's
undulations were producing a breeze that bore its psychic
odor through the air. Eliot began to picture it as a loony,
shy old uncle who liked to sit under the basement steps and
eat flies and cackle to himself, but who could tell when the
first frost was due and knew how to fix the tail on your kite.
Weird, yet harmless. The Khaa stretched out an arm: the
arm just peeled away from its torso, its hand a thumbless
black mitten. Eliot edged back. He wasn't quite prepared
to believe it was harmless. But the arm stretched farther
than he had thought possible and enveloped his wrist. It
was soft, ticklish, a river of furry moths crawling over his
skin.

In the instant before he jumped away, Eliot heard a
whining note inside his skull, and that whining—seeming
to flow through his brain with the same suppleness that the
Khaa's arm had displayed—was translated into a wordless
plea. From it he understood that the Khaa was afraid. Terribly afraid. Suddenly it melted downward and went rolling,
bunching, flowing up the stairs; it stopped on the first landing, rolled halfway down, then up again, repeating the
process over and over. It came clear to Eliot (*Oh, Jesus!
This is nuts!*) that it was trying to convince him to follow.
Just like Lassie or some other ridiculous TV animal, it was
trying to tell him something, to lead him to where the

wounded forest ranger had fallen, where the nest of baby ducks was being threatened by the brush fire. He should walk over, rumple its head, and say, "What's the matter, girl? Those squirrels been teasing you?" This time his laughter had a sobering effect, acting to settle his thoughts. One likelihood was that his experience with Michaela had been sufficient to snap his frayed connection with consensus reality; but there was no point in buying that. Even if that were the case, he might as well go with it. He crossed to the stairs and climbed toward the rippling shadow on the landing.

"Okay, Bongo," he said. "Let's see what's got you so excited."

On the third floor, the Khaa turned down a hallway, moving fast, and Eliot didn't see it again until he was approaching the room that housed Mr. Chatterji's collection. It was standing beside the door, flapping its arms, apparently indicating that he should enter. Eliot remembered the crate.

"No, thanks," he said. A drop of sweat slid down his rib cage, and he realized that it was unusually warm next to the door.

The Khaa's hand flowed over the doorknob, enveloping it, and when the hand pulled back, it was bulging, oddly deformed, and there was a hole through the wood where the lock mechanism had been. The door swung open a couple of inches. Darkness leaked out of the room, adding an oily essence to the air. Eliot took a backward step. The Khaa dropped the lock mechanism—it materialized from beneath the formless black hand and clattered to the floor —and latched onto Eliot's arm. Once again he heard the whining, the plea for help, and, since he did not jump away, he had a clearer understanding of the process of translation. He could feel the whining as a cold fluid coursing through his brain, and as the whining died, the message simply appeared—the way an image might appear in a crystal ball. There was an undertone of reassurance to the

Khaa's fear, and though Eliot knew this was the mistake people in horror movies were always making, he reached inside the room and fumbled for the wall switch, half expecting to be snatched up and savaged. He flicked on the light and pushed the door open with his foot.

And wished that he hadn't.

The crates had exploded. Splinters and shards of wood were scattered everywhere, and the bricks had been heaped at the center of the room. They were dark red, friable bricks like crumbling cakes of dried blood, and each was marked with black letters and numbers that signified its original position in the fireplace. But none were in their proper position now, though they were quite artfully arranged. They had been piled into the shape of a mountain, one that—despite the crudity of its building blocks—duplicated the sheer faces and chimneys and gentle slopes of a real mountain. Eliot recognized it from its photograph. The Eiger. It towered to the ceiling, and under the glare of the lights it gave off a radiation of ugliness and barbarity. It seemed alive, a fang of dark red meat, and the charred smell of the bricks was like a hum in Eliot's nostrils.

Ignoring the Khaa, who was again flapping its arms, Eliot broke for the landing; there he paused, and after a brief struggle between fear and conscience, he sprinted up the stairs to the bedroom, taking them three at a time. Michaela was gone! He stared at the starlit billows of the sheets. Where the hell . . . her room! He hurtled down the stairs and fell sprawling on the second-floor landing. Pain lanced through his kneecap, but he came to his feet running, certain that something was behind him.

A seam of reddish orange light—not lamplight—edged the bottom of Michaela's door, and he heard a crispy chuckling in a hearth. The wood was warm to the touch. Eliot's hand hovered over the doorknob. His heart seemed to have swelled to the size of a basketball and was doing a fancy dribble against his chest wall. The sensible thing to do would be to get out quick, because whatever lay beyond the door was bound to be too much for him to handle. But instead he did the stupid thing and burst into the room.

His first impression was that the room was burning, but then he saw that though the fire looked real, it did not spread; the flames clung to the outlines of things that were themselves unreal, that had no substance of their own and were made of the ghostly fire: belted drapes, an overstuffed chair and sofa, a carved mantelpiece, all of antique design. The actual furniture—production-line junk—was undamaged. Intense reddish-orange light glowed around the bed, and at its heart lay Michaela. Naked, her back arched. Lengths of her hair lifted into the air and tangled, floating in an invisible current; the muscles of her legs and abdomen were coiling, bunching, as if she were shedding her skin. The crackling grew louder, and the light began to rise from the bed to form into a column of even brighter light; it narrowed at the midpoint, bulged in an approximation of hips and breasts, gradually assuming the shape of a burning woman. She was faceless, a fiery silhouette. Her flickering gown shifted as with the movements of walking, and flames leapt out behind her head like windblown hair.

Eliot was pumped full of terror, too afraid to scream or run. Her aura of heat and power wrapped around him. Though she was within arm's length, she seemed a long way off, inset into a great distance and walking toward him down a tunnel that conformed exactly to her shape. She stretched out a hand, brushing his cheek with a finger. The touch brought more pain than he had ever known. It was luminous, lighting every circuit of his body. He could feel his skin crisping, cracking, fluids leaking forth and sizzling. He heard himself moan: a gush of rotten sound like something trapped in a drain.

Then she jerked back her hand, as if *he* had burned *her*.

Dazed, his nerves screaming, Eliot slumped to the floor and—through blurred eyes—caught sight of a blackness rippling by the door. The Khaa. The burning woman stood facing it a few feet away. It was such an uncanny scene, this confrontation of fire and darkness, of two supernatural systems, that Eliot was shocked to alertness. He had the idea that neither of them knew what to do. Surrounded by its patch of disturbed air, the Khaa undulated; the burning woman crackled and flickered, embedded in her eerie distance. Tentatively, she lifted her hand; but before she could complete the gesture, the Khaa reached with blinding swiftness and its hand enveloped hers.

A shriek like tortured metal issued from them, as if some ironclad principle had been breached. Dark tendrils wound through the burning woman's arm, seams of fire striped the Khaa, and there was a high-pitched humming, a vibration that jarred Eliot's teeth. For a moment he was afraid that spiritual versions of antimatter and matter had been brought into conjunction, that the room would explode. But the hum was sheared off as the Khaa snatched back its hand: a scrap of reddish-orange flame glimmered within it. The Khaa melted downward and went rolling out the door. The burning woman—and every bit of flame in the room— shrank to an incandescent point and vanished.

Still dazed, Eliot touched his face. It felt burned, but there was no apparent damage. He hauled himself to his feet, staggered to bed, and collapsed next to Michaela. She was breathing deeply, unconscious. "Michaela!" He shook her. She moaned, her head rolled from side to side. He heaved her over his shoulder in a fireman's lift and crept out into the hall. Moving stealthily, he eased along the hall to the balcony overlooking the courtyard and peered over the edge . . . and bit his lip to stifle a cry. Clearly visible in the electric-blue air of the predawn darkness, standing in the middle of the courtyard, was a tall, pale woman wearing a white nightgown. Her black hair fanned across her back. She snapped her head around to stare at him, her cameo features twisted by a gloating smile, and that smile told Eliot everything he had wanted to know about the possibility of escape. Just try to leave, Aimée Cousineau was saying. Go ahead and try. I'd like that. A shadow sprang erect about a dozen feet away from her, and she turned to it. Suddenly there was a wind in the courtyard: a violent, whirling wind of which she was the calm center. Plants went flapping up into the well like leathery birds; pots shattered, and the shards flew toward the Khaa. Slowed by Michaela's weight, wanting to get as far as he could from the battle, Eliot headed up the stairs toward Mr. Chatterji's bedroom.

It was an hour later, an hour of peeking down into the courtyard, watching the game of hide-and-seek that the Khaa was playing with Aimée Cousineau, realizing that the Khaa was protecting them by keeping her busy . . . it was then that Eliot remembered the book. He retrieved it from the shelf and began to skim through it, hoping to learn something helpful. There was nothing else to do. He picked up at the point of Aimée's rap about her marriage to Happiness, passed over the transformation of Ginny Whitcomb into a teenage monster, and found a second section dealing with Aimée.

In 1895 a wealthy Swiss-American named Armand Cousineau had returned to St. Berenice—his birthplace—for a visit. He was smitten with Aimée Vuillemont, and her family, seizing the opportunity to be rid of her, allowed Cousineau to marry Aimée and sail her off to his home in Carversville, New Hampshire. Aimée's taste for seduction had not been curbed by the move. Lawyers, deacons, merchants, farmers: they were all grist for her mill. But in the winter of 1905 she fell in love—obsessively, passionately in love—with a young schoolmaster. She believed that the schoolmaster had saved her from her unholy marriage, and her gratitude knew no bounds. Unfortunately, when the schoolmaster fell in love with another woman, neither did her fury. One night while passing the Cousineau mansion, the town doctor spotted a woman walking the grounds. "A woman of flame, not burning but composed of flame, her every particular a fiery construct. . . ." Smoke was curling from a window; the doctor rushed inside and discovered the schoolmaster wrapped in chains, burning like a log in the vast fireplace. He put out the small blaze spreading from the hearth, and on going back onto the grounds, he stumbled over Aimée's charred corpse.

It was not clear whether Aimée's death had been accidental, a stray spark catching on her nightgown, or the result of suicide; but it *was* clear that thereafter the mansion had been haunted by a spirit who delighted in possessing women and driving them to kill their men. The spirit's supernatural powers were limited by the flesh, but were augmented by immense physical strength. Ginny Whitcomb, for example, had killed her brother Tim by twisting off his arm, and then had gone after her other brother and her father, a harrowing chase that had lasted a day and a night: while in possession of a body, the spirit was not limited to nocturnal activity. . . .

Christ!

The light coming through the skylight was gray.

They were safe!

Eliot went to the bed and began shaking Michaela. She moaned, her eyes blinked open. "Wake up!" he said. "We've got to get out!"

"What?" She batted at his hands. "What are you talking about?"

"Don't you remember?"

"Remember what?" She swung her legs onto the floor, sitting with her head down, stunned by wakefulness; she stood, swayed, and said, "God, what did you do to me? I feel. . . ." A dull, suspicious expression washed over her face.

"We have to leave." He walked around the bed to her. "Ranjeesh hit the jackpot. Those crates of his had an honest-to-God spirit packed in with the bricks. Last night it tried to possess you." He saw her disbelief. "You must have blanked out. Here." He offered the book. "This'll explain. . . ."

"Oh, God!" she shouted. "What did you do? I'm all raw inside!" She backed away, eyes wide with fright.

"I didn't do anything." He held out his palms as if to prove he had no weapons.

"You raped me! While I was asleep!" She looked left, right, in a panic.

"That's ridiculous!"

"You must have drugged me or something! Oh, God! Go away!"

"I won't argue," he said. "We have to get out. After that you can turn me in for rape or whatever. But we're leaving, even if I have to drag you."

Some of her desperation evaporated, her shoulders sagged.

"Look," he said, moving closer. "I didn't rape you. What you're feeling is something that goddamn spirit did to you. It was. . . ."

She brought her knee up into his groin.

As he writhed on the floor, curled up around the pain, Eliot heard the door open and her footsteps receding. He caught at the edge of the bed, hauled himself to his knees, and vomited all over the sheets. He fell back and lay there for several minutes, until the pain had dwindled to a powerful throbbing, a throbbing that jolted his heart into the same rhythm; then, gingerly, he stood and shuffled out into the hall. Leaning on the railing, he eased down the stairs to Michaela's room and lowered himself into a sitting position. He let out a shuddering sigh. Actinic flashes burst in front of his eyes.

"Michaela," he said. "Listen to me." His voice sounded feeble: the voice of an old, old man.

"I've got a knife," she said from just behind the door. "I'll use it if you try to break in."

"I wouldn't worry about that," he said. "And I sure as hell wouldn't worry about being raped. Now, will you listen?"

No response.

He told her everything, and when he was done, she said, "You're insane. You raped me."

"I wouldn't hurt you. I . . . ." He had been on the verge of telling her he loved her, but decided it probably wasn't true. He probably just wished that he had a good, clean truth like love. The pain was making him nauseated again, as if the blackish-purple stain of his bruises were seeping up into his stomach and filling him with bad gases. He struggled to his feet and leaned against the wall. There was no point in arguing, and there was not much hope that she would leave the house on her own, not if she reacted to Aimée like Ginny Whitcomb. The only solution was to go to the police, accuse her of some crime. Assault. She would accuse him of rape, but with luck they would both be held overnight. And he would have time to wire Mr. Chatterji . . . who would believe him. Mr. Chatterji was by nature a believer: it simply hadn't fit his notion of sophistication to give credence to his native spirits. He'd be on the first flight from Delhi, eager to document the Terror.

Himself eager to get it over, Eliot negotiated the stairs and hobbled across the courtyard; but the Khaa was waiting, flapping its arms in the shadowed alcove that led to the street. Whether it was an effect of the light or of its battle with Aimée, or, specifically, of the pale scrap of fire visible within its hand, the Khaa looked less substantial. Its blackness was somewhat opaque, and the air around it was blurred, smeary, like waves over a lens: it was as if the Khaa were being submerged more deeply in its own medium. Eliot felt no compunction about allowing it to touch him; he was grateful to it, and his relaxed attitude seemed to intensify the communication. He began to see images in his mind's eye: Michaela's face, Aimée's, and then the two faces were superimposed. He was shown this over and over, and he understood from it that the Khaa wanted the possession to take place. But he didn't understand why. More images. Himself running, Michaela running, Durbar Square, the mask of White Bhairab, the Khaa. Lots of Khaa. Little black hieroglyphs. These images were repeated, too, and after each sequence the Khaa would hold its hand up to his face and display the glimmering scrap of Aimée's fire. Eliot thought he understood, but whenever he tried to convey that he wasn't sure, the Khaa merely repeated the images.

At last, realizing that the Khaa had reached the limits of its ability to communicate, Eliot headed for the street. The Khaa melted down, reared up in the doorway to block his path, and flapped its arms desperately. Once again Eliot had a sense of its weird-old-man-ness. It went against logic to put his trust in such an erratic creature, especially in such a dangerous plan; but logic had little hold on him, and this was a permanent solution. If it worked. If he hadn't misread it. He laughed. The hell with it!

"Take it easy, Bongo," he said. "I'll be back as soon as I get my shootin' iron fixed."

The waiting room of Sam Chipley's clinic was crowded with Newari mothers and children, who giggled as Eliot did a bowlegged shuffle through their midst. Sam's wife led him into the examination room, where Sam—a burly, bearded man, his long hair tied in a ponytail—helped him onto a surgical table.

"Holy shit!" he said after inspecting the injury. "What you been into, man?" He began rubbing ointment into the bruises.

"Accident," gritted Eliot, trying not to cry out.

"Yeah, I bet," said Sam. "Maybe a sexy little accident who had a change of heart when it come down to strokes. You know, not gettin' it steady might tend to make you a tad intense for some ladies, man. Ever think about that?"

"That's not how it was. Am I all right?"

"Yeah, but you ain't gonna be superstud for a while." Sam went to the sink and washed his hands. "Don't gimme that innocent bullshit. You were tryin' to slip it to Chatterji's new squeeze, right?"

"You know her?"

"He brought her over one day, showin' her off. She's a head case, man. You should know better."

"Will I be able to run?"

Sam laughed. "Not hardly."

"Listen, Sam." Eliot sat up, winced. "Chatterji's lady. She's in bad trouble, and I'm the only one who can help her. I have to be able to run, and I need something to keep me awake. I haven't slept for a couple of days."

"I ain't givin' you pills, Eliot. You can stagger through your doper phase without my help." Sam finished drying his hands and went to sit on a stool beside the window; beyond the window was a brick wall, and atop it a string of prayer flags snapped in the breeze.

"I'm not after a supply, dammit! Just enough to keep me going tonight. This is important, Sam!"

Sam scratched his neck. "What kind of trouble she in?"

"I can't tell you now," said Eliot, knowing that Sam would laugh at the idea of something as metaphysically suspect as the Khaa. "But I will tomorrow. It's not illegal. Come on, man! There's got to be something you can give me."

"Oh, I can fix you up. I can make you feel like King Shit on Coronation Day." Sam mulled it over. "Okay, Eliot. But you get your ass back here tomorrow and tell me what's happenin'." He gave a snort of amusement. "All I can say is it must be some strange damn trouble for you to be the only one who can save her."

After wiring Mr. Chatterji, urging him to come home at once, Eliot returned to the house and unscrewed the hinges of the front door. He was not certain that Aimée would be able to control the house, to slam doors and make windows stick as she had with her house in New Hampshire, but he didn't want to take any chances. As he lifted the door and set it against the wall of the alcove, he was amazed by its lightness; he felt possessed of a giddy strength, capable of heaving the door up through the well of the courtyard and over the roofs. The cocktail of painkillers and speed was working wonders. His groin ached, but the ache was distant, far removed from the center of his consciousness, which was a fount of well-being. When he had finished with the door, he grabbed some fruit juice from the kitchen and went back to the alcove to wait.

In midafternoon Michaela came downstairs. Eliot tried to talk to her, to convince her to leave, but she warned him to keep away and scuttled back to her room. Then, around five o'clock, the burning woman appeared, floating a few feet above the courtyard floor. The sun had withdrawn to the upper third of the well, and her fiery silhouette was inset into slate-blue shadow, the flames of her hair dancing about her head. Eliot, who had been hitting the painkillers heavily, was dazzled by her: had she been a hallucination, she would have made his all-time top ten. But even realizing that she was not, he was too drugged to relate to her as a threat. He snickered and shied a piece of broken pot at her. She shrank to an incandescent point, vanished, and that brought home to him his foolhardiness. He took more speed to counteract his euphoria, and did stretching exercises to loosen the kinks and to rid himself of the cramped sensation in his chest.

Twilight blended the shadows in the courtyard, celebrants passed in the street, and he could hear distant drums and cymbals. He felt cut off from the city, the festival. Afraid. Not even the presence of the Khaa, half merged with the shadows along the wall, served to comfort him. Near dusk, Aimée Cousineau walked into the courtyard and stopped about twenty feet away, staring at him. He had no desire to laugh or throw things. At this distance he could see that her eyes had no whites or pupils or irises. They were dead black. One moment they seemed to be the bulging head of black screws threaded into her skull; the next they seemed to recede into blackness, into a cave beneath a mountain where something waited to teach the joys of hell to whoever wandered in. Eliot sidled closer to the door. But she turned, climbed the stairs to the second landing, and walked down Michaela's hallway.

Eliot's waiting began in earnest.

An hour passed. He paced between the door and the courtyard. His mouth was cottony; his joints felt brittle, held together by frail wires of speed and adrenaline. This was insane! All he had done was to put them in worse danger. Finally, he heard a door close upstairs. He backed into the street, bumping into two Newari girls, who giggled and skipped away. Crowds of people were moving toward Durbar Square.

"Eliot!"

Michaela's voice. He'd expected a hoarse, demon voice, and when she walked into the alcove, her white scarf glowing palely against the dark air, he was surprised to see that she was unchanged. Her features held no trace of anything other than her usual listlessness.

"I'm sorry I hurt you," she said, walking toward him. "I know you didn't do anything. I was just upset about last night."

Eliot continued to back away.

"What's wrong?" She stopped in the doorway.

It might have been his imagination, the drugs, but Eliot could have sworn that her eyes were much darker than normal. He trotted off a dozen yards or so and stood looking at her.

"Eliot!"

It was a scream of rage and frustration, and he could scarcely believe the speed with which she darted toward him. He ran full tilt at first, leaping sideways to avoid collisions, veering past alarmed, dark-skinned faces; but after a couple of blocks he found a more efficient rhythm and began to anticipate obstacles, to glide in and out of the crowd. Angry shouts were raised behind him. He glanced back. Michaela was closing the distance, beelining for him, knocking people sprawling with what seemed effortless blows. He ran harder. The crowd grew thicker, and he kept near the walls of the houses, where it was thinnest; but even there it was hard to maintain a good pace. Torches were waved in his face; young men—singing, their arms linked —posed barriers that slowed him further. He could no longer see Michaela, but he could see the wake of her passage. Fists shaking, heads jerking. The entire scene was starting to lose cohesiveness to Eliot. There were screams of torchlight, bright shards of deranged shouts, jostling waves of incense and ordure. He felt like the only solid chunk in a glittering soup that was being poured through a stone trough.

At the edge of Durbar Square, he had a brief glimpse of a shadow standing by the massive gilt doors of Degutale Temple. It was larger and a more anthracitic black than Mr. Chatterji's Khaa: one of the old ones, the powerful ones. The sight buoyed his confidence and restored his equilibrium. He had not misread the plan. But he knew that this was the most dangerous part. He had lost track of Michaela, and the crowd was sweeping him along; if she caught up to him now, he would not be able to run. Fighting for elbow room, struggling to keep his feet, he was borne into the temple complex. The pagoda roofs sloped up into darkness like strangely carved mountains, their peaks hidden by a moonless night; the cobbled paths were narrow, barely ten feet across, and the crowd was being squeezed along them, a lava flow of humanity. Torches bobbed everywhere, sending wild licks of shadow and orange light up the walls, revealing scowling faces on the eaves. Atop its pedestal, the gilt statue of Hanuman—the monkey god—looked to be swaying. Clashing cymbals and arrhythmic drumming scattered Eliot's heartbeat; the sinewy wail of oboes seemed to be graphing the fluctuations of his nerves.

As he swept past Hanuman Dhoka Temple, he caught sight of the brass mask of White Bhairab shining over the heads of the crowd like the face of an evil clown. It was less than a hundred feet away, set in a huge niche in a temple wall and illuminated by light bulbs that hung down among strings of prayer flags. The crowd surged faster, knocking him this way and that; but he managed to spot two more Khaa in the doorway of Hanuman Dhoka. Both melted downward, vanishing, and Eliot's hopes soared. They must have located Michaela, they must be attacking! By the time he had been carried to within a few yards of the mask, he was sure that he was safe. They must have finished her exorcism by now. The only problem left was to find her. That, he realized, had been the weak link in the plan. He'd been an idiot not to have foreseen it. Who knows what might happen if she were to fall in the midst of the crowd. Suddenly he was beneath the pipe that stuck out of the god's mouth; the stream of rice beer arching from it looked translucent under the lights, and as it splashed his face (no fish), its coldness acted to wash away his veneer of chemical strength. He was dizzy, his groin throbbed. The great face, with its fierce fangs and goofy, startled eyes, appeared to be swelling and rocking back and forth. He took a deep breath. The thing to do would be to find a place next to a wall where he could wedge himself against the flow of the crowd, wait until it had thinned, and then search for her. He was about to do that very thing, when two powerful hands gripped his elbows from behind.

Unable to turn, he craned his neck and peered over his shoulder. Michaela smiled at him: a gloating "gotcha!" smile. Her eyes were dead-black ovals. She shaped his name with her mouth, her voice inaudible above the music and shouting, and she began to push him ahead of her, using him as a battering ram to forge a path through the crowd. To anyone watching, it might have appeared that he was running interference for her, but his feet were dangling just off the ground. Angry Newar yelled at him as he knocked them aside. He yelled too. No one noticed. Within seconds they had gotten clear into a side street, threading between groups of drunkards. People laughed at Eliot's cries for help, and one guy imitated the funny, loose-limbed way he was running.

Michaela turned into a doorway, carrying him down a

dirt-floored corridor whose walls were carved into ornate screens; the dusky orange lamplight shining through the screens cast a lacework of shadow on the dirt. The corridor widened to a small courtyard, the age-darkened wood of its walls and doors inlaid with intricate mosaics of ivory. Michaela stopped and slammed him against a wall. He was stunned, but he recognized the place to be one of the old Buddhist temples that surrounded the square. Except for a life-size statue of a golden cow, the courtyard was empty.

"Eliot." The way she said it, it was more of a curse than a name.

He opened his mouth to scream, but she drew him into an embrace; her grip on his right elbow tightened, and her other hand squeezed the back of his neck, pinching off the scream.

"Don't be afraid," she said. "I only want to kiss you."

Her breasts crushed into his chest, her pelvis ground against him in a mockery of passion, and inch by inch she forced his face down to hers. Her lips parted, and—*oh, Christ Jesus!*—Eliot writhed in her grasp, enlivened by a new horror. The inside of her mouth was as black as her eyes. She wanted him to kiss that blackness, the same she had kissed beneath the Eiger. He kicked and clawed with his free hand, but she was irresistible, her hands like iron. His elbow cracked, and brilliant pain shot through his arm. Something else was cracking in his neck. Yet none of that compared to what he felt as her tongue—a burning black poker—pushed between his lips. His chest was bursting with the need to scream, and everything was going dark. Thinking this was death, he experienced a peevish resentment that death was not—as he'd been led to believe—an end to pain, that it merely added a tickling sensation to all his other pain. Then the searing heat in his mouth diminished, and he thought that death must just have been a bit slower than usual.

Several seconds passed before he realized that he was lying on the ground, several more before he noticed Michaela lying beside him, and—because darkness was tattering the edges of his vision—it was considerably longer before he distinguished the six undulating darknesses that had ringed Aimée Cousineau. They towered over her; their blackness gleamed like thick fur, and the air around them was awash with vibration. In her fluted white nightgown, her cameo face composed in an expression of calm, Aimée looked the antithesis of the vaguely male giants that were menacing her, delicate and finely worked in contrast to their crudity. Her eyes appeared to mirror their negative color. After a moment, a little wind kicked up, swirling about her. The undulations of the Khaa increased, becoming rhythmic, the movements of boneless dancers, and the wind subsided. Puzzled, she darted between two of them and took a defensive stance next to the golden cow; she lowered her head and stared up through her brows at the Khaa. They melted downward, rolled forward, sprang erect, and hemmed her in against the statue. But the stare was doing its damage. Pieces of ivory and wood were splintering, flying off the walls toward the Khaa, and one of them was fading, a mist of black particles accumulating around its body; then, with a shrill noise that reminded Eliot of a jet passing overhead, it misted away.

Five Khaa remained in the courtyard. Aimée smiled and turned her stare on another. Before the stare could take effect, however, the Khaa moved close, blocking Eliot's view of her; and when they pulled back, it was Aimée who showed signs of damage. Rills of blackness were leading from her eyes, webbing her cheeks, making it look as if her face were cracking. Her nightgown caught fire, her hair began to leap. Flames danced on her fingertips, spread to her arms, her breast, and she assumed the form of the burning woman.

As soon as the transformation was complete, she tried to shrink, to dwindle to her vanishing point; but, acting in unison, the Khaa extended their hands and touched her. There was that shriek of tortured metal, lapsing to a high-pitched hum, and to Eliot's amazement the Khaa were

sucked inside her. It was a rapid process. The Khaa faded
to a haze, to nothing, and veins of black marbled the burning woman's fire; the blackness coalesced, forming into five
tiny stick figures, a hieroglyphic design patterning her gown.
With a fuming sound, she expanded again, regaining her
normal dimensions, and the Khaa flowed back out, surrounding her. For an instant she stood motionless, dwarfed:
a schoolgirl helpless amidst a circle of bullies. Then she
clawed at the nearest of them. Though she had no features
with which to express emotion, it seemed to Eliot there was
desperation in gesture, in the agitated leaping of her fiery
hair. Unperturbed, the Khaa stretched out their enormous
mitten hands, hands that spread like oil and enveloped her.

The destruction of the burning woman, of Aimée Cousineau, lasted only a matter of seconds; but to Eliot it occurred within a bubble of slow time, a time during which
he achieved a speculative distance. He wondered if—as the
Khaa stole portions of her fire and secreted it within their
bodies—they were removing disparate elements of her soul,
if she consisted of psychologically distinct fragments: the
girl who had wandered into the cave, the girl who had
returned from it, the betrayed lover. Did she embody gradations of innocence and sinfulness, or was she a contam-
inated essence, an unfractionated evil? While still involved
in this speculation, half a reaction to pain, half to the
metallic shriek of her losing battle, he lost consciousness,
and when he reopened his eyes, the courtyard was deserted.
He could hear music and shouting from Durbar Square.
The golden cow stared contentedly into nowhere.

He had the idea that if he moved, he would further break
all the broken things inside him; but he inched his left hand
across the dirt and rested it on Michaela's breast. It was
rising and falling with a steady rhythm. That made him
happy, and he kept his hand there, exulting in the hits of
her life against his palm. Something shadowy above him.
He strained to see it. One of the Khaa . . . No! It was Mr.
Chatterji's Khaa. Opaquely black, scrap of fire glimmering

in its hand. Compared to its big brothers, it had the look of a skinny, sorry mutt. Eliot felt a camaraderie toward it.

"Hey, Bongo," he said weakly. "We won."

A tickling at the top of his head, a whining note, and he had an impression not of gratitude—as he might have expected—but of intense curiosity. The tickling stopped, and Eliot suddenly felt clear in his mind. Strange. He was passing out once again, his consciousness whirling, darkening, and yet he was calm and unafraid. A roar came from the direction of the square. Somebody—the luckiest somebody in the Katmandu Valley—had caught the fish. But as Eliot's eyelids fluttered shut, as he had a last glimpse of the Khaa looming above them and felt the warm measure of Michaela's heartbeat, he thought maybe that the crowd was cheering the wrong man.

Three weeks after the night of White Bhairab, Ranjeesh Chatterji divested himself of all worldly possessions (including the gift of a year's free rent at his house to Eliot) and took up residence at Swayambhunath where—according to Sam Chipley, who visited Eliot in the hospital—he was attempting to visualize the Avalokitesvara Buddha. It was then that Eliot understood the nature of his newfound clarity. Just as it had done long ago with the woman's goiters, the Khaa had tried his habituation to meditation on for size, had not cared for it, and had sloughed it off in a handy respository: Ranjeesh Chatterji.

It was such a delicious irony that Eliot had to restrain himself from telling Michaela when she visited that same afternoon; she had no memory of the Khaa, and news of it tended to unsettle her. But otherwise she had been healing right along with Eliot. All her listlessness had eroded over the weeks, her capacity for love was returning and was focused solely on Eliot. "I guess I needed someone to show me that I was worth an effort," she told him. "I'll never stop trying to repay you." She kissed him. "I can hardly wait till you come home." She brought him books and candy and flowers; she sat with him each day until the nurses shooed her away. Yet being the center of her devotion disturbed him. He was still uncertain whether or not he loved her. Clarity, it seemed, made a man dangerously versatile, his conscience flexible, and instituted a cautious approach to commitment. At least this was the substance of Eliot's clarity. He didn't want to rush into anything.

When at last he did come home, he and Michaela made love beneath the starlight glory of Mr. Chatterji's skylight. Because of Eliot's neck brace and cast, they had to manage the act with extreme care, but despite that, despite the ambivalence of his feelings, this time it *was* love they made. Afterward, lying with his good arm around her, he edged nearer to commitment. Whether or not he loved her, there was no way this part of things could be improved by any increment of emotion. Maybe he'd give it a try with her. If it didn't work out, well, he was not going to be responsible for her mental health. She would have to learn to live without him.

"Happy?" he asked, caressing her shoulder.

She nodded and cuddled closer and whispered something that was partially drowned out by the crinkling of the pillow. He was sure he had misheard her, but the mere thought that he hadn't was enough to lodge a nugget of chill between his shoulder blades.

"What did you say?" he asked.

She turned to him and propped herself on an elbow, silhouetted by the starlight, her features obscured. But when she spoke, he realized that Mr. Chatterji's Khaa had been true to its erratic traditions on the night of White Bhairab; and he knew that if she were to tip back her head ever so slightly and let the light shine into her eyes, he would be able to resolve all his speculations about the composition of Aimée Cousineau's soul.

"I'm wed to Happiness," she said.

SALVAGE RITES

IAN WATSON

British writer Ian Watson is one of the most significant writers and critics to emerge in the last twenty years. From the publication in 1974 of his first novel, *The Embedding,* for which he was runner-up for the John W. Campbell Award, he has been lauded for his excellent and thought-provoking writing. In much of his writing reality often appears to be a subjective matter, and one could interpret "Salvage Rites" from this perspective. On first glance, "Salvage Rites" is the story of an innocent foray to the town dump. Quite obviously, however, Ian Watson has considered the matter of rubbish and comes up with a dark vision indeed of a trip to the junkyard.

Tim and Rosy had cleared out their spare room ruthlessly. They had almost emptied it of the various categories of things that haunt spare rooms: surplus things, fatigued things, souvenir things, exiled things, scraps of things, things that might conceivably be repaired or cannibalized, things that might one day come in handy—all the time vault of twenty years.

"Trouble with being poor," Rosy said while they were loading the car, "is the way you store rubbish like treasure." As if she blamed him for the accumulation.

"We aren't exactly poor," Tim said awkwardly. "Compared with, say, someone in Africa, we're well off. We get by."

Yes, they got by, on the income from the grocery shop. They were able to pay the interest on their debts, which lodged with them like a greedy, infirm uncle; like a senile, crippled mother who stopped them from ever going on vacation. Tim's poetry earned a bit of extra money. His short, fierce lyrics could be roughed out during slack half hours—jotted down like customers' grocery lists—then polished before bed. Two small collections had been published and well received. And of course he was working on his sustained mock epic set in an imaginary Central European country, forever adding ten lines, crossing out five. The country in question needed to be imaginary since he and Rosy couldn't afford to travel abroad.

"Modern life is rubbish," said Rosy. "I saw that sprayed on the front of the cinema. It's perfectly true."

"It's the fault of the recession," he replied.

"It always costs more to be poor, doesn't it? We buy the cheapest, so it's trash. We wear clothes from charity shops, so we look like paupers and people try to swindle us. The poor always rob the poor. This car's a heap of junk; it costs more to keep on the road than a Rolls."

Their car was over ten years old, and rust was eating the bottoms of the doors. The hydraulics of the hatchback had

failed; thus the hatch had to be propped up with a broom
handle when open. The erratic engine guzzled oil.

When the car, with its rear seats lowered, had been
crammed with off cuts of carpet, underfelt, old curtains and
coats, bags of lank sweaters and sad shoes, tatty toys, a sick
television set, and such, Tim felt oddly refreshed and clean.
Whenever he scraped out the last smears of marmalade or
pickle from a jar, whenever he emptied out a cereal box,
he would feel a similar minor surge of satisfaction, as though
now something new and different might happen. Freud
might explain this as a babyish pleasure in the expulsion of
feces. True, Freud also spoke about anal retention. Next to
nothing had been retained in the spare room.

The clearout coincided with Daughter Emma's departure
to college. Her choice of geography to study wasn't so much
a poignant comment on her parents' immobility as due to
geography being regarded academically as an easy option.
Emma would probably become an underpaid teacher in a
mediocre school; she might marry another teacher. Emma
didn't know this yet. Kids were as bouncy as bunnies, before
the fox ate them or the winter froze them. Nature pumped
the hormone of optimism into each generation. In recent
years, Tim had reconciled himself at last to dwelling in the
geography of the imagination.

So the house above the shop was doubly empty. It was
empty of accumulated clutter; and empty of Emma. Sadly,
yet somehow refreshingly empty, like the late-autumn Sunday itself. The sun shone brightly on the empty street.
People were still in bed, sleeping in. But the public dump
five miles away would be open. Dawn till dusk.

"Junk," repeated Rosy. Tim hoped she wasn't going to
turn bitter when it came time to throw their past away.

He removed the broom handle, let the hatchback slam
itself, and patted it reassuringly. "Don't discourage the old
thing."

Rosy plucked at a loop in her saggy sweater and eyed a
box of Emma's childhood toys inside.

"Well, we've got rid of her at last," she said, apparently changing the subject. "Now we can start living, I suppose. If we still know how. Before we're too old."

Automatically, Tim smoothed his hair around the tonsure of his bald patch. They climbed into the car, which started without too much fuss.

As they drove off, Rosy said, "If we won a fortune, I shouldn't be able to spend it, you know. I could never bring myself to buy a coat at *new* prices. Or a meal in a restaurant. Or a proper hairdo. It would seem obscene. I've been trained."

"Me too. I wonder how we'd win a fortune." He spoke flatly, not asking. Most houses and gardens they passed were blank and lifeless, but one man was out washing a car with last year's registration. Tim hardly knew what model it was. He failed to imagine himself driving it. He and Rosy had originally started the shop with help from parents, back in the days when he had dreamed of becoming an internationally regarded poet who traveled places. Parents were now all dead. Legacies had gone to assuage the upward-creeping debts.

"Beautiful day."

Rosy said nothing in reply. She pulled down the sun visor briefly and sought wrinkles in the mirror on the back.

"My hair needs cutting," she said presently.

"Go to a hairdresser's," he murmured.

"I'll do it myself. As usual."

Tim thought he needed a haircut too. When you wore cheap old clothes, short hair was best.

"The roots are showing," she said.

"That's fashionable nowadays. Look, you said we ought to start living. If you couldn't ever splash out in a restaurant, how can we start living? A bit of a contradiction, isn't it?"

"An economic contradiction. Why should we have to own a shop? The state should own everything. There shouldn't be private cars either. There should be enough good buses and railways."

"True. But there aren't. The services have been castrated."

A poem occurred to him: about eunuchs in Arabian robes driving harems of passengers who peered not through windows but through intricate lattices.

The dump would be open today because the dump was a market too. A bazaar of sorts. Just as charity shops sprouted like fungi in any temporarily empty commercial premises in town, selling the rags of richer people to poorer people to send aid to the totally poor in the Third World, so, with the deliberate decline of the economy, rubbish dumps had changed their nature. Concessionaires bid for the salvage rights. Anything reusable was sold back to the public. Ecological recycling? Logic of poverty? One or the other.

Tim and Rosy had visited the dump outside town a year before and bought a washing machine for a song. The machine worked for three months before breaking down. Cheaper than renting with an option to buy. Now the carcass, with holes cut in it, acted as a compost bin in their patch of back garden. According to gossips visiting the shop, the dump had since undergone a further metamorphosis. A hot-drink vending machine had been installed so that browsers could refresh themselves with a plastic cup of coffee. That summer an ice cream van had visited the dump most weekends.

"Next thing," he said, "people will be having picnics at the dump. There'll be a play area for kids. Tours of the infill. Bulldozer rides. Déjeuner sur le dump."

"What?"

"The Manet painting. Imagine that fellow and his naked mistress sitting on the dump drinking champagne. I presume she'd have to wear a bikini."

A poem? "Manet at the dump." Maybe. What word rhymed with "rubbish"?

Driving along the two-lane road between the first plowed empty fields of the countryside, Tim spotted a cloud of gulls milling in the sky over the sprawling infill acres of the dump, like so many scraps of white paper. Rusty corrugated iron sheets walled off the visitors' zone.

Which they entered, in low gear, the suspension creaking ominously as the car humped itself over the sleeping-policeman ramp.

A large concrete yard was lined with bulky rubbish bins into which their car could probably have fit. Down one side the high bins were already loaded with rubble. Those along the opposite side were empty; however, most were roped off with a notice prohibiting use. An arrow pointed to the far end, where several bins stood behind notice boards indicating "glass," "garden refuse," "metal." Those bins were already full; sunlight glared from a pile of windows.

A battered bulk-shipping container the size of a railway carriage blocked the view beyond, though another mounted wooden arrow pointed behind it.

Nearer to hand stood a black oil sump, and a bottle bank painted camouflage green that resembled an armored car, with slots for clear and colored bottles reminiscent of muzzles from which howitzer shells could be fired. A score of ripped-off doors were stacked against one end.

Tim stopped the car by a truck trailer that was packed with a mound of old clothes and rags. Shirt-sleeves hung down as if they had tried to climb out and failed, all the breath crushed out of them.

Beside this trailer, another huge shipping container, open at one end, was labeled "shop." Within, Tim saw clothes on racks, shelves of paperback books, electrical goods. A fat, vacant-faced woman of indeterminate middle age, wearing a pink parka, occupied a deck chair outside. The shop forecourt displayed collections of tools, lamp bases and shades, mirrors, ambiguous metal paraphernalia, a cocktail cabinet with the veneer peeling.

Inside a makeshift pen, cobbled together from car roof racks, an Alsatian guard bitch woke to life when Tim opened his door. The powerful animal reared, barking, raving.

"Jilly!" screamed the fat woman. She ignored Tim. The Alsatian slumped, and whined.

Apart from their own car, the yard was deserted. Too early in the day, perhaps. By this afternoon the bazaar of rubbish might be buzzing; then the beast wouldn't be on edge. Tim stepped nervously round to the hatchback, raised it, and inserted the broom handle. He carried the first plastic bag of clothes to the open trailer, and swung. The bag landed high up the hill of garments, jamming against the roof. He noticed a movement in the inner gloom. Some rags shifting, knocked off balance?

Rosy wound her window down. "Why can't you save the bags?"

"Oh," he said stupidly, measuring the height of the trailer floor, the incline of the clothes hill. Should he climb up and empty the bag? "There's no space left at the front. Our stuff would fall out."

Supposing you tried to repossess a coat you'd thrown away—having changed your mind about discarding it— would the Alsatian be within its rights to rip your throat out? Because you no longer owned that coat? A sign fixed to the dog pen forbade visitors from taking anything, except by way of the shop. Salvage rights had been granted. To a firm called Griffiths Scavenging. Associates of the fat woman in the deck chair.

"Tim, come back here!"

He hurried to the car window.

"Someone inside there," Rosy whispered.

In the dim interior of the trailer, almost hidden by the summit of fabrics, Tim spotted a skinny girl with ratty hair. As he watched, she ripped open the bag he had thrown, and tossed the contents this way and that, examining, sorting.

"It's obscene," said Rosy, "having your socks and knickers picked over before your very eyes."

"Maybe we should have washed all our old clothes before we threw them away?"

"That isn't funny. Find somewhere else, will you? Down there by those signs."

Leaving the hatchback propped, Tim got in and started the engine. He drove down toward the other freight container and followed the arrow round behind it.

Another arrow pointed the way down a long lane lined by bins. As Tim and Rosy entered the lane, shadow fell upon them from the high metal sides and suddenly the day was cold. The occasional freestanding notice announced "plastic," "rubber & tires." As well as being inconveniently tall, the bins were mostly full.

Heeding a further arrow, he turned the car along a side lane similarly walled with bins and intermittent notices.

"Carpeting," he read. "Here we are. Get rid of *that*, at any rate."

On his second attempt, he managed to raise their rolled threadbare carpet to head height and tumble it over the metal lip. It fell dully within. From the car, he hauled the first bundle of heavy underfelt, which they had stored for years on the off chance.

"That isn't exactly *carpet*," called Rosy.

"Undercarpet. Same thing. What do they expect? We should sort out everything for them? Bother that. I'll toss the lot in here, clothes and all. Who cares?"

Another plump, empty-faced woman, in raggy woolens and baggy trousers—an obvious sister of the deck chair occupant—squeezed her way from between two bins and stood watching. A boy of five or six in shorts and black zipper jacket followed her, clutching a torn picture book.

Tim walked over to the woman. "Is it all right if I throw underfelt in that one?" Her skin oozed grease.

"Wha'?" she said after a while.

He repeated himself.

"Uh," she said, which might have meant anything. He realized that the woman was stupid, moronic. Maybe she had no connection with Griffiths Scavenging, after all. She might just be wandering around.

"Well, I will, then." So Tim disposed of all the underfelt, awkwardly heaving and hurling aloft while the woman stared silently at him.

He got back into the car. "There'll be bins for clothes and stuff farther on."

True enough. The next arrow directed them into another long, narrow roadway of bins, all brimful of different categories of clothing. Signs were hardly necessary. Suits. Shirts. Skirts. Underwear. Boots and shoes. Buttons; there was even a bin full of buttons, a mountain height of multicolored shingle.

He cruised at walking pace. "Must be their storeroom, hmm? Maybe they export to poor countries. Or places hit by disaster. Cyclones, earthquakes. We oughtn't to have come so far. We should have dumped the lot back in the yard."

A pair of acne-scarred youths in jeans, heavy steel-tipped boots, and bomber jackets emerged. One slapped a hand on the front of the car, forcing Tim to brake. The other strolled grinning round to the open backside.

"Yelp yer, mate?" The youth tore a bag open and pulled out an old skirt of Rosy's. He ran and tossed this up into a bin of skirts, returned, and burrowed, while his companion joined him.

"Hey," objected Tim. "Get out of our car. Now."

As though instinctively alert to the contents, the youths grabbed the other clothes bags out of the back and ripped them open to sort on the ground. Tim immediately drove on and soon rounded another corner. Yet another lane of bins—all apparently empty—stretched ahead, with an arrow indicating a turning halfway along.

"Stop and reverse," said Rosy. "Go back the way we came."

"We still have the TV to dump, and the—"

"Stop! Back up and turn. Unload the rest in the yard. Anywhere! Drive away. Home."

Home. That house above a shop that fed them and im-

prisoned them. The house with an empty daughter's room.
And now with an empty spare room. Tim experienced an
odd feeling of certainty that before leaving that morning
they had emptied the entire house—of furniture, stove,
refrigerator, everything—and that there was nothing left any
longer to connect them to the place. As if they had cleared
all the shelves in the shop, too, leaving bare boards. They
were free; they had escaped—hadn't they? Something new
could begin.

Vacant shop, vacant house, vacant debts. As vacant as
this street of empty bins; as vacant as the rear of the car was
fast becoming. He wished he had closed the hatchback
down. Otherwise something more precious than junk might
escape, might be snatched or simply drift away into the
chilly air here between these looming steel boxes that mock-
ingly imitated a decrepit city street—from the future, perhaps, after a war.

He halted the car and shook his head to clear a cold fog
of apprehension from his brain. Before he could engage
reverse gear, he saw in the rearview mirror the high front
of a truck loom around the corner behind. Piston arms, at
attention, dangled chains embracing the steel bin on its
flatbed back. Somehow the bin truck negotiated the turn.
He wondered how it could ever maneuver to pick up or
deposit any of the bins ranged on either side. Maybe there
was a turntable built into the chassis. Standing in the bin
as though navigating the vehicle was the moronic woman.
Suddenly the sight of her terrified him. The truck slowly
approached, and honked.

"It must be one-way-only, Rosy." Tim drove forward to
the next intersection and swung down a lane of close-packed
bins containing scrap metal. By the time they reached another arrow, and another turn, the bin truck had already
entered the scrap metal street.

Tim took another turn, then another, losing the truck
way behind. *If* it had been deliberately following, to begin
with.

Arrow followed arrow. Turn followed turn. Lane of bins succeeded lane of bins. Once they turned into the street of clothing bins, yet this led to a street of scrap metal bins, not a street where the bins were empty. Unless his memory was deceiving him. No, it wasn't. The clothes bins must have been different ones. They were lost in a maze.

"This is ridiculous," he told Rosy. "There isn't space for all these lanes."

"We've entered the world of rubbish," Rōsy whispered back. "Where we've been heading for the past twenty years."

The engine coughed and missed a couple of times. Tim pulled the choke half out, racing the engine, though of necessity still driving slowly.

"It's all this damn crawling in first gear. The plugs soot up."

The very next lane opened into a long concrete yard walled in by bins. It wasn't the yard that housed the shop. Slamming the choke back in, Tim gunned the car toward the arrow marking the exit at the far end, hoping to burn the plugs clean. He braked violently in time to enter the next narrow alley.

Six lanes later the engine quit. Tim couldn't restart the car.

"What do we do now?" asked Rosy.

"Walk. I'll leave the keys in the ignition."

The bins on either side stood shoulder to shoulder. They seemed twice as large as previously. You couldn't even squeeze sideways between bins, though you might just manage to crawl on your belly. The only route was the concrete road.

"I wonder if this was once an old airfield?"

Then Tim remembered the gulls flocking above the infill. But no gulls flapped in the sky now.

"What's in the bins, Tim?"

Not since that second yard had they passed a single sign announcing the contents. He peered up. Suddenly he understood the assorted shapes peering over the lips of the containers.

Car doors.

Farther along . . . a forest of exhaust pipes like several church organs jumbled by a bomb blast.

"Bits of cars," he said, opening his door.

Two lanes later they heard from somewhere behind them the whine of a power tool, then the clanging of metal. He felt sure that their stalled car was being broken up into parts. Taking Rosy's hand, he hurried her onward and along another lane. Faintly, he heard a thump of boots and a silly, idiotic giggling.

Clothes bins again! Jackets, shirts, sandals, nightdresses loomed over bin tops. Before they could reach the next corner, the moronic woman waddled out from it ahead of them. She was accompanied by a big, bony, overall-clad man in his mid-forties, his thick black hair slicked back in waves, his nose an absurdly small squash blob in a large, battered face.

"Yer need a hand, squire?"

Tim jerked around. One of the youths sat perched on the edge of a shirt bin behind them. The youth dropped to the ground just as his partner came wading over the bin of summer dresses opposite. He leapt down too.

"Show us the way out of here!" cried Rosy. "No, go away! Leave us alone!"

The two youths rushed and clamped Rosy by the arms. At the same moment the man seized Tim, who struggled uselessly; the grip was like granite.

"Yer need a hand," the youth repeated.

The plump woman ambled forward. While the man manipulated Tim like a toy or a life-size doll, the woman undressed him, taking her time about it, tossing his clothes up into various bins. Soon Tim shivered nakedly, still held tight.

Then it was Rosy's turn.

•

Their captors led Tim and Rosy, both stripped naked, to the turn and released them, thrusting them into the next steel and concrete lane.

"Ge' on, now, squire!"

The woman and her three companions remained at the intersection, blocking any return to the bins where Tim's and Rosy's clothes and shoes had been discarded. Shaking with cold and shock, Tim and Rosy ran along numbly to the next turn, as much to hide their nakedness from the blankly watchful eyes and chilly breeze as to escape.

· Tim's teeth chattered. "We'll f-find something to wear. F-farther on. Any old rags. Or c-curtains."

The bins in this new lane were loaded with sheets of cardboard, rolls of wallpaper, bundles of old magazines. Tim wondered whether he could scale the side of a bin with bare feet. He would have to!

Rosy wailed, "I thought they were going to rape—!" Her breast bounced. "They did! They did. It was the same."

"Listen, this is all a vicious joke. Next we'll come across some rags to put on. Then we'll reach the yard where the shop is, looking like scarecrows. And we'll find our car waiting for us—with our clothes folded on the seats. Nobody will believe us, but . . ." He had to believe it. "They could have hurt us. They didn't."

"You think they didn't hurt us? I'm hurt forever."

The bins in the next lane all looked empty; nothing peeped over the tops. Tim rapped his knuckles against several; all rang hollowly. He didn't feel inclined to try to climb, to check.

They walked in cold shade. Whichever direction a lane led, sunlight seemed excluded. At last an arrow pointed the way down between rows of bins full of broken furniture, to a concrete-surfaced yard.

"It's the way out," he said. "We've arrived."

However, the yard, lined with more giant bins, was only as large as a tennis court, and no arrow pointed to an exit.

There was only an entrance. Half of the yard was bathed in sunshine, where Rosy ran to warm herself. Her bare flesh quivering, the breeze still nipped her. Whatever these bins contained couldn't be seen from ground level. A car roof rack rested against one. Side-on, its metal bars were steps.

"I'll see the way out!" Wincing, then planting her feet sideways so as to spread her weight along the thin steel bars, Rosy ascended.

Shading her eyes, she stared around helplessly.

She looked down inside the bin itself. And screamed. Screamed.

Tim scaled the bars; there was room alongside. Clutching her cold shoulders with a chilly arm, he, too, gazed down.

For a few seconds he hardly understood what he saw. A layer of slime-coated Ping-Pong balls? Hundreds of hard-boiled eggs?

No. Eyes. The optic cords sprouted like tiny lengths of electric cord torn out of plugs.

Sheep's eyes? No, he didn't think so. Not the eyes of sheep, or any other animal. Rosy had stopped screaming, out of breath. She shook convulsively, clutching the top of the bin, screwing her own eyes tight shut as if to hide them.

He could see into the neighboring bin as well. A heap of french fries? Baby parsnips? No.

Fingers. Chopped-off human fingers.

He stared wildly around the yard. What did all the other bins hide in their depths? Toes, tongues, lungs? Arms and loins and brains? The parts of the body, sorted out . . . Yes! He knew this was so, even before the grind of an engine dragged his gaze to the entrance of the little yard.

The bin truck heaved into view and halted in the entrance, completing the circuit of metal walls. The front jutted sufficiently into the yard that the truck doors would be free to open. Crowded side by side in the cab were the man, at the wheel; the two youths; the moronic woman with her boy on her knee; the blank-faced fat woman in the pink parka; and the skinny, ratty girl. All of the passengers,

even the little boy, were clutching assorted tools. Saws.
Pincers. A gouge. A small ax.

The truck engine died.

"For God's sake, climb on top, Rosy!! Walk along the
side of the bin beyond. We must get out of here."

Beyond the yard for as far as he could see in all directions
were endless rows of bins.

Desperately, bruising his naked body, almost crippling a
toe, Tim scrambled on top, struggling to balance, half helping, half dragging Rosy with him. The top edge was far too
narrow ever to walk along with bare feet, tightrope-style.
Nude, he knew they couldn't even slide along, astride. That
would be like riding a blunt steel blade. After a while it
would cut up through them, between their legs. Instead, he
slid down inside, pulling Rosy howling with him.

"We'll climb out the back way into the next one! And
the next!"

Jelly lumps squelched underfoot. He skidded in the six-
inch-deep pool of eyes and fell, nauseated. Scrambling up,
he waded, then leapt at the high rear edge of the bin. He
did catch hold, with outstretched fingers, his front smashing
against the metal, but he couldn't pull himself up. He hadn't
enough of a grip. There was no purchase. His feet were
slipping on soft marbles.

"Yer need a hand?"

A crowd of heads popped up behind. Vacant faces smiled
vaguely. The man, the women, the youths, the ratty girl,
even the little boy.

Hands rose into view, displaying a gouge, an ax, pincers,
saws.

TEST

THEODORE L. THOMAS

Theodore L. Thomas, patent attorney, science columnist and lecturer, and scuba diver, began publishing in 1952 both under his own name and under the pseudonym of Leonard Lockhardt. In addition to his short stories, he has written two novels in collaboration with Kate Wilhelm, *The Clone* (1965) and *The Year of the Cloud* (1970). "Test," first published in *F & SF* in 1962, is a curt and chilling tale which, despite its brevity, is one of the best action stories you will ever read. It poses a question that —once asked—readers will recognize as having echoed in their own minds forever.

Robert Proctor was a good driver for so young a man. The turnpike curved gently ahead of him, lightly traveled on this cool morning in May. He felt relaxed and alert. Two hours of driving had not yet produced the twinges of fatigue that appeared first in the muscles in the base of the neck. The sun was bright but not glaring, and the air smelled fresh and clean. He breathed it deeply, and blew it out noisily. It was a good day for driving.

He glanced quickly at the slim, gray-haired woman sitting in the front seat with him. Her mouth was curved in a quiet smile. She watched the trees and the fields slip by on her side of the pike. Robert Proctor immediately looked back at the road. He said, "Enjoying it, Mom?"

"Yes, Robert." Her voice was as cool as the morning. "It is very pleasant to sit here. I was thinking of the driving I did for you when you were little. I wonder if you enjoyed it as much as I enjoy this."

He smiled, embarrassed. "Sure I did."

She reached over and patted him gently on the arm, and then turned back to the scenery.

He listened to the smooth purr of the engine. Up ahead he saw a great truck, spouting a geyser of smoke as it sped along the turnpike. Behind it, not passing it, was a long blue convertible, content to drive in the wake of the truck. Robert Proctor noted the arrangement and filed it in the back of his mind. He was slowly overtaking them, but he would not reach them for another minute or two.

He listened to the purr of the engine, and he was pleased with the sound. He had tuned that engine himself over the objections of the mechanic. The engine idled rough now, but it ran smoothly at high speed. You needed a special feel to do good work on engines, and Robert Proctor knew he had it. No one in the world had a feel like his for the tune of an engine.

It was a good morning for driving, and his mind was filled with good thoughts. He pulled nearly abreast of the blue convertible and began to pass it. His speed was a few miles per hour above the turnpike limit, but his car was under perfect control. The blue convertible suddenly swung out from behind the truck. It swung out without warning and struck his car near the right front fender, knocking his car to the shoulder on the left side of the turnpike lane.

Robert Proctor was a good driver, too wise to slam on the brakes. He fought the steering wheel to hold the car on a straight path. The left wheels sank into the soft left shoulder, and the car tugged to pull to the left and cross the island and enter the lanes carrying the cars heading in the opposite direction. He held it, then the wheel struck a rock buried in the soft dirt, and the left front tire blew out. The car slewed, and it was then that his mother began to scream.

The car turned sideways and skidded part of the way out into the other lanes. Robert Proctor fought against the steering wheel to straighten the car, but the drag of the blown tire was too much. The scream ran steadily in his ears, and even as he strained at the wheel one part of his mind wondered coolly how a scream could so long be sustained without a breath. An oncoming car struck his radiator from the side and spun him viciously, full into the left-hand lanes.

He was flung into his mother's lap, and she was thrown against the right door. It held. With his left hand he reached for the steering wheel and pulled himself erect against the force of the spin. He turned the wheel to the left, and tried to stop the spin and careen out of the lanes of oncoming traffic. His mother was unable to right herself; she lay against the door, her cry rising and falling with the eccentric spin of the car.

The car lost some of its momentum. During one of the spins he twisted the wheel straight, and the car wobblingly stopped spinning and headed down the lane. Before Robert Proctor could turn it off the pike to safety, a car loomed ahead of him, bearing down on him. There was a man at the wheel of that other car, sitting rigid, unable to move, eyes wide and staring and filled with fright. Alongside the man was a girl, her head against the back of the seat, soft curls framing a lovely face, her eyes closed in easy sleep. It was not the fear in the man that reached into Robert Proctor; it was the trusting helplessness in the face of the sleeping girl. The two cars sped closer to each other, and Robert Proctor could not change the direction of his car. The driver of the other car remained frozen at the wheel. At the last moment Robert Proctor sat motionless, staring into the face of the onrushing, sleeping girl, his mother's cry still sounding in his ears. He heard no crash when the two cars collided head-on at a high rate of speed. He felt something push into his stomach, and the world began to go gray. Just before he lost consciousness he heard the scream stop, and he knew then that he had been hearing a single, short-lived scream that had only seemed to drag on and on. There came a painless wrench, and then darkness.

Robert Proctor seemed to be at the bottom of a deep black well. There was a spot of faint light in the far distance, and he could hear the rumble of a distant voice. He tried to pull himself toward the light and the sound, but the effort was too great. He lay still and gathered himself and tried again. The light grew brighter and the voice louder. He tried harder, again, and he drew closer. Then he opened his eyes full and looked at the man sitting in front of him.

"You all right, son?" asked the man. He wore a blue uniform, and his round, beefy face was familiar.

Robert Proctor tentatively moved his head, and discovered he was seated in a reclining chair, unharmed, and able to move his arms and legs with no trouble. He looked around the room, and he remembered.

The man in the uniform saw the growing intelligence in his eyes and he said, "No harm done, son. You just took the last part of your driver's test."

Robert Proctor focused his eyes on the man. Though he saw the man clearly, he seemed to see the faint face of the sleeping girl in front of him.

The uniformed man continued to speak. "We put you through an accident under hypnosis—do it to everybody these days before they can get their driver's licenses. Makes better drivers of them, more careful drivers the rest of their lives. Remember it now? Coming in here and all?"

Robert Proctor nodded, thinking of the sleeping girl. She never would have awakened; she would have passed right from a sweet, temporary sleep into the dark heavy sleep of death, nothing in between. His mother would have been bad enough; after all, she was pretty old. The sleeping girl was downright waste.

The uniformed man was still speaking. "So you're all set now. You pay me the ten-dollar fee, and sign this application, and we'll have your license in the mail in a day or two." He did not look up.

Robert Proctor placed a ten-dollar bill on the table in front of him, glanced over the application, and signed it. He looked up to find two white-uniformed men, standing one on each side of him, and he frowned in annoyance. He started to speak, but the uniformed man spoke first. "Sorry, son. You failed. You're sick; you need treatment."

The two men lifted Robert Proctor to his feet, and he said, "Take your hands off me. What is this?"

The uniformed man said, "Nobody should want to drive a car after going through what you just went through. It should take months before you can even think of driving again, but you're ready right now. Killing people doesn't bother you. We don't let your kind run around loose in society anymore. But don't you worry now, son. They'll take good care of you, and they'll fix you up." He nodded to the two men, and they began to march Robert Proctor out.

At the door he spoke, and his voice was so urgent the two men paused. Robert Proctor said, "You can't really mean this. I'm still dreaming, aren't I? This is still part of the test, isn't it?"

The uniformed man said, *"How do any of us know?"* And they dragged Robert Proctor out the door, knees stiff, feet dragging, his rubber heels sliding along the two grooves worn into the floor.

THE LITTLE BLACK TRAIN

MANLY WADE WELLMAN

When Manly Wade Wellman died in 1986, the world of American fiction was lessened. Manly Wade Wellman began publishing in 1927, capturing the southern American spirit in all his tales. His most famous sequence of tales, of which "The Little Black Train" is but one, concerned the roving ballad singer, John. These stories were published in *F & SF* from 1951 to 1962 and collected as *Who Fears the Devil?* (1963). John is a character who seems just bound to meet up with odd people in odder places. We find these tales particularly attractive both for Manly Wade Wellman's faithful recording of one type of regional speech and for his rewarding explorations in American folklore. "The Little Black Train" is one of Manly Wade Wellman's most compelling tales. In it, John once again confronts evil in an attempt to turn aside—with his silver-stringed guitar—a curse of twenty years.

There in the High Fork country, with peaks saw-toothing into the sky and hollows diving away down and trees thicketed every which way, you'd think human foot had never stepped. Walking the trail between high pines, I touched my guitar's silver strings for company of the sound. But then a man squandered into sight around a bend—younglike, red-faced, baldy-headed. Gentlemen, he was as drunk as a hoot. I gave him good evening.

"Can you play that thing?" he gobbled at me and, second grab of his shaky hand, he got hold of my hickory shirtsleeve. "Come to the party, friend. Our fiddle band, last moment, they got scared out. We got just only a mouth harp to play for us."

"What way was the fiddle band scared?" I asked him to tell.

"Party's at Miss Donie Carawan's," he said, without replying me. "Bobbycue pig and chicken, bar'l of good stumphole whiskey."

"Listen," I said, "ever hear tell of the man invited a stranger fiddler, he turned out to be Satan?"

"Shoo," he snickered, "Satan plays the fiddle, you play the guitar, I don't pay your guitar no worry. What's your name, friend?"

"John. What's yours?"

But he'd started up a narrow, grown-over, snaky-turny path you'd not notice. I reckoned the party'd be at a house, where I could sleep the night that was coming, so I followed. He nearly fell back top of me, he was so stone drunk, but we got to a notch on the ridge, and the far side was a valley of trees, dark and secret-looking. Going down, I began to hear loud laughing talk. Finally we reached a yard at the bottom. There was a house there, and it looked like enough men and women to swing a primary election.

They whooped at us; so loud it rang my ears. The drunk man waved both his hands. "This here's my friend John," he bawled out, "and he's a-going to play us some music!"

They whooped louder at that, and easiest thing for me

to do was start picking "Hell Broke Loose in Georgia"; and, gentlemen, right away they danced up a storm.

Wildlike, they whipped and whirled. Most of them were young folks dressed their best. One side, a great big man called the dance, but you couldn't much hear him, everybody laughed and hollered so loud. It got in my mind that children laugh and yell thataway, passing an old burying ground where ghosts could be. It was the way they might be trying to dance down the nervouses; I jumped myself, between picks, when something started moaning beside me. But it was just a middling-old fellow with a thin face, playing his mouth harp along with my guitar.

I looked to the house—it was new and wide and solid, with whitewashed clay chinking between the squared logs of it. Through a dog-trot from front to back I saw clear down valley, west to where the sunball dropped red toward a far string of mountains. The valley bottom's trees were spaced out with a kind of path or road, the whole length. The house windows began to light up as I played. Somebody was putting a match to lamps, against the night's fall.

End of the tune, everybody clapped me loud and long. "More! More!" they hollered, bunched among the yard trees, still fighting their nervouses.

"Friends," I managed to be heard, "let me make my manners to the one who's giving this party."

"Hi, Miss Donie!" yelled out the drunk man. "Come meet John!"

From the house she walked through the crowded-around folks, stepping so proud, she looked taller than she was. A right much stripy skirt swished to her high heels; but she hadn't such a much dress above, and none at all on her round arms and shoulders. The butter yellow of her hair must have come from a bottle, and the doll pink of her face from a box. She smiled up to me, and her perfume tingled my nose. Behind her followed that big dance-caller, with his dead black hair and wide teeth, and his heavy hands swinging like balance weights.

"Glad you came, John," she said, deep in her round throat.

I looked at her robin-egg-blue eyes and her butter hair and her red mouth and her bare pink shoulders. She was maybe thirty-five, maybe forty, maybe more and not looking it. "Proud to be here," I said, my politest. "Is this a birthday, Miss Donie Carawan?"

Folks fell quiet, swapping looks. An open cooking fire blazed up as the night sneaked in. Donie Carawan laughed deep.

"Birthday of a curse," and she widened her blue eyes. "End of the curse, too, I reckon. All tonight."

Some mouths came open, but didn't let words out. I reckoned that whatever had scared out the fiddle band was nothing usual. She held out a slim hand, with green-stoned rings on it.

"Come eat and drink, John," she bade me.

"Thanks," I said, for I hadn't eaten ary mouthful since crack of day.

Off she led me, her fingers pressing mine, her eye corners watching me. The big dance-caller glittered a glare after us. He was purely jealoused up that she'd made me so welcome.

Two dark-faced old men stood at an iron rack over a pit of coals, where lay two halves of a slow-cooking hog. One old man dipped a stick with a rag ball into a kettle of sauce and painted it over the brown roast meat. From a big pot of fat over yet another fire, an old woman forked hush puppies into pans set ready on a plank table.

"Line up!" called Donie Carawan out, like a bugle. They lined up, talking and hollering again, smiles back on their faces. It was some way like dreams you have, folks carrying on loud and excited, and something bad coming on to happen.

Donie Carawan put her bare arm through my blue-sleeved elbow while an old man sliced chunks of barbecued hog on paper plates for us. The old woman forked on a hush puppy and a big hobby of cole slaw. Eating, I wondered how they made the barbecue sauce—wondered, too, if all these folks really wanted to be here for what Donie Carawan called the birthday of a curse.

"John," she said, the way you'd think she read what I wondered, "don't they say a witch's curse can't work on a pure heart?"

"They say that," I agreed her, and she laughed her laugh. The big dance-caller and the skinny mouth harp man looked up from their barbecue.

"An old witch cursed me for guilty twenty years back," said Donie Carawan. "The law said I was innocent. Who was right?"

"Don't know how to answer that," I had to say, and again she laughed, and bit into her hush puppy.

"Look around you, John," she said. "This house is my house, and this valley is my valley, and these folks are my friends, come to help me pleasure myself."

Again I reckoned, she's the only one here that's pleasured, maybe not even her.

"Law me," she laughed, "it's rough on a few folks, holding their breath all these years to see the curse light on me. Since it wouldn't light, I figured how to shoo it away." Her blue eyes looked up. "But what are you doing around High Fork, John?"

The dance-caller listened, and the thin mouth harp man. "Just passing through," I said. "Looking for songs. I heard about a High Fork song, something about a little black train."

Silence quick stretched all around, the way you'd think I'd been impolite. Yet again she broke the silence with a laugh.

"Why," she said, "I've known that song as long as I've known about the curse, near to. Want me to sing it for you?"

Folks were watching, and, "Please, ma'am," I asked her.

She sang, there in the yellow lamplight and red firelight, among the shady-shadowy trees and the mountain dark, without ary slice of moon overhead. Her voice was a good voice. I put down my plate and, a line or two along, I made out to follow her with the guitar.

> *I heard a voice of warning,*
> *A message from on high,*
> *"Go put your house in order*
> *For thou shalt surely die.*
> *Tell all your friends a long farewell*
> *And get your business right—*
> *The little black train is rolling in*
> *To call for you tonight."*

"Miss Donie, that's a tuneful thing," I said. "Sounds right like a train rolling."

"My voice isn't high enough to sound the whistle part," she smiled at me, red-mouthed.

"I might could do that," said the mouth harp man, coming close and speaking soft. And folks were craning at us, looking sick, embarrassed, purely distasted. I began to wonder why I shouldn't have given a name to that black train song.

But then rose up a big holler near the house, where a barrel was set. The drunk man that'd fetched me was yelling mad at another man near about as drunk, and they were trying to grab a drinking gourd from each other. Two, three other men on each side hoorawed them on to squabble more.

"Jeth!" called Donie Carawan to the big dance-caller. "Let's stop that before they spill the whiskey, Jeth."

Jeth and she headed for the bunch by the barrel, and everybody else was crowding to watch.

"John," said a quiet somebody—the mouth harp man, with firelight showing lines in his thin face, salty gray in his hair. "What you really doing here?"

"Watching," I said, while big Jeth hauled those two drunk men off from each other, and Donie Carawan scolded them.

"And listening," I said. "Wanting to know what way the black train song fits in with this party and the tale about the curse. You know about it?"

"I know," he said.

We carried out food out of the firelight. Folks were crowding to the barrel, laughing and yelling.

"Donie Carawan was to marry Trevis Jones," the mouth harp man told me. "He owned the High Fork Railroad to freight the timber from this valley. He'd a lavish of money, is how he got to marry her. But"—and he swallowed hard—"another young fellow loved her. Cobb Richardson, who ran Trevis Jones's train on the High Fork Railroad. And he killed Trevis Jones."

"For love?" I asked.

"Folks reckoned that Donie Carawan decided against Trevis and love-talked Cobb into the killing; for Trevis had made a will and heired her all his money and property—the railroad and all. But Cobb made confession. Said Donie had no part in it. The law let her go, and killed Cobb in the electric chair, down at the state capital."

"I declare to never," I said.

"Fact. And Cobb's mother—Mrs. Amanda Richardson —spoke the curse."

"Oh," I said, "is she the witch that—"

"She was no witch"—he broke me off—"but she cursed Donie Carawan, that the train that Cobb had engine drove, and Trevis had heired to her, would be her death and destruction. Donie laughed. You've heard her laugh. And folks started the song, the black train song."

"Who made it?" I asked him.

"Reckon I did," he said, looking long at me. He waited to let me feel that news. Then he said, "Maybe it was the song decided Donie Carawan to deal with the Hickory River Railroad, agreeing for an income of money not to run the High Fork train no more."

I'd finished my barbecue. I could have had more, but I didn't feel like it. "I see," I told him. "She reckoned that if no train ran on the High Fork tracks, it couldn't be her death and destruction."

He and I put our paper plates on one of the fires. I didn't look at the other folks, but it seemed to me they were quieting their laughing and talking as the night got darker.

"Only thing is," the mouth harp man went on, "folks say the train runs on that track. Or it did. A black train runs some nights at midnight, they say, and when it runs a sinner dies."

"You ever see it run?"

"No, John, but I've sure God heard it. And only Donie Carawan laughs about it."

She laughed right then, joking the two men who'd feathered up to fight. Ary man's neck craned at her, and women looked the way you'd figure they didn't relish that. My neck craned some itself.

"Twenty years back, the height of her bloom," said the mouth harp man, "law me, you'd never call to look at anything else."

"What does she mean, no more curse?"

"She made another deal, John. She sold off the rails of the High Fork Road, that's stood idle for twenty years. Today the last of them was torn up and carried off. Meanwhile, she's had this house built, across where the right of way used to be. Looky yonder, through the dog-trot. That's where the road ran."

So it was the old road bed made that dark dip amongst the trees. Just now it didn't look so wide a dip.

"No rails," he said. "She figures no black train at midnight. Folks came at her invite—some because they rent her land, some because they owe her money, and some— men folks—because they'll do arything she bids them."

"And she never married?" I asked.

"If she done that, she'd lose the money and land she heired from Trevis Jones. It was in his will. She just takes men without marrying, one and then another. I've known men kill theirselves because she'd put her heart back in her pocket on them. Lately, it's been big Jeth. She acts tonight like picking herself a new beau lover."

She walked back through the lamplight and firelight. "John," she said, "these folks want to dance again."

What I played them was "Many Thousands Gone," with the mouth harp to help, and they danced and stomped the way you'd think it was a many thousands dancing. In its thick, Donie Carawan promenaded left and right and do-si-doed with a fair-haired young fellow, and Jeth the dance-caller looked pickle sour. When I'd done, Donie Carawan came swishing back.

"Let the mouth harp play," she said, "and dance with me."

"Can't dance no shakes," I told her. "Just now, I'd relish to practice the black train song."

Her blue eyes crinkled. "All right. Play, and I'll sing."

She did. The mouth harp man blew whistle moanings to my guitar, and folks listened, goggling like frogs.

> *A bold young man kept mocking,*
> *Cared not for the warning word,*
> *When the wild and lonely whistle*
> *Of the little black train he heard.*
> *"Have mercy, Lord, forgive me!*
> *I'm cut down in my sin!*
> *O death, will you not spare me?"*
> *But the little black train rolled in.*

When she'd sung that much, Donie Carawan laughed like before, deep and bantering. Jeth the dance-caller made a funny sound in his bull throat.

"What I don't figure," he said, "was how you all made the train sound like coming in, closer and closer."

"Just by changing the music," I said. "Changing the pitch."

"Fact," said the mouth harp man. "I played the change with him."

A woman laughed, nervous. "Now, I think, that's true. A train whistle sounds higher and higher while it comes up to you. Then it passes and goes off, sounding lower and lower."

"But I didn't hear the train go away in the song," allowed a man beside her. "It just kept coming." He shrugged, maybe he shivered.

"Donie," said the woman, "reckon I'll go along."

"Stay on, Lettie," began Donie Carawan, telling her instead of asking.

"Got a right much walking to do, and no moon," said the woman. "Reuben, you come too."

She left. The man looked back just once at Donie Carawan, and followed. Another couple, and then another, went with them from the firelight. Maybe more would have gone, but Donie Carawan snorted, like a horse, to stop them.

"Let's drink," she said. "Plenty for all, now those folks I reckoned to be my friends are gone."

Maybe two, three others faded away, between there and the barrel. Donie Carawan dipped herself a drink, watching me over the gourd's edge. Then she dipped more and held it out.

"You drink after a lady," she whispered, "and get a kiss."

I drank. It was good stump-hole whiskey. "Tasty," I said.

"The kiss?" she laughed. But the dance-caller didn't laugh, or either the mouth harp man, or either me.

"Let's dance," said Donie Carawan, and I picked "Sourwood Mountain" and the mouth harp moaned.

The dancers had got to be few, just in a short while. But the trees they danced through looked bigger, and more of them. It minded me of how I'd heard, when I was a chap, about day-trees and night-trees, they weren't the same things at all; and the night-trees can crowd all round a house they don't like, pound the shingles off the roof, bust in the window glass and the door panels; and that's the sort of night you'd better never set your foot outside. . . .

Not so much clapping at the end of "Sourwood Mountain." Not such a holler of "More!" Folks went to take another drink at the barrel, but the mouth harp man held me back.

"Tell me," he said, "about that business. The noise sounding higher when the train comes close."

"It was explained out to me by a man I know, place in Tennessee called Oak Ridge," I said. "It's about what they call sound waves, and some way it works with light too. Don't rightly catch on how, but they can measure how far it is to the stars thataway."

He thought, frowning. "Something like what's called radar?"

I shook my head. "No, no machinery to it. Just what they name a principle. Fellow named Doppler—Christian Doppler, a foreigner—got it up."

"His name was Christian," the mouth harp man repeated me. "Then I reckon it's no witch stuff."

"Why you worrying it?" I asked him.

"I watched through the dog-trot while we were playing the black train song, changing pitch, making it sound like coming near," he said. "Looky yonder, see for yourself."

I looked. There was a streaky shine down the valley. Two streaky shines, though nary moon. I saw what he meant— it looked like those pulled-up rails were still there, where they hadn't been before.

"That second verse Miss Donie sang," I said. "Was it about—"

"Yes," he said before I'd finished. "That was the verse about Cobb Richardson. How he prayed for God's forgiveness, night before he died."

Donie Carawan came and poked her hand under my arm. I could tell that good strong liquor was feeling its way around her insides. She laughed at almost nothing whatever. "You're not leaving, anyway." She smiled at me.

"Don't have anyplace special to go," I said.

She upped on her pointed toes. "Stay here tonight," she said in my ear. "The rest of them will be gone by midnight."

"You invite men like that?" I said, looking into her blue eyes. "When you don't know them?"

"I know men well enough," she said. "Knowing men keeps a woman young." Her finger touched my guitar where it hung behind my shoulder, and the strings whispered a reply. "Sing me something, John."

"I still want to learn the black train song."

"I've sung you both verses," she said.

"Then," I told her, "I'll sing a verse I've just made up inside my head." I looked at the mouth harp man. "Help me with this."

Together we played, raising pitch gradually, and I sang the new verse I'd made, with my eyes on Donie Carawan.

> *Go tell that laughing lady*
> *All filled with worldly pride,*
> *The little black train is coming,*
> *Get ready to take a ride.*
> *With a little black coach and engine*
> *And a little black baggage car,*
> *The words and deeds she has said and done*
> *Must roll to the judgment bar.*

When I was through, I looked up at those who'd stayed. They weren't more than half a dozen now, bunched up together like cows in a storm; all but Big Jeth, standing to one side with eyes stabbing at me, and Donie Carawan, leaning tiredlike against a tree with hanging branches.

"Jeth," she said, "stomp his guitar to pieces."

I switched the carrying cord off my neck and held the guitar at my side. "Don't try such a thing, Jeth," I warned him.

His big square teeth grinned, with dark spaces between them. He looked twice as wide as me.

"I'll stomp you and your guitar both," he said.

I put the guitar on the ground, glad I'd had but the one drink. Jeth ran and stooped for it, and I put my fist hard under his ear. He hopped two steps away to keep his feet.

Shouldn't anybody name me what he did then, and I hit him twice more, harder yet. His nose flatted out under my knuckles and when he pulled back away, blood trickled.

The mouth harp man grabbed up my guitar. "This here'll be a square fight!" he yelled, louder than he'd spoken so far. "Ain't a fair one, seeing Jeth's so big, but it'll be square! Just them two in it, and no more!"

"I'll settle you later," Jeth promised him, mean.

"Settle me first," I said, and got betwixt them.

Jeth ran at me. I stepped sidewise and got him under the ear again as he went shammocking past. He turned, and I dug my fist right into his belly-middle, to stir up all that stump-hole whiskey he'd been drinking, then the other fist under the ear yet once more, then on the chin and the mouth, under the ear, on the broken nose—ten licks like that, as fast and hard as I could fetch them in, and eighth or ninth he went slack, and the tenth he just fell flat and loose, like a coat from a nail. I stood waiting, but he didn't move.

"Gentlemen," said the drunk man who'd fetched me, "looky yonder at Jeth laying there! Never figured to see the day! Maybe that stranger-man calls himself John is Satan, after all!"

Donie Carawan walked across, slow, and gouged Jeth's ribs with the pointy toe of her high-heeled shoe. "Get up," she bade him.

He grunted and mumbled and opened his eyes. Then he got up, joint by joint, careful and sore, like a sick bull. He tried to stop the blood from his nose with the back of his big hand. Donie Carawan looked at him and then she looked at me.

"Get out of here, Jeth," she ordered him. "Off my place."

He went, cripplylike, with his knees bent and his hands

swinging and his back humped, the way you'd think he carried something heavy.

The drunk man hiccuped. "I reckon to go too," he said, maybe just to himself.

"Then go!" Donie Carawan yelled at him. "Everybody can go, right now, this minute! I thought you were my friends—now I see I don't have a friend among the whole bunch! Hurry up, get going! Everybody!"

Hands on hips, she blared it out. Folks moved off through the trees, a sight faster than Jeth had gone. But I stood where I was. The mouth harp man gave me back my guitar, and I touched a chord of its strings. Donie Carawan spun around like on a swivel to set her blue eyes on me.

"You stayed," she said, the way she thought there was something funny about it.

"It's not midnight yet," I told her.

"But near to," added the mouth harp man. "Just a few minutes off. And it's at midnight the little black train runs."

She lifted her round bare shoulders. She made to laugh again, but didn't.

"That's all gone. If it ever was true, it's not true anymore. The rails were taken up—"

"Looky yonder through the dog-trot," the mouth harp man broke in. "See the two rails in place, streaking along the valley."

Again she swung around and she looked, and seemed to me she swayed in the light of the dying fires. She could see those streaky rails, all right.

"And listen," said the mouth harp man. "Don't you all hear something?"

I heard it, and so did Donie Carawan, for she flinched. It was a wild and lonely whistle, soft but plain, far down valley.

"Are you doing that, John?" she squealed at me in a voice gone all of a sudden high and weak and old. Then she ran at the house and into the dog-trot, staring down along what looked like railroad track.

I followed her, and the mouth harp man followed me. Inside the dog-trot was a floor of dirt, stomped hard as brick. Donie Carawan looked back at us. Lamplight came through a window, to make her face look bright pale, with the painted red of the mouth gone almost black against it.

"John," she said, "you're playing a trick, making it sound like—"

"Not me," I swore to her.

It whistled again, *woooooeeeee*! And I, too, looked along the two rails, shining plain as plain in the dark, moonless night, to curve off around a valley bend. A second later the engine itself sounded, *chukchukchukchuk*, and the whistle, *woooooeeeee*!

"Miss Donie," I said, close behind her, "you'd better go away."

I pushed her gently.

"No!" She lifted her fists, and I saw cordy lines on their backs—they weren't a young woman's fists. "This is my house and my land, and it's my railroad!"

"But—" I started to say.

"If it comes here," she broke me off, "where can I run to from it?"

The mouth harp man tugged my sleeve. "I'm going," he said. "You and me raised the pitch and brought the black train. Thought I could stay, watch it, and glory in it. But I'm not man enough."

Going, he blew a whistle moan on his mouth harp, and the other whistle blew back an answer, louder and nearer.

And higher in the pitch.

"That's a real train coming," I told Donie Carawan, but she shook her yellow head.

"No," she said, deadlike. "It's coming, but it's no real train. It's heading right to this dog-trot. Look, John. On the ground."

Rails looked to run there, right through the dog-trot like through a tunnel. Maybe it was some peculiar way of the light. They lay close together, like narrow-gauge rails. I didn't feel like touching them with my toe to make sure of them, but I saw them. Holding my guitar under one arm, I put out my other hand to take Donie Carawan's elbow. "We'd better go," I said again.

"I can't!"

She said it loud and sharp and purely scared. And taking hold of her arm was like grabbing the rail of a fence, it was so stiff and unmoving.

"I own this land," she was saying. "I can't leave it."

I tried to pick her up, and that couldn't be done. You'd have thought she'd grown to the ground inside that dog-trot, spang between what looked like the rails, the way you'd figure roots had come from her pointy toes and high heels. Out yonder, where the track marks curved off, the sound rose louder, higher, *chukchukchukchuk—wooooooe eeee!* And light was coming from round the curve, like a headlight maybe, only it had some blue to its yellow.

The sound of the coming engine made the notes of the song in my head:

> Go put your house in order
> For thou shalt surely die—

Getting higher, getting higher, changing pitch as it came close and closer—

I don't know when I began picking the tune on my guitar, but I was playing as I stood there next to Donie Carawan. She couldn't flee. She was rooted there, or frozen there, and the train was going to come in sight in just a second.

The mouth harp man credited us, him and me, with bringing it, by that pitch-changing. And, whatever anybody deserved, wasn't for me to bring their deservings on them. I thought things like that. Also:

Christian Doppler was the name of the fellow who'd thought out the why and wherefore of how pitch makes the sound closeness. Like what the mouth harp man said, his name showed it wasn't witch stuff. An honest man could try . . .

I slid my fingers back up the guitar neck, little by little, as I picked the music, and the pitch sneaked down.

"Here it comes, John," whimpered Donie Carawan, standing solid as a stump.

"No," I said. "It's going—listen!"

I played so soft you could pick up the train noise with your ear. And the pitch was dropping, like with my guitar, and the whistle sounded *wooooooeeeee!* Lower it sounded.

"The light—dimmer—" she said. "Oh, if I could have the chance to live different—"

She moaned and swayed.

Words came for me to sing as I picked.

> *Oh, see her standing helpless,*
> *Oh, hear her shedding tears.*
> *She's counting these last moments*
> *As once she counted years.*
> *She'd turn from proud and wicked ways,*
> *She'd leave her sin, O Lord!*
> *If the little black train would just back up*
> *And not take her aboard.*

For she was weeping, all right. I heard her breath catch and strangle and shake her body, the way you'd look for it to tear her ribs loose from her backbone. I picked on, strummed on, lower and lower.

Just for once, I thought I could glimpse what might have come at us.

It was little, all right, and black under that funny cold-blue light it carried. And the cars weren't any bigger than coffins, and some way the shape of coffins. Or maybe I just sort of imagined that, dreamed it up while I stood there. Anyway, the light grew dim, and the *chukchukchukchuk* went softer and lower, and you'd guess the train was backing off, out of hearing.

I stopped my hand on the silver strings. We stood there

THE LITTLE BLACK TRAIN   215

in a silence like what there must be in some lifeless, airless place like on the moon.

Then Donie Carawan gave out one big, broken sob, and I caught her with my free arm as she fell.

She was soft enough then. All the tight was gone from her. She lifted one weak, round, bare arm around my neck, and her tears wet my hickory shirt.

"You saved me, John," she kept saying. "You turned the curse away."

"Reckon I did," I said, though that sounded like bragging. I looked down at the rails, and they weren't there, in the dog-trot or beyond. Just the dark of the valley. The cooking fires had burned out, and the lamps in the house were low.

Her arm tightened around my neck. "Come in," she said. "Come in, John. You and me, alone in there."

"It's time for me to head off away," I said.

Her arm dropped from me. "What's the matter? Don't you like me?" she asked.

I didn't even answer that one, she sounded so pitiful. "Miss Donie," I said, "you told a true thing. I turned the curse from you. It hadn't died. You can't kill it by laughing at it, or saying there aren't such things, or pulling up rails. If it held off tonight, it might come back."

"Oh!" She half raised her arms to me again, then put them down.

"What must I do?" she begged me.

"Stop being a sinner."

Her blue eyes got round in her pale face.

"You want me to live," she said, hopeful.

"It's better for you to live. You told me that folks owe you money, rent land from you, and such. How'd they get along if you got carried off?"

She could see what I meant, maybe the first time in her life.

"You'd be gone," I minded her, "but the folks would stay behind, needing your help. Well, you're still here, Miss Donie. Try to help the folks. There's a thousand ways to do it. I don't have to name them to you. And you act right, you won't be so apt to hear that whistle at midnight."

I started out of the dog-trot.

"John!" My name sounded like a wail in her mouth.

"Stay here tonight, John," she begged me. "Stay with me! I want you here, John, I need you here!"

"No, you don't need me, Miss Donie," I said. "You've got a right much of thinking and planning to do. Around about the up of sun, you'll have done enough, maybe, to start living different from this on."

She started to cry. As I walked away I noticed how, farther I got, lower her voice-pitch sounded.

I sort of stumbled on the trail. The mouth harp man sat on a chopped-down old log.

"I listened, John," he said. "Think you done right?"

"Did the closest I could to right. Maybe the black train was bound to roll, on orders from whatever station it starts from; maybe it was you and me, raising the pitch the way we did, brought it here tonight."

"I left when I did, dreading that thought." He nodded.

"The same thought made me back it out again," I said.

"Anyway, I kind of glimmer the idea you all can look for a new Donie Carawan hereabouts, from now forward."

He got up and turned to go up trail. "I never said who I was."

"No, sir," I agreed him. "And I never asked."

"I'm Cobb Richardson's brother. Wyatt Richardson. Dying, my mother swore me to even things with Donie Carawan for what happened to Cobb. Doubt if she meant this sort of turnout, but I reckon it would suit her fine."

We walked into the dark together.

"Come stay at my house tonight, John," he made the offer. "Ain't much there, but you're welcome to what there is."

"Thank you kindly," I said. "I'd be proud to stay."

THE AUTOPSY

MICHAEL SHEA

Californian Michael Shea often mixes science fiction with horror in his writings to produce (paradoxically) literate, rational terror. His novel *Nifft the Lean* (1982) is set in the future, yet it is a horrific future. "The Autopsy" uses a similar mix of sf and horror. This story—in which Dr. Carl Winters, a fifty-seven-year-old pathologist, arrives at a mountain town to perform autopsies on the victims of a suspicious mining explosion—is about the business of death; and so be warned that it is in some ways a grim tale. However, it is ultimately a positive, even touching story. You won't soon forget Dr. Winters and what he finds in a defunct ice plant on the edge of the town known as Bailey.

Dr. Winters stepped out of the tiny Greyhound station and into the midnight street that smelt of pines and the river, though the street was in the heart of the town. But then, it was a town of only five main streets in breadth, and these extended scarcely a mile and a half along the rim of the gorge. Deep in that gorge though the river ran, its blurred roar flowed, perfectly distinct, between the banks of dark shop windows. The station's window showed the only light, save for a luminous clock face several doors down and a little neon beer logo two blocks farther on. When he had walked a short distance, Dr. Winters set his suitcase down, pocketed his hands, and looked at the stars —thick as cobblestones in the black gulf.

"A mountain hamlet—a mining town," he said. "Stars. No moon. We are in Bailey."

He was talking to his cancer. It was in his stomach. Since learning of it, he had developed this habit of wry communion with it. He meant to show courtesy to this uninvited guest, Death. It would not find him churlish, for that would make its victory absolute. Except, of course, that its victory would *be* absolute, with or without his ironies.

He picked up his suitcase and walked on. The starlight made faint mirrors of the windows' blackness and showed him the man who passed: lizard-lean, white-haired (at fifty-seven), a man traveling on death's business, carrying his own death in him, and even bearing death's wardrobe in his suitcase. For this was filled—aside from his medical kit and some scant necessities—with mortuary bags. The sheriff had told him on the phone of the improvisations that presently enveloped the corpses, and so the doctor had packed these, laying them in his case with bitter amusement, checking the last one's breadth against his chest before the mirror, as a woman will gauge a dress before donning it, and telling his cancer: "Oh, yes, that's plenty roomy enough for both of us!"

The case was heavy and he stopped frequently to rest and scan the sky. What a night's work to do, probing soulless filth, eyes earthward, beneath such a ceiling of stars! It had taken five days to dig them out. The autumnal equinox had passed, but the weather here had been uniformly hot. And warmer still, no doubt, so deep in the earth.

He entered the courthouse by a side door. His heels knocked on the linoleum corridor. A door at the end of it, on which was lettered NATE CRAVEN, COUNTY SHERIFF, opened well before he reached it, and his friend stepped out to meet him.

"Dammit, Carl, you're *still* so thin they could use you for a whip. Gimme that. You're in too good a shape already. You don't need the exercise."

The case hung weightless from his hand, imparting no tilt at all to his bull shoulders. Despite his implied self-derogation, he was only moderately paunched for a man his age and size. He had a rough-hewn face and the bulk of brow, nose, and jaw made his greenish eyes look small until one engaged them and felt the snap and penetration of their intelligence. He half filled two cups from a coffee urn and topped both off with bourbon from a bottle in his desk. When they had finished these, they had finished trading news of mutual friends. The sheriff mixed another round, and sipped from his in a silence clearly prefatory to the work at hand.

"They talk about rough justice," he said. "I've sure seen it now. One of those . . . patients of yours that you'll be working on? He was a killer. 'Killer' don't even half say it, really. You could say that *he* got justly executed in that blast. That much was justice for damn sure. But rough as hell on those other nine. And the rough don't just stop with their being dead either. That kiss-ass boss of yours! He's breaking his goddamned back touching his toes for Fordham Mutual. How much of the picture did he give you?"

"You refer, I take it, to the estimable Coroner Waddleton of Fordham County." Dr. Winters paused to sip his drink. With a delicate flaring of his nostrils he communicated all the disgust, contempt, and amusement he had felt in his four years as pathologist in Waddleton's office. The sheriff laughed.

"Clear pictures seldom emerge from anything the coroner says," the doctor continued. "He took your name in vain. Vigorously and repeatedly. These expressions formed his opening remarks. He then developed the theme of our office's strict responsibility to the letter of the law, and of the workmen's compensation law in particular. Death benefits accrue only to the dependents of decedents whose death arise *out of the course of* their employment, not merely *in* the course of it. Victims of a maniacal assault, though they die on the job, are by no means necessarily compensable under the law. We then contemplated the tragic injustice of an insurance company—*any* insurance company—having to pay benefits to unentitled persons, solely through the laxity and incompetence of investigating officers. Your name came up again."

Craven uttered a bark of mirth and fury. "The impartial public servant! Ha! The impartial brown-nose, flimflam and bullshit man is what he *is*. Ten to one, Fordham Mutual will slip out of it *without* his help, and those widows won't see a goddamn nickel." Words were an insufficient vent; the sheriff turned and spat into his wastebasket. He drained his cup, and sighed. "I beg your pardon, Carl. We've been five days digging those men out and the last two days sifting half that mountain for explosive traces, with those insurance investigators hanging on our elbows, and the most they could say was that there was 'strong presumptive evidence' of a bomb. Well, I don't budge for that because I don't have to. Waddleton can shove his 'extraordinary circumstances.' If you don't find anything in those bodies, then that's all the autopsy there is to it, and they get buried right here where their families want 'em."

The doctor was smiling at his friend. He finished his cup and spoke with his previous wry detachment, as if the sheriff had not interrupted.

"The honorable coroner then spoke with remarkable vol-

ubility on the subject of autopsy consent forms and the
malicious subversion of private citizens by vested officers of
the law. He had, as it happened, a sheaf of such forms on
his desk, all signed, all with a rider clause typed in above
the signatures. A cogent paragraph. It had, among its other
qualities, the property of turning the coroner's face purple
when he read it aloud. He read it aloud to me three times.
It appeared that the survivors' consent was contingent on
two conditions: that the autopsy be performed *in locem
mortis*, that is to say in Bailey, and that only if the coroner's
pathologist found concrete evidence of homicide should the
decedents be subject either to removal from Bailey or to
further necropsy. It was well written. I remember wondering
who wrote it."

The sheriff nodded musingly. He took Dr. Winters's empty
cup, set it by his own, filled both two thirds with bourbon,
and added a splash of coffee to the doctor's. The two friends
exchanged a level stare, rather like poker players in the
clinch. The sheriff regarded his cup, sipped from it.

"*In locem mortis*. What-all does that mean exactly?"

" 'In the place of death'."

"Oh. Freshen that up for you?"

"I've just started it, thank you."

Both men laughed, paused, and laughed again, some
might have said immoderately.

"He all but told me that I *had* to find something to compel
a second autopsy," the doctor said at length. "He would
have sold his soul—or taken out a second mortgage on it
—for a mobile X-ray unit. He's right, of course. If those
bodies have trapped any bomb fragments, that would be the
surest and quickest way of finding them. It still amazes me
your Dr. Parsons could let his X ray go unfixed for so long."

"He sets bones, stitches wounds, writes prescriptions, and
sends anything tricky down the mountain. Just barely man-
ages that. Drunks don't get much done."

"He's gotten that bad?"

"He hangs on and no more. Waddleton was right there,

not deputizing him pathologist. I doubt he could find a cannonball in a dead rat. I wouldn't say it where it could hurt him, as long as he's still managing, but everyone here knows it. His patients sort of look after *him* half the time. But Waddleton would have sent you, no matter who was here. Nothing but his best for party contributors like Fordham Mutual."

The doctor looked at his hands and shrugged. "So. There's a killer in the batch. *Was* there a bomb?"

Slowly, the sheriff planted his elbows on the desk and pressed his hands against his temples, as if the question had raised a turbulence of memories. For the first time the doctor—half harkening throughout to the never-quite-muted stirrings of the death within him—saw his friend's exhaustion: the tremor of hand, the bruised look under the eyes.

"I'm going to give you what I have, Carl. I told you I don't think you'll find a damn thing in those bodies. You're probably going to end up assuming what I do about it, but assuming is as far as anyone's going to get with this one. It is truly one of those nightmare specials that the good Lord tortures lawmen with and then hides the answers to forever.

"All right then. About two months ago, we had a man disappear—Ronald Hanley. Mine worker, rock steady, family man. He didn't come home one night, and we never found a trace of him. Okay, that happens sometimes. About a week later, the lady that ran the Laundromat, Sharon Starker, *she* disappeared, no trace. We got edgy then. I made an announcement on the local radio about a possible weirdo at large, spelled out special precautions everybody should take. We put both our squad cars on the night beat, and by day we set to work knocking on every door in town collecting alibis for the two times of disappearance.

"No good. Maybe you're fooled by this uniform and think I'm a law officer, protector of the people, and all that? A natural mistake. A lot of people were fooled. In less than seven weeks, six people vanished, just like that. Me and my deputies might as well have stayed in bed round the clock, for all the good we did." The sheriff drained his cup.

"Anyway, at last we got lucky. Don't get me wrong now. We didn't go all hog wild and actually prevent a crime or anything. But we *did* find a body—except it wasn't the body of any of the seven people that had disappeared. We'd took to combing the woods nearest town, with temporary deputies from the miners to help. Well, one of those boys was out there with us last week. It was hot—like it's been for a while now—and it was real quiet. He heard this buzzing noise and looked around for it, and he saw a bee swarm up in the crotch of a tree. Except he was smart enough to know that that's not usual around here—beehives. So it wasn't bees. It was bluebottle flies, a goddamned big cloud of them, all over a bundle that was wrapped in a tarp."

The sheriff studied his knuckles. He had, in his eventful life, occasionally met men literate enough to understand his last name and rash enough to be openly amused by it, and the knuckles—scarred knobs—were eloquent of his reactions. He looked back into his old friend's eyes.

"We got that thing down and unwrapped it. Billy Lee Davis, one of my deputies, he was in Vietnam, been near some bad, bad things and held on. Billy Lee blew his lunch all over the ground when we unwrapped that thing. It was a man. Some of a man. We knew he'd stood six-two because all the bones were there, and he'd probably weighed between two fifteen and two twenty-five, but he folded up no bigger than a big-size laundry package. Still had his face, both shoulders, and the left arm, but all the rest was clean. It wasn't animal work. It was knife work, all the edges neat as butcher cuts. Except butchered meat, even when you drain it all you can, will bleed a good deal afterward, and there wasn't one goddamned drop of blood on the tarp, nor in that meat. It was just as pale as fish meat."

Deep in his body's center, the doctor's cancer touched him. Not a ravening attack—it sank one fang of pain, ques-

tioningly, into new, untasted flesh, probing the scope for
its appetite there. He disguised his tremor with a shake of
the head.

"A cache, then."

The sheriff nodded. "Like you might keep a pot roast in
the icebox for making lunches. I took some pictures of his
face, then we put him back and erased our traces. Two of
the miners I'd deputized did a lot of hunting, were woods-
smart. So I left them on the first watch. We worked out
positions and cover for them, and drove back.

"We got right on tracing him, sent out descriptions to
every town within a hundred miles. He was no one I'd ever
seen in Bailey, nor anyone else either, it began to look like,
after we'd combed the town all day with the photos. Then,
out of the blue, Billy Lee Davis smacks himself on the
forehead and says, 'Sheriff, I seen this man somewhere in
town, and not long ago!'

"He'd been shook all day since throwing up, and then
all of a sudden he just snapped to. Was dead sure. Except
he couldn't remember where or when. We went over and
over it and he tried and tried. It got to where I wanted to
grab him by the ankles and hang him upside down and
shake him till it dropped out of him. But it was no damn
use. Just after dark we went back to that tree—we'd worked
out a place to hide the cars and a route to it through the
woods. When we were close we walkie-talkied the men we'd
left for an all-clear to come up. No answer at all. And when
we got there, all that was left of our trap was the tree. No
body, no tarp, no special assistant deputies. Nothing."

This time Dr. Winters poured the coffee and bourbon.
"Too much coffee," the sheriff muttered, but drank anyway.
"Part of me wanted to chew nails and break necks. And
part of me was scared shitless. When we got back I got on
the radio station again and made an emergency broadcast
and then had the man at the station rebroadcast it every
hour. Told everyone to do everything in groups of three,
to stay together at night in threes at least, to go out little as

possible, keep armed, and keep checking up on each other. It had such a damn-fool sound to it, but just pairing up was no protection if half of one of those pairs was the killer. I deputized more men and put them on the streets to beef up the night patrol.

"It was next morning that things broke. The sheriff of Rakehell called—he's over in the next county. He said our corpse sounded a lot like a man named Abel Dougherty, a mill hand with Con Wood over there. I left Billy Lee in charge and drove right out.

"This Dougherty had a crippled older sister he always checked back to by phone whenever he left town for long, a habit no one knew about, probably embarrassed him. Sheriff Peck there only found out about it when the woman called him, said her brother'd been four days gone for vacation and not rung her once. Without that Peck might not've thought of Dougherty just from our description, though the photo I showed him clinched it, and one would've reached him by mail soon enough. Well, he'd hardly set it down again, when a call came through for me. It was Billy Lee. He'd remembered.

"When he'd seen Dougherty was the Sunday night three days before we found him. Where he'd seen him was the Trucker's Tavern outside the north end of town. The man had made a stir by being jolly drunk and latching on to a miner who was drinking there, man named Joe Allen, who'd started at the mine about two months back. Dougherty kept telling him that he wasn't Joe Allen, but Dougherty's old buddy named Sykes that had worked with him at Con Wood for a coon's age, and what the hell kind of joke was this, come have a beer old buddy and tell me why you took off so sudden and what the hell you been doing with yourself.

"Allen took it laughing. Dougherty'd clap him on the shoulder, Allen'd clap him right back and make every kind of joke about it, say 'Give this man another beer, I'm standing in for a long-lost friend of his.' Dougherty was so big and loud and stubborn, Billy Lee was worried about a fight starting, and he wasn't the only one worried. But this Joe Allen was a natural good ol' boy, handled it perfect. We'd checked him out weeks back along with everyone else, and he was real popular with the other miners. Finally Dougherty swore he was going to take him on to another bar to help celebrate the vacation Dougherty was starting out on. Joe Allen got up grinning, said goddammit, he couldn't accommodate Dougherty by being this fellow Sykes, but he could sure as hell have a glass with any serious drinking man that was treating. He went out with him, and gave everyone a wink as he left, to the general satisfaction of the audience."

Craven paused. Dr. Winters met his eyes and knew his thought, two images: the jolly wink that roused the room to laughter, and the thing in the tarp aboil with bright blue flies.

"It was plain enough for me," the sheriff said. "I told Billy Lee to search Allen's room at the Skettles' boarding-house and then go straight to the mine and take him. We could fine-polish things once we had him. Since I was already in Rakehell, I saw to some of the loose ends before I started back. I went with Sheriff Peck down to Con Wood and we found a picture of Eddie Sykes in the personnel files. I'd seen Joe Allen often enough, and it was his picture in that file.

"We found out Sykes lived alone, was an on-again off-again worker, private in his comings and goings, and hadn't been around for a while. But one of the sawyers there could be pretty sure of when Sykes left Rakehell because he'd gone to Sykes's cabin the morning after a big meteor shower they had out there about nine weeks back, since some thought the shower might have reached the ground, and not far from Sykes's side of the mountain. He wasn't in that morning, and the sawyer hadn't seen him since.

"It looked sewed up. It *was* sewed up. After all those weeks, I was less than a mile out of Bailey, had the pedal floored. Full of rage and revenge. I felt . . . like a *bullet*, like I was one big thirty-caliber slug that was going to go right through that blood-sucking cannibal, tear the whole truth right out of his heart, enough to hang him a hundred times. That was the closest I got. So close that I *heard* it when it all blew to shit.

"I sound squirrelly. I know I do. Maybe all this gave me something I'll never shake off. We had to put together what happened. Billy Lee didn't have my other deputy with him. Travis was out with some men on the mountain dragnetting around that tree for clues. By luck, he was back at the car when Billy Lee was trying to raise him. He said he'd just been through Allen's room and had gotten something we could maybe hold him on. It was a sphere, half again big as a basketball, heavy, made of something that wasn't metal or glass but was a little like both. He could half-see into it and it looked to be full of some kind of circuitry and components. If someone tried to spring Allen, we could make a theft rap out of this thing, or say we suspected it was a bomb. Jesus! Anyway, he said it was the only strange thing he found, but it was plenty strange. He told Travis to get up to the mine for backup. He'd be there first and should already have Allen by the time Travis arrived.

"Tierney, the shift boss up there, had an assistant that told us the rest. Billy Lee parked behind the offices where the men in the yard wouldn't see the car. He went upstairs to arrange the arrest with Tierney. They got half a dozen men together. Just as they came out of the building, they saw Allen take off running from the squad car with the sphere under his arm.

"The whole compound's fenced in and Tierney'd already phoned to have all the gates shut. Allen zigged and zagged some but caught on quick to the trap. The sphere slowed him, but he still had a good lead. He hesitated a minute and then ran straight for the main shaft. A cage was just going down with a crew, and he risked every bone in him jumping down after it, but he got safe on top. By the time they got to the switches, the cage was down to the second

level, and Allen and the crew had got out. Tierney got it
back up. Billy Lee ordered the rest back to get weapons and
follow, and him and Tierney rode the cage right back down.
And about two minutes later half the goddamned mine blew
up."

The sheriff stopped as if cut off, his lips parted to say
more, his eyes registering for perhaps the hundredth time
his amazement that there was no more, that the weeks of
death and mystification ended here, with this split-second
recapitulation: more death, more answerless dark, sealing
all.

"Nate."

"What."

"Wrap it up and go to bed. I don't need your help. You're
dead on your feet."

"I'm not on my feet. And I'm coming along."

"Give me a picture of the victims' position relative to the
blast. I'm going to work and you're going to bed."

The sheriff shook his head absently. "They're mining in
shrinkage stopes. The adits—levels—branch off lateral from
the vertical shaft. From one level they hollow out overhand
up to the one above. Scoop out big chambers and let most
of the broken rock stay inside so they can stand on the heaps
to cut the ceilings higher. They leave sections of support
wall between stopes, and those men were buried several
stopes in from the shaft. The cave-in killed *them*. The
mountain just folded them up in their own hill of tailings.
No kind of fragments reached them. I'm dead sure. The
only ones they *found* were of some standard charges that
the main blast set off, and those didn't even get close. The
big one blew out where the adit joined the shaft, right where,
and right when Billy Lee and Tierney got out of the cage.
And there is *nothing* left there, Carl. No sphere, no cage,
no Tierney, no Billy Lee Davis. Just rock blown fine as
flour."

Dr. Winters nodded and, after a moment, stood up.

"Come on, Nate. I've got to get started. I'll be lucky to

have even a few of them done before morning. Drop me off and go to sleep, till then at least. You'll still be there to witness most of the work."

The sheriff rose, took up the doctor's suitcase, and led him out of the office without a word, concession in his silence.

The patrol car was behind the building. The doctor saw a crueller beauty in the stars than he had an hour before. They got in, and Craven swung them out onto the empty street. The doctor opened the window and harkened, but the motor's surge drowned out the river sound. Before the thrust of their headlights, ranks of old-fashioned parking meters sprouted shadows tall across the sidewalks, shadows which shrank and were cut down by the lights' passage. The sheriff said: "All those extra dead. For nothing! Not even to . . . *feed* him! If it *was* a bomb, and he made it, he'd know how powerful it was. He wouldn't try some stupid escape stunt with it. And how did he even know the thing was there? We worked it out that Allen was just ending a shift, but he wasn't even up out of the ground before Billy Lee'd parked out of sight."

"Let it rest, Nate. I want to hear more, but after you've slept. I know you. All the photos will be there, and the report complete, all the evidence neatly boxed and carefully described. When I've looked things over I'll know exactly how to proceed by myself."

Bailey had neither hospital nor morgue, and the bodies were in a defunct ice plant on the edge of town. A generator had been brought down from the mine, lighting improvised, and the refrigeration system reactivated. Dr. Parsons's office, and the tiny examining room that served the sheriff's station in place of a morgue, had furnished this makeshift with all the equipment that Dr. Winters would need beyond what he carried with him. A quarter-mile outside the main body of the town, they drew up to it. Tree-flanked, unneighbored by any other structure, it was a double building; the smaller half—the office—was illuminated. The bodies would be in the big, windowless refrigerator segment. Craven pulled up beside a second squad car parked near the office door. A short, rake-thin man wearing a large white Stetson got out of the car and came over. Craven rolled down his window.

"Trav. This here's Dr. Winters."

" 'Lo, Nate. Dr. Winters. Everything's shipshape inside. Felt more comfortable out here. Last of those newshounds left two hours ago."

"They sure do hang on. You take off now, Trav. Get some sleep and be back at sunup. What temperature we getting?"

The pale Stetson, far clearer in the starlight than the shadow face beneath it, wagged dubiously. "Thirty-six. She won't get lower—some kind of leak."

"That should be cold enough," the doctor said.

Travis drove off and the sheriff unlocked the padlock on the office door. Waiting behind him, Dr. Winters heard the river again—a cold balm, a whisper of freedom—and overlying this, the stutter and soft snarl of the generator behind the building, a gnawing, remorseless sound that somehow fed the obscure anguish which the other soothed. They went in.

The preparations had been thoughtful and complete. "You can wheel 'em out of the fridge on this and do the examining in here," the sheriff said, indicating a table and a gurney. "You should find all the gear you need on this big table here, and you can write up your reports on that desk. The phone's not hooked up—there's a pay phone at that last gas station if you have to call me."

The doctor nodded, checking over the material on the larger table: scalpels, post-mortem and cartilage knives, intestine scissors, rib shears, forceps, probes, mallet and chisels, a blade saw and electric bone saw, scale, jars for specimens, needles and suture, sterilizer, gloves. . . . Beside this array were a few boxes and envelopes with descriptive sheets attached, containing the photographs and such evidentiary objects as had been found associated with the bodies.

"Excellent," he muttered.

"The overhead light's fluorescent, full spectrum or whatever they call it. Better for colors. There's a pint of decent bourbon in that top desk drawer. Ready to look at 'em?"

"Yes."

The sheriff unbarred and slid back the big metal door to the refrigeration chamber. Icy, tainted air boiled out of the doorway. The light within was dimmer than that provided in the office—a yellow gloom wherein ten oblong heaps lay on trestles.

The two stood silent for a time, their stillness a kind of unpremeditated homage paid the eternal mystery at its threshold. As if the cold room were in fact a shrine, the doctor found a peculiar awe in the row of veiled forms. The awful unison of their dying, the titan's grave that had been made for them, conferred on them a stern authority, death's chosen ones. His stomach hurt, and he found he had his hand pressed to his abdomen. He glanced at Craven and was relieved to see that his friend, staring wearily at the bodies, had missed the gesture.

"Nate. Help me uncover them."

Starting at opposite ends of the row, they stripped the tarps off and piled them in a corner. Both were brusque now, not pausing over the revelation of the swelled, pulpy faces—most three-lipped with the gaseous burgeoning of their tongues—and the fat, livid hands sprouting from the filthy sleeves. But at one of the bodies Craven stopped. The doctor saw him look, and his mouth twist. Then he flung the tarp on the heap and moved to the next trestle.

When they came out Dr. Winters took out the bottle and glasses Craven had put in the desk, and they had a drink together. The sheriff made as if he would speak, but shook his head and sighed.

"I *will* get some sleep, Carl. I'm getting crazy thoughts with this thing." The doctor wanted to ask those thoughts. Instead, he laid a hand on his friend's shoulder.

"Go home, Sheriff Craven. Take off the badge and lie down. The dead won't run off on you. We'll all still be here in the morning."

When the sound of the patrol car faded, the doctor stood listening to the generator's growl and the silence of the dead, resurgent now. Both the sound and the silence seemed to mock him. The after-echo of his last words made him uneasy. He said to his cancer: "What about it, dear colleague? We *will* still be here tomorrow? All of us?"

He smiled, but felt an odd discomfort, as if he had ventured a jest in company and roused a hostile silence. He went to the refrigerator door, rolled it back, and viewed the corpses in their ordered rank, with their strange tribunal air. "What, sirs?" he murmured. "Do you judge me? Just who is to examine whom tonight, if I may ask?"

He went back into the office, where his first step was to examine the photographs made by the sheriff, in order to see how the dead had lain at their uncovering. The earth had seized them with terrible suddenness. Some crouched, some partly stood, others sprawled in crazy, free-fall postures. Each successive photo showed more of the jumble as the shovels continued their work between shots. The doctor studied them closely, noting the identifications inked on the bodies as they came completely into view.

One man, Roger Willet, had died some yards from the main cluster. It appeared he had just straggled into the stope from the adit at the moment of the explosion. He should thus have received, more directly than any of the others, the shockwaves of the blast. If bomb fragments were to be found in any of the corpses, Mr. Willet's seemed likeliest to contain them. Dr. Winters pulled on a pair of surgical gloves.

He lay at one end of the line of trestles. He wore a thermal shirt and overalls that were strikingly new beneath the filth of burial. Their tough fabrics jarred with that of his flesh —blue, swollen, seeming easily torn or burst, like ripe fruit. In life Willet had grease-combed his hair. Now it was a sculpture of dust, spikes, and whorls shaped by the head's last grindings against the mountain that clenched it.

Rigor had come and gone—Willet rolled laxly onto the gurney. As the doctor wheeled him past the others, he felt a slight self-consciousness. The sense of some judgment flowing from the dead assembly—unlike most such vagrant emotional embellishments of experience—had an odd tenacity in him. This stubborn unease began to irritate him with himself, and he moved more briskly.

He put Willet on the examining table and cut the clothes off him with shears, storing the pieces in an evidence box. The overalls were soiled with agonal waste expulsions. The doctor stared a moment with unwilling pity at his naked subject.

"You won't ride down to Fordham in any case," he said to the corpse. "Not unless I find something pretty damned obvious." He pulled his gloves tighter and arranged his implements.

Waddleton had said more to him than he had reported to the sheriff. The doctor was to find, and forcefully to record that he had found, strong "indications" absolutely requiring the decedents' removal to Fordham for X ray and an exhaustive second post mortem. The doctor's continued employment with the coroner's office depended entirely on his compliance in this. He had received this stipulation with a silence Waddleton had not thought it necessary to break. His present resolution was all but made at that moment. Let the obvious be taken as such. If the others showed as plainly as Willet did the external signs of death by asphyxiation, they would receive no more than a thorough external exam. Willet he would examine internally as well, merely to establish in depth for this one what should appear obvious in all. Otherwise, only when the external exam revealed a clearly anomalous feature—and clear and suggestive it must be—would he look deeper.

He rinsed the caked hair in a basin, poured the sediment into a flask, and labeled it. Starting with the scalp, he began a minute scrutiny of the body's surfaces, recording his observations as he went.

The characteristic signs of asphyxial death were evident, despite the complicating effects of autolysis and putrefaction. The eyeballs' bulge and the tongue's protrusion were by now at least partly due to gas pressure as well as the mode of death, but the latter organ was clamped between locked teeth, leaving little doubt as to that mode. The coloration of degenerative change—a greenish-yellow tint, a darkening and mapping-out of superficial veins—was marked, but not sufficient to obscure the blue of syanosis on the face and neck, nor the pinpoint hemorrhages freckling neck, chest, and shoulders. From the mouth and nose the doctor scraped matter he was confident was the blood-tinged mucus typically ejected in the airless agony.

He began to find a kind of comedy in his work. What a buffoon death made of a man! A blue, popeyed, three-lipped thing. And there was himself, his curious, solicitous intimacy with this clownish carrion. Excuse me, Mr. Willet, while I probe this laceration. How does it feel when I do this? Nothing? Nothing at all? Fine, now what about these nails. Split them clawing at the earth, did you? Yes. A nice blood blister under this thumbnail I see—got it on the job a few days before your accident no doubt? Remarkable calluses here, still quite tough. . . .

The doctor looked for an unanalytic moment at the hands—puffed, dark paws, gestureless, having renounced all touch and grasp. He felt the wastage of the man concentrated in the hands. The painful futility of the body's fine articulation when it is seen in death—this poignancy he had long learned not to acknowledge when he worked. But now he let it move him a little. This Roger Willet, plodding to his work one afternoon, had suddenly been scrapped, crushed to a nonfunctional heap of perishable materials. It simply happened that his life had chanced to move too close to the passage of a more powerful life, one of those inexorable and hungry lives that leave human wreckage—known or undiscovered—in their wakes. Bad luck, Mr. Willet. Naturally, we feel very sorry about this. But this Joe Allen, your coworker. Apparently he was some sort of . . . cannibal. It's complicated. We don't understand it all. But the fact is we have to dismantle you now to a certain extent. There's really no hope of your using these parts of yourself again, I'm afraid. Ready now?

The doctor proceeded to the internal exam with a vague eagerness for Willet's fragmentation, for the disarticulation of that sadness in his natural form. He grasped Willet by the jaw and took up the post-mortem knife. He sank its point beneath the chin and began the long, gently sawing incision that opened Willet from throat to groin.

In the painstaking separation of the body's laminae, Dr. Winters found absorption and pleasure. And yet throughout he felt, marginal but insistent, the movement of a stream of irrelevant images. These were of the building that contained him, and of the night containing it. As from outside, he saw the plant—bleached planks, iron roofing—and the trees crowding it, all in starlight, a ghost-town image. And he saw the refrigerator vault beyond the wall as from within, feeling the stillness of murdered men in a cold yellow light. And at length a question formed itself, darting in and out of the weave of his concentration as the images did: Why did he still feel, like some stir of the air, that sense of mute vigilance surrounding his action, furtively touching his nerves with its inquiry as he worked? He shrugged, overtly angry now. Who else was attending but Death? Wasn't he Death's hireling, and this Death's place? Then let the master look on.

Peeling back Willet's cover of hemorrhage-stippled skin, Dr. Winters read the corpse with an increasing dispassion, a mortuary text. He confined his inspection to the lungs and mediastinum and found there unequivocal testimony to Willet's asphyxial death. The pleurae of the lungs exhibited the expected ecchymoses—bruised spots in the glassy, enveloping membrane. Beneath, the polyhedral surface lobules of the lungs themselves were bubbled and blistered—the expected interstitial emphysema. The lungs, on section, were intensely and bloodily congested. The left half of the heart he found contracted and empty, while the right was overdistended and engorged with dark blood, as were the large veins of the upper mediastinum. It was a classic picture of death by suffocation, and at length the doctor, with needle and suture, closed up the text again.

He returned the corpse to the gurney and draped one of his mortuary bags over it in the manner of a shroud. When he had help in the morning, he would weigh the bodies on a platform scale the office contained and afterward bag them properly. He came to the refrigerator door, and hesitated. He stared at the door, not moving, not understanding why.

Run. Get out, now.

The thought was his own, but it came to him so urgently, he turned around as if someone behind him had spoken. Across the room a thin man in smock and gloves, his eyes shadows, glared at the doctor from the black windows. Behind the man was a shrouded cart, behind that, a wide metal door.

Quietly, wonderingly, the doctor asked, "Run from what?" The eyeless man in the glass was still half crouched, afraid.

Then, a moment later, the man straightened, threw back his head, and laughed. The doctor walked to the desk and sat down shoulder to shoulder with him. He pulled out the bottle and they had a drink together, regarding each other with identical bemused smiles. Then the doctor said, "Let me pour you another. You need it old fellow. It makes a man himself again."

Nevertheless, his reentry of the vault was difficult, toilsome, each step seeming to require a new summoning of the will to move. In the freezing half light, all movement felt like defiance. His body lagged behind his craving to be quick, to be done with this molestation of the gathered dead. He returned Willet to his pallet and took his neighbor. The name on the tag wired to his boot was Ed Moses. Dr. Winters wheeled him back to the office and closed the big door behind him.

With Moses his work gained momentum. He expected to perform no further internal necropsies. He thought of his employer, rejoicing now in his seeming submission to Waddleton's ultimatum. The impact would be dire. He pictured the coroner in shock, a sheaf of pathologist's reports in one hand, and smiled.

Waddleton could probably make a plausible case for incomplete examination. Still, a pathologist's discretionary powers were not well defined. Many good ones would approve the adequacy of the doctor's method, given his working conditions. The inevitable litigation with a coalition of compensation claimants would be strenuous and protracted. Win or lose, Waddleton's venal devotion to the insurance company's interest would be abundantly displayed. Further, immediately on his dismissal the doctor would formally disclose its occult cause to the press. A libel action would ensue, which he would have as little cause to fear as he had to fear his firing. Both his savings and the lawsuit would long outlast his life.

Externally, Ed Moses exhibited a condition as typically asphyxial as Willet's had been, with no slightest mark of fragment entry. The doctor finished his report and returned Moses to the vault, his movements brisk and precise. His unease was all but gone. That queasy stirring of the air— had he really felt it? It had been, perhaps, some new reverberation of the death at work in him, a psychic shudder of response to the cancer's stealthy probing for his life. He brought out the body next to Moses in the line.

Walter Lou Jackson was big, six-two from heel to crown, and would surely weigh out at more than two hundred pounds. He had writhed mightily against his million-ton coffin with an agonal strength that had torn his face and hands. Death had mauled him like a lion. The doctor set to work.

His hands were fully themselves now—fleet, exact, intricately testing the corpse's character as other fingers might explore a keyboard for its latent melodies. And the doctor watched them with an old pleasure, one of the few that had never failed him, his mind at one remove from their busy intelligence. All the hard deaths! A worldful of them, time without end. Lives wrenched kicking from their snug meat frames. Walter Lou Jackson had died very hard. Joe Allen brought this on you, Mr. Jackson. We think it was part of his attempt to escape the law.

But what a botched flight! The unreason of it—more than baffling—was eerie in its colossal futility. Beyond question, Allen had been cunning. A ghoul with a psychopath's social finesse. A good old boy who could make a tavernful of men laugh with delight while he cut his victim from their midst, make them applaud his exit with the prey, who stepped jovially into the darkness with murder at his side clapping him on the shoulder. Intelligent, certainly, with a strange technical sophistication as well, suggested by the sphere. Then what of the lunacy yet more strongly suggested by the same object? In the sphere was concentrated all the lethal mystery of Bailey's long nightmare.

Why the explosion? Its location implied an ambush for Allen's pursuers, a purposeful detonation. Had he aimed at a limited cave-in from which he schemed some inconceivable escape? Folly enough in this—far more if, as seemed sure, Allen had made the bomb himself, for then he would have to know its power was grossly inordinate to the need.

But if it was not a bomb, had a different function and only incidentally an explosive potential, Allen might underestimate the blast. It appeared the object was somehow remotely monitored by him, for the timing of events showed he had gone straight for it the instant he emerged from the shaft—shunned the bus waiting to take his shift back to town and made a beeline across the compound for a patrol car that was hidden from his view by the office building. This suggested something more complex than a mere explosive device, something, perhaps, whose destruction was itself more Allen's aim than the explosion produced thereby.

The fact that he risked the sphere's retrieval at all pointed to this interpretation. For the moment he sensed its presence at the mine, he must have guessed that the murder investigation had led to its discovery and removal from his room. But then, knowing himself already liable to the extreme penalty, why should Allen go to such lengths to recapture evidence incriminatory of a lesser offense, possession of an explosive device?

Then grant that the sphere was something more, something instrumental to his murders that could guarantee a conviction he might otherwise evade. Still, his gambit made no sense. Since the sphere—and thus the lawmen he could assume to have taken it—were already at the mine office, he must expect the compound to be sealed at any moment. Meanwhile, the gate was open, escape into the mountains a strong possibility for a man capable of stalking and destroying two experienced and well-armed woodsmen lying in ambush for him. Why had he all but insured his capture to weaken a case against himself that his escape would have rendered irrelevant? Dr. Winters saw his fingers, like a hunting pack round a covert, converge on a small puncture wound below Walter Lou Jackson's xiphoid process, between the eighth ribs.

His left hand touched its borders, the fingers' inquiry quick and tender. The right hand introduced a probe, and both together eased it into the wound. It inched unobstructed deep into the body, curving upward through the diaphragm toward the heart. The doctor's own heart accelerated. He watched his hands move to record the observation, watched them pause, watched them return to their survey of the corpse, leaving pen and page untouched.

Inspection revealed no further anomaly. All else he ob-

served the doctor recorded faithfully, wondering throughout
at the distress he felt. When he had finished, he understood
it. Its cause was not the discovery of an entry wound that
might bolster Waddleton's case. For the find had, within
moments, revealed to him that, should he encounter anything he thought to be a mark of fragment penetration, he
was going to ignore it. The damage Joe Allen had done was
going to end here, with this last grand slaughter, and would
not extend to the impoverishment of his victims' survivors.
No more internals. The externals, will they nill-they, would
from now on explicitly contraindicate the need for them.

The problem was that he did not believe the puncture
in Jackson's thorax *was* a mark of fragment entry. Why?
And, finding no answer to this question, why was he, once
again, afraid? Slowly, he signed the report on Jackson, set
it aside, and took up the post-mortem knife.

First the long, sawing slice, unzipping the mortal overcoat. Next, two great, square flaps of flesh reflected, scrolled
laterally to the armpits' line, disrobing the chest: one hand
grasping the flap's skirt, the other sweeping beneath it with
the knife, flensing through the glassy tissue that joined it to
the chest wall, and shaving all muscles from their anchor-
ages to bone and cartilage beneath. Then the dismantling
of the strongbox within. Rib shears—so frank and forward
a tool, like a gardener's. The steel beak bit through each
rib's gristle anchor to the sternum's centerplate. At the sternum's crownpiece the collarbones' ends were knifed, pried,
and sprung free from their sockets. The coffer unhasped,
unhinged, a knife teased beneath the lid and levered it off.

Some minutes later the doctor straightened up and stepped
back from his subject. He moved almost drunkenly, and
his age seemed scored more deeply in his face. With loath-
ing haste he stripped his gloves off. He went to the desk,
sat down, and poured another drink. If there was something
like horror in his face, there was also a hardening in his
mouth's line, and the muscles of his jaw. He spoke to his

glass: "So be it, Your Excellency. Something new for your humble servant. Testing my nerve?"

Jackson's pericardium, the shapely capsule containing his heart, should have been all but hidden between the big blood-fat loaves of his lungs. The doctor had found it fully exposed, the lungs flanking it wrinkled lumps less than a third their natural bulk. Not only they, but the left heart and the superior mediastinal veins—all the regions that should have been grossly engorged with blood—were utterly drained of it.

The doctor swallowed his drink and got out the photographs again. He found that Jackson had died on his stomach across the body of another worker, with the upper part of a third trapped between them. Neither these two subjacent corpses nor the surrounding earth showed any stain of a blood loss that must have amounted to two liters.

Possibly the pictures, by some trick of shadow, had failed to pick it up. He turned to the investigator's report, where Craven would surely have mentioned any significant amounts of bloody earth uncovered during the disinterment. The sheriff recorded nothing of the kind. Dr. Winters returned to the pictures.

Ronald Pollack, Jackson's most intimate associate in the grave, had died on his back, beneath and slightly askew of Jackson, placing most of their torsos in contact, save where the head and shoulder of the third interposed. It seemed inconceivable Pollock's clothing should lack any trace of such massive drainage from a death mate thus embraced.

The doctor rose abruptly, pulled on fresh gloves, and returned to Jackson. His hands showed a more brutal speed now, closing the great incision temporarily with a few widely spaced sutures. He replaced him in the vault and brought out Pollock, striding, heaving hard at the dead shapes in the shifting of them, thrusting always—so it seemed to him—just a step ahead of urgent thoughts he did not want to have, deformities that whispered at his back, emitting faint, chill gusts of putrid breath. He shook his head—denying, delaying—and pushed the new corpse onto the worktable. The scissors undressed Pollock in greedy bites.

But at length, when he had scanned each scrap of fabric and found nothing like the stain of blood, he came to rest again, relinquishing that simplest, desired resolution he had made such haste to reach. He stood at the instrument table, not seeing it, submitting to the approach of the half-formed things at his mind's periphery.

The revelation of Jackson's shriveled lungs had been more than a shock. He had felt a stab of panic, too, in fact that same curiously explicit terror of this place that had urged him to flee earlier. He acknowledged now that the germ of that quickly suppressed terror had been a premonition of this failure to find any trace of the missing blood. Whence the premonition? It had to do with a problem he had steadfastly refused to consider: the mechanics of so complete a drainage of the lungs' densely reticulated vascular structure. Could the earth's crude pressure by itself work so thoroughly, given only a single vent both slender and strangely curved? And then the photograph he had studied. It frightened him now to recall the image—some covert meaning stirred within it, struggling to be seen. Dr. Winters picked the probe up from the table and turned again to the corpse. As surely and exactly as if he had already ascertained the wound's presence, he leaned forward and touched it: a small, neat puncture, just beneath the xiphoid process. He introduced the probe. The wound received it deeply, in a familiar direction.

The doctor went to the desk, and took up the photograph again. Pollock's and Jackson's wounded areas were not in contact. The third man's head was sandwiched between their bodies at just that point. He searched out another picture, in which this third man was more central, and found his name inked in below his image: Joe Allen.

Dreamingly, Dr. Winters went to the wide metal door, shoved it aside, entered the vault. He did not search, but went straight to the trestle, where his friend had paused some hours before, and found the same name on its tag.

The body, beneath decay's spurious obesity, was trim and well muscled. The face was square cut, shelf-browed, with a vulpine nose skewed by an old fracture. The swollen tongue lay behind the teeth, and the bulge of decomposition did not obscure what the man's initial impact must have been—handsome and open, his now-waxen black eyes sly and convivial. Say, good buddy, got a minute? I see you comin' on the swing shift every day, don't I? Yeah, Joe Allen. Look, I know it's late, you want to get home, tell the wife you ain't been in there drinkin' since you got off, right? Oh, yeah, I hear that. But this damn disappearance thing's got me so edgy, and I'd swear to God just as I was coming here I seen someone moving around back of that frame house up the street. See how the trees thin out a little down back of the yard, where the moonlight gets in? That's right. Well, I got me this little popper here. Oh, yeah, that's a beauty, we'll have it covered between us. I knew I could spot a man ready for some trouble—couldn't find a patrol car anywhere on the street. Yeah, just down in here now, to that clump of pine. Step careful, you can barely see. That's right. . . .

The doctor's face ran with sweat. He turned on his heel and walked out of the vault, heaving the door shut behind him. In the office's greater warmth he felt the perspiration soaking his shirt under the smock. His stomach rasped with steady oscillations of pain, but he scarcely attended it. He went to Pollock and seized up the post-mortem knife.

The work was done with surreal speed, the laminae of flesh and bone recoiling smoothly beneath his desperate but unerring hands, until the thoracic cavity lay exposed, and in it, the vampire-stricken lungs, two gnarled lumps of gray tissue.

He searched no deeper, knowing what the heart and ve'
would show. He returned to sit at the desk, weakly dr
the knife, forgotten, still in his left hand. He loo'

window, and it seemed his thoughts originated with that fainter, more tenuous Dr. Winters hanging like a ghost outside.

What was this world he lived in? Surely, in a lifetime, he had not begun to guess. To feed in such a way! There was horror enough in this alone. But to feed thus *in his own grave.* How had he accomplished it—leaving aside how he had fought suffocation long enough to do anything at all? How was it to be comprehended, a greed that raged so hotly it would glut itself at the very threshold of its own destruction? That last feast was surely in his stomach still. Dr. Winters looked at the photograph, at Allen's head snugged into the others' middles like a hungry suckling nuzzling to the sow. Then he looked at the knife in his hand. The hand felt empty of all technique. Its one impulse was to slash, cleave, obliterate the remains of this gluttonous thing, this Joe Allen. He must do this, or flee it utterly. There was no course between. He did not move.

"I *will* examine him," said the ghost in the glass, and did not move. Inside the refrigeration vault there was a slight noise.

No. It had been some hitch in the generator's murmur. Nothing in there could move. There was another noise, a brief friction against the vault's inner wall. The two old men shook their heads at each other. A catch clicked and the metal door slid open. Behind the staring image of his own amazement, the doctor saw that a filthy shape stood in the doorway and raised its arms toward him in a gesture of supplication. The doctor turned in his chair. From the shape came a whistling groan, the decayed fragment of a human voice.

Pleadingly, Joe Allen worked his jaw and spread his purple hands. As if speech were a maggot struggling to emerge from his mouth, the blue, tumescent face toiled, the huge tongue wallowed helplessly between the viscid lips. The doctor reached for the telephone, lifted the reciever.

Its deadness to his ear meant nothing—he could not have spoken. The thing confronting him, with each least move-ment that it made, destroyed the very frame of sanity in which words might have meaning, reduced the world itself around him to a waste of dark and silence, a starlit ruin where already, everywhere, the alien and unimaginable was awakening to its new dominion. The corpse raised and reached out one hand as if to stay him—turned, and walked toward the instrument table. Its legs were leaden, it rocked its shoulders like a swimmer, fighting to make its passage through gravity's dense medium. It reached the table and grasped it exhaustedly. The doctor found himself on his feet, crouched slightly, weightlessly still. The knife in his hand was the only part of himself he clearly felt, and it was like a tongue of fire, a crematory flame. Joe Allen's corpse thrust one hand among the instruments. The thick fingers, with a queer simian ineptitude, brought up a scalpel. Both hands clasped the little handle and plunged the blade be-tween the lips, as a thirsty child might a Popsicle, then jerked it out again, slashing the tongue. Turbid fluid splashed down to the floor. The jaw worked stiffly, the mouth brought out words in a wet, ragged hiss: "Please. Help me. Trapped in this." One dead hand struck the dead chest. "Starving."

"What are you?"

"Traveler. Not of earth."

"An eater of human flesh. A drinker of human blood."

"No. No. Hiding only. Am small. Shape hideous to you. Feared death."

"You brought death." The doctor spoke with the calm of perfect disbelief, himself as incredible to him as the thing he spoke with. It shook its head, the dull, popped eyes glaring with an agony of thwarted expression.

"Killed none. Hid in this. Hid in this not to be killed. Five days now. Drowning in decay. Free me. Please."

"No. You have come to feed on us, you are not hidi[ng] in fear. We are your food, your meat and drink. Yo[u] on those two men within your grave. *Their grave.* For you, a delay. In fact, a diversion that has ended the hunt for you."

"No! No! Used men already dead. For me, five days, starvation. Even less. Fed only from necessity. Horrible necessity!"

The spoiled vocal instrument made a mangled gasp of the last word—an inhuman, snake-pit noise the doctor felt as a cold flicker of ophidian tongues within his ears—while the dead arms moved in a sodden approximation of the body language that swears truth.

"No," the doctor said. "You killed them all. Including your . . . tool—this man. *What are you?*" Panic erupted in the question which he tried to bury by answering himself instantly. "Resolute, yes. That surely. You used death for an escape route. You need no oxygen perhaps."

"Extracted more than my need from gasses of decay. A lesser component of our metabolism."

The voice was gaining distinctness, developing makeshifts for tones lost in the agonal rupturing of the valves and stops of speech, more effectively wrestling vowel and consonant from the putrid tongue and lips. At the same time, the body's crudity of movement did not quite obscure a subtle, incessant experimentation. Fingers flexed and stirred, testing the give of tendons, groping the palm for the old points of purchase and counterpressure there. The knees, with cautious repetitions, assessed the new limits of their articulation.

"What was the sphere?"

"My ship. Its destruction our first duty facing discovery." (Fear touched the doctor, like a slug climbing his neck; he had seen, as it spoke, a sharp, spastic activity of the tongue, a pleating and shrinkage of its bulk as at the tug of some inward adjustment.) "No chance to reenter. Leaving this take far too long. Not even time to set for destruct—must extrude a cilium, chemical key to broach hull shield. In shaft my only chance to halt host."

The right arm tested the wrist, and the scalpel the hand still held cut white sparks from the air, while the word "host" seemed itself a little knife prick, a teasing abandonment of fiction—though the dead mask showed no irony—prelim-inary to attack.

But he found that fear had gone from him. The impos-sibility with which he conversed, and was about to struggle, was working in him an overwhelming amplification of his life's long, helpless rage at death. He found his parochial pity for earth alone stretched to the transstellar scope this traveler commanded, to the whole cosmic trash yard with its bulldozed multitudes of corpses; galactic wheels of car-nage—stars, planets with their most majestic generations—all trash, cracked bones and foul rags that pooled, settled, reconcatenated in futile symmetries gravid with new mul-titudes of briefly animate trash.

And this, standing before him now, was the death it was given him particularly to deal—his mite was being called in by the universal Treasury of death, and Dr. Winters found himself, an old healer, on fire to pay. His own, more lethal blade, tugged at his hand with its own sharp appetite. He felt entirely the Examiner once more, knew the precise cuts he would make, swiftly and without error. *Very soon now*, he thought, and coolly probed for some further insight before its onslaught.

"Why must your ship be destroyed, even at the cost of your host's life?"

"We must not be understood."

"The livestock must not understand what is devouring them."

"Yes, Doctor. Not all at once. But one by one. You will understand what is devouring you. That is essential to my feast."

The doctor shook his head. "You are in your grave al-ready, Traveler. That body will be your coffin. You will be buried in it a second time, for all time."

The thing came one step nearer and opened its mouth.

The flabby throat wrestled as with speech, but what sprang out was a slender white filament, more than whip-fast. Dr. Winters saw only the first flicker of its eruption, and then his brain novaed, thinning out at light-speed to a white nullity.

When the doctor came to himself, it was in fact to a part of himself only. Before he had opened his eyes he found that his wakened mind had repossessed proprioceptively only a bizarre truncation of his body. His head, neck, left shoulder, arm, and hand declared themselves—the rest was si-lence.

When he opened his eyes, he found that he lay supine on the gurney, and naked. Something propped his head. A strap bound his left elbow to the gurney's edge, a strap he could feel. His chest was also anchored by a strap, and this he could not feel. Indeed, save for its active remnant, his entire body might have been bound in a block of ice, so numb was it, and so powerless was he to compel the slightest movement from the least part of it.

The room was empty, but from the open door of the vault there came slight sounds: the creak and soft frictions of heavy tarpaulin shifted to accommodate some business involving small clicking and kissing noises.

Tears of fury filled the doctor's eyes. Clenching his one fist at the starry engine of creation that he could not see, he ground his teeth and whispered in the hot breath of strangled weeping: "Take it back, this dirty little shred of life! I throw it off gladly like the filth it is." The slow knock of boot soles loudened from within the vault, and he turned his head. From the vault door Joe Allen's corpse approached him.

It moved with new energy, though its gait was grotesque, a ducking, hitching progress, jerky with circumventions of decayed muscle, while above this galvanized, struggling frame, the bruise-colored face hung inanimate, an image of detachment. With terrible clarity it revealed the thing for what it was—a damaged hand puppet vigorously worked from within. And when that frozen face was brought to hang above the doctor, the reeking hands, with the light, solicitous touch of friends at sickbeds, rested on his naked thigh.

The absence of sensation made the touch more dreadful than it felt. It showed him that the nightmare he still desperately denied at heart had annexed his body while he—holding head and arm free—had already more than half drowned in its mortal paralysis. There lay his nightmare part, a nothingness freely possessed by an unspeakability. The corpse said: "Rotten blood. Thin nourishment. Only one hour alone before you came. Fed from neighbor to my left—barely had strength to extend siphon. Fed from the right while you worked. Tricky going—you are alert. Expected Dr. Parsons. Energy needs of animating this"—one hand left the doctor's thigh and smote the dusty overalls—"and of host-transfer, very high. Once I have you synapsed, will be near starvation again."

A sequence of unbearable images unfolded in the doctor's mind, even as the robot carrion turned from the gurney and walked to the instrument table: the sheriff's arrival just after dawn, alone, of course, since Craven always took thought for his deputies' rest and because on this errand he would want privacy to consider any indiscretion on behalf of the miners' survivors that the situation might call for; his finding his old friend, supine and alarmingly weak; his hurrying over, his leaning near. Then, somewhat later, a police car containing a rack of still-wet bones might plunge off the highway above some deep spot in the gorge.

The corpse took an evidence box from the table and put the scalpel in it. Then it turned and retrieved the mortuary knife from the floor and put that in as well, saying as it did so, without turning, "The sheriff will come in the morning. You spoke like close friends. He will probably come alone."

The coincidence with his thoughts had to be accident, but the intent to terrify and appall him was clear. The tone and timing of that patched-up voice were unmistakably deliberate—sly probes that sought his anguish specifically, sought his mind's personal center. He watched the corpse—back at the table—dipping an apish but accurate hand and plucking up rib shears, scissors, clamps, adding all to the box. He stared, momentarily emptied by shock of all but the will to know finally the full extent of the horror that had appropriated his life. Joe Allen's body carried the box to the worktable beside the gurney, and the expressionless eyes met the doctor's.

"I have gambled. A grave gamble. But now I have won. At risk of personal discovery we are obliged to disconnect, contract, hide as well as possible in host body. Suicide in effect. I disregarded situational imperatives, despite starvation before disinterment and subsequent autopsy all but certain. I caught up with crew, tackled Pollock and Jackson microseconds before blast. Computed five days' survival from this cache, could disconnect at limit of strength to do so, but otherwise would chance autopsy, knowing doctor was alcoholic incompetent. And now see my gain. You are a prize host, can feed with near impunity even when killing too dangerous. Safe meals delivered to you still warm."

The corpse had painstakingly aligned the gurney parallel to the worktable but offset, the table's foot extending past the gurney's, and separated from it by a distance somewhat less than the reach of Joe Allen's right arm. Now the dead hands distributed the implements along the right edge of the table, save for the scissors and the box. These the corpse took to the table's foot, where it set it down the box and slid the scissors' jaws round one strap of its overalls. It began to speak again, and as it did, the scissors dismembered its ceremonies in unhesitating strokes.

"The cut must be medical, forensically right, though a smaller one easier. Must be careful of the pectoral muscles or arms will not convey me. I am no larva anymore—over fifteen hundred grams."

To ease the nightmare's suffocating pressure, to thrust

out some flicker of his own will against its engulfment, the doctor flung a question, his voice more cracked than the other's now was: "Why is my arm free?"

"The last, fine neural splicing needs a sensory-motor standard, to perfect my brain's fit to yours. Lacking this eye–hand coordinating check, much coarser motor control of host. This done, I flush out the paralytic, unbind us, and we are free together."

The grave clothes had fallen in a puzzle of fragments, and the cadaver stood naked, its dark, gas-rounded contours making it seem some sleek marine creature, ruddered with the black-veined, gas-distended sex. Again the voice had teased for his fear, had uttered the last word with a savoring protraction, and now the doctor's cup of anguish brimmed over; horror and outrage wrenched his spirit in brutal alternation as if trying to tear it naked from its captive frame. He rolled his head in this deadlock, his mouth beginning to split with the slow birth of a mind-emptying outcry.

The corpse watched this, giving a single nod that might have been approbation. Then it mounted the worktable and, with the concentrated caution of some practiced convalescent reentering his bed, lay on its back. The dead eyes again sought the living and found the doctor staring back, grinning insanely.

"Clever corpse!" the doctor cried. "Clever, carnivorous corpse! Able alien! Please don't think I'm criticizing. Who am I to criticize? A mere arm and shoulder, a talking hand, just a small piece of a pathologist. But I'm confused." He paused, savoring the monster's attentive silence and his own buoyancy in the hysterical levity that had unexpectedly liberated him. "You're going to use your puppet there to pluck you out of itself and put you on me. But once he's pulled you from your driver's seat, won't he go dead, so to speak, and drop you? You could get a nasty knock. Why not set a plank between the tables—the puppet opens the door, and you scuttle, ooze, lurch, flop, slither, as the case may be, across the bridge. No messy spills. And in any case,

isn't this an odd, rather clumsy way to get around among
your cattle? Shouldn't you at least carry your own scalpels
when you travel? There's always the risk you'll run across
that one host in a million that isn't carrying one with him."

He knew his gibes would be answered to his own despair.
He exulted, but solely in the momentary bafflement of the
predator—in having, for just a moment, mocked its gloating
assurance to silence and marred its feast.

Its right hand picked up the post-mortem knife beside it,
and the left hand wedged a roll of gauze beneath Allen's neck,
lifting the throat to a more prominent arch. The mouth
told the ceiling: "We retain larval form till entry of the host.
As larvae we have locomotor structures, and sense buds
usable outside our ships' sensory amplifiers. I waited coiled
round Joe Allen's bed leg till night, entered by his mouth
as he slept." Allen's hand lifted the knife, held it high above
the dull, quick eyes, turning it in the light. "Once lodged,
we have three instars to adult form," the voice continued
absently—the knife might have been a mirror from which
the corpse read its features. "Larvally we have only a sketch
of our full neural tap. Our metamorphosis cued and determined by host's endosomatic ecology. I matured in three
days." Allen's wrist flexed, tipping the knife's point down-
most. "Most supreme adaptations purchased at the cost of
inessential capacities." The elbow pronated and slowly flexed,
hooking the knife body-wards. "Our hosts are all sentients,
eco-dominants, are already carrying the baggage of coping
structures for the planetary environment. Limbs, sensory
portals"—the fist planted the fang of its tool under the chin,
tilted it and rode it smoothly down the throat, the voice
proceeding unmarred from under the furrow that the steel
plowed—"somatic envelopes, instrumentalities"—down the
sternum, diaphragm, abdomen the stainless blade painted
its stripe of gaping, muddy tissue—"with a host's brain we
inherit all these, the mastery of any planet, netted in its
dominant's cerebral nexus. Thus our genetic codings are
now all but disencumbered of such provisions."

So swiftly the doctor flinched, Joe Allen's hand slashed four lateral cuts from the great wound's axis. The seeming butchery left two flawlessly drawn thoracic flaps cleanly outlined. The left hand raised the left flap's hem, and the right coaxed the knife into the aperture, deepening it with small stabs and slices. The posture was a man's who searches a breast pocket, with the dead eyes studying the slow recoil of flesh. The voice, when it resumed, had geared up to an intenser pitch.

"Galactically, the chordate nerve/brain paradigm abounds, and the neural labyrinth is our dominion. Are we to make plank bridges and worm across them to our food? Are cockroaches greater than we for having legs to run up walls and antennae to grope their way! All the quaint, hinged crutches that life sports! The stilts, fins, fans, springs, stalks, flippers, and feathers, all in turn so variously terminating in hooks, clamps, suckers, scissors, forks, or little cages of digits! And besides all the gadgets it concocts for wrestling through its worlds, it is all knobbed, whiskered, crested, plumed, vented, spiked, or measeled over with perceptual gear for combing pittances of noise or color from the environing plenitude."

Invincibly calm and sure, the hands traded tool and tasks. The right flap eased back, revealing ropes of ingeniously spared muscle while promising a genuine appearance once sutured back in place. Helplessly the doctor felt his delirious defiance bleed away and a bleak fascination rebind him.

"We are the taps and relays that share the host's aggregate of afferent nerve impulse precisely at its nodes of integration. We are the brains that peruse these integrations, integrate them with our existing banks of host-specific data, and, lastly, let their consequences flow down the motor pathway—either the consequences they seek spontaneously, or those we wish to graft upon them. We are besides a streamlined alimentary/circulatory system and a reproductive apparatus. And more than this we need not be."

The corpse had spread its bloody vest, and the feculent hands now took up the rib shears. The voice's sinister coloration of pitch and stress grew yet more marked—the phrases slid from the tongue with a cobra's seeking sway, winding their liquid rhythms round the doctor till a gap in his resistance should let them pour through to slaughter the little courage left him.

"For in his form we have inhabited the densest brainweb of three hundred races, lain intricately snug within them like thriving vine on trelliswork. We've looked out from too many variously windowed masks to regret our own vestigial senses. None read their worlds definitely. Far better then our nomad's range and choice than an unvarying tenancy of one poor set of structures. Far better to slip on as we do whole living beings and wear at once all of their limbs and organs, memories and powers—wear all as tightly congruent to our wills as a glove is to the hand that fills it."

The shears clipped through the gristle, stolid, bloody jaws monotonously feeding, stopping short of the sternoclavicular joint in the manubrium where the muscles of the pectoral girdle have an important anchorage.

"No consciousness of the chordate type that we have found has been impermeable to our finesse—no dendritic pattern so elaborate we could not read its stitchwork and thread ourselves to match, precisely map its each synaptic seam till we could loosen it and retailor all to suit ourselves. We have strutted costumed in the bodies of planetary autarchs, venerable manikins of moral fashion, but cut out of the universal cloth: the weave of fleet electric filaments of experience which we easily reshuffled to the warp of our wishes. Whereafter—newly hemmed and gathered—their living fabric hung obedient to our bias, investing us with honor and influence unlimited."

The tricky verbal melody, through the corpse's deft, unfaltering self-dismemberment—the sheer neuromuscular orchestration of the compound activity—struck Dr. Winters with the detached enthrallment great keyboard performers could bring him. He glimpsed the alien's perspective—a Gulliver waiting in a brobdingnagian grave, then marshaling a dead giant against a living, like a dwarf in a huge mechanical crane, feverishly programming combat on a battery of levers and pedals, waiting for the robot arms' enactments, the remote, titanic impact of the foes—and he marveled, filled with a bleak wonder at life's infinite strategy and plasticity. Joe Allen's hands reached into his half-opened abdominal cavity, reached deep below the uncut anterior muscle that was exposed by the shallow, spurious incision of the epidermis, till by external measure they were extended far enough to be touching his thighs. The voice was still as the forearms advertised a delicate rummaging with the buried fingers. The shoulders drew back. As the steady with-drawal brought the wrists into view, the dead legs tremored and quaked with diffuse spasms.

"You called your kind out food and drink, Doctor. If you were merely that, an elementary usurpation of your motor tracts alone would satisfy us, give us perfect cattle-control—for what rarest word or subtlest behavior is more than a flurry of varied muscles? That trifling skill was ours long ago. It is not mere blood that feeds this lust I feel now to tenant you, this craving for an intimacy that years will not stale. My truest feast lies in compelling you to feed in that way and in the utter deformation of your will this will involve. Had gross nourishment been my prime need, then my gravemates—Pollock and Jackson—could have eked out two weeks of life for me or more. But I scorned a cowardly parsimony in the face of death. I reinvested more than half the energy that their blood gave me in fabricating chemicals to keep their brains alive, and fluid-bathed with oxygenated nutriment."

Out of the chasmed midriff the smeared hands dragged two long tresses of silvery filament that writhed and sparkled with a million simultaneous coilings and contractions. The legs jittered with faint, chaotic pulses throughout their mus-culature, until the bright vermiculate tresses had gathered into two spheric masses which the hands laid carefully within the incision. Then the legs lay still as death.

"I had accessory neural taps only to spare, but I could access much memory, and all of their cognitive responses, and having in my banks all the organ of Cott's electro-chemical conversions of English words, I could whisper anything to them directly into the eighth cranial nerve. Those are our true feast, Doctor, such bodiless electric storms of impotent cognition as I tickled up in those two little bone globes. I was forced to drain them yesterday, just before disinterment. They lived till then and understood everything—*everything* I did to them."

When the voice paused, the dead and living eyes were locked together. They remained so a moment, and then the dead face smiled.

It recapitulated all the horror of Allen's first resurrection—this waking of expressive soul from those grave-mound contours. And it was a demon-soul the doctor saw awaken: the smile was barbed with fine, sharp hooks of cruelty at the corners of the mouth, while the barbed eyes beamed fond, languorous anticipation of his pain. Remotely, Dr. Winters heard the flat sound of his own voice asking, "And Joe Allen?"

"Oh, yes, Doctor. He is with us now, has been through-out. I grieve to abandon so rare a host! He is a true hermit-philosopher, well-read in four languages. He is writing a translation of Marcus Aurelius—he was, I mean, in his free time. . . ."

Long minutes succeeded of the voice accompanying the surreal self-autopsy, but the doctor lay stilled, emptied of reactive power. Still, the full understanding of his fate re-verberated in his mind—an empty room through which the voice, not heard exactly but somehow implanted directly as in the subterranean torture it had just described, sent af-tershocks of realization, amplifications of the Unspeakable. The parasite had traced and tapped the complex interface between cortical integration of input and the consequent neural output shaping response. It had interposed its brain between, sharing consciousness while solely commanding the pathways of reaction. The host, the bottled personality, was mute and limbless for any least expression of its own will, while hellishly articulate and agile in the service of the parasite's. It was the host's own hands that bound and wrenched the life half out of his prey, his own loins that experienced the repeated orgasms crowning his other despoliations of their bodies. And when they lay, bound and shrieking still, ready for the consummation, it was his own strength that hauled the smoking entrails from them, and his own intimate tongue and guzzling mouth he plunged into the rank, palpitating feast.

And the doctor had glimpses of the history behind this predation, that of a race so far advanced in the essentializing, the inexorable abstraction of their own mental fabric that through scientific commitment and genetic self-cultivation they had come to embody their own model of perfected consciousness, streamlined to permit the entry of other beings and the direct acquisition of their experiential worlds. All strictest scholarship at first, until there matured in the dis-embodied scholars their long-germinal and now blazing, jealous hatred for all 'lesser' minds rooted and clothed in the soil and sunlight of solid, particular worlds. The parasite spoke of the "cerebral music," the "symphonies of agonized paradox" that were its invasion's chief plunder. The doctor felt the truth behind this grandiloquence: its actual harvest from the systematic violation of enconfined personalities was the experience of a barren supremacy of means over lives more primitive, perhaps, but vastly wealthier in the vivid-ness and passionate concern with which life for them was imbued.

Joe Allen's hands had scooped up the bunched skeins of alien nerve, with the wrinkled brain node couched amidst them, and for some time had waited the slow retraction of a last major trunkline which seemingly had followed the spine's axis. At last, when only a slender subfiber of this remained implanted, the corpse, smiling once more, held up for him to view its reconcatenated master. The doctor looked into its eyes then and spoke—not to their controller, but to the captive who shared them with it, and who now, the doctor knew, neared his final death.

"Good-bye, Joe Allen. Eddie Sykes. You are guiltless. Peace be with you at last."

The demon smile remained fixed, the right hand reached its viscid cargo across the gap and over the doctor's groin. He watched the hand set the glittering medusa's head—his new self—upon his flesh, return to the table, take up the scalpel, and reach back to cut in his groin a four-inch incision—all in eerie absence of tactile stimulus. The line that had remained plunged into the corpse suddenly whipped free of the mediastinal crevice, retracted across the gap, and shortened to a taut stub on the seething organism atop the doctor.

Joe Allen's body collapsed, emptied, all slack. He was a corpse again entirely, but with one anomalous feature to his posture. His right arm had not dropped to the nearly vertical hang that would have been natural. At the instant of the alien's unplugging, the shoulder had given a fierce shrug and wrenching of its angle, flinging the arm upward as it died so that it now lay in the orientation of an arm that reaches up for a ladder's next rung. The slightest tremor would unfix the joints and dump the arm back into the gravitational bias; it would also serve to dump the scalpel from the proffered, upturned palm that implement still precariously occupied.

The man had repossessed himself one microsecond before his end. The doctor's heart stirred, woke, and sang within him, for he saw that the scalpel was just in reach of his fingers at his forearm's fullest stretch from the bound elbow. The horror crouched on him and, even now slowly feeding its trunkline into his groin incision, at first stopped the doctor's hand with a pang of terror. Then he reminded himself that, until implanted, the enemy was a senseless mass, bristling with plugs, with input jacks for senses, but, until installed in the physical amplifiers of eyes and ears, an utterly deaf, blind monad that waited in a perfect solipsism between two captive sensory envelopes.

He saw his straining fingers above the bright tool of freedom, thought with an insane smile of God and Adam on the Sistine ceiling, and then, with a life span of surgeon's fine control, plucked up the scalpel. The arm fell and hung.

"Sleep." The doctor said. "Sleep revenged."

But he found his retaliation harshly reined in by the alien's careful provisions. His elbow had been fixed with his upper arm almost at right angles to his body's long axis; his forearm could reach his hand inward and present it closely to the face, suiting the parasite's need of an eye-hand coordinative check, but could not, even with the scal-pel's added reach, bring its point within four inches of his groin. Steadily the parasite fed in its tap line. It would usurp motor control in three or four minutes at most, to judge by the time its extrication from Allen had taken.

Frantically the doctor bent his wrist inward to its limit, trying to pick through the strap where it crossed his inner elbow. Sufficient pressure was impossible, and the hold so awkward that even feeble attempts threatened the loss of the scalpel! Smoothly the root of alien control sank into him. It was a defenseless thing of jelly against which he lay lethally armed, and he was still doomed—a preview of all his thrall's impotence-to-be.

But of course there was a way. Not to survive. But to escape, and to have vengeance. For a moment he stared at his captor, hardening his mettle in the blaze of hate it lit in him. Then, swiftly, he determined the order of his moves, and began.

He reached the scalpel to his neck and opened his superior thyroid vein—his inkwell. He laid the scalpel by his ear, dipped his finger in his blood, and began to write on the metal surface of the gurney, beginning by his thigh and moving toward his armpit. Oddly, the incision of his neck, though this was muscularly awake, had been painless, which gave him hopes that raised his courage for what remained to do.

When he had done the message read:

MIND PARASITE
I'M ALIEN IN ME
CUT ALL TILL
FIND
1500 GM MASS
NERVE FIBER

He wanted to write good-bye to his friend, but the alien had begun to pay out smaller, auxiliary filaments collaterally with the main one, and all now lay in speed.

He took up the scalpel, rolled his head to the left, and plunged the blade deep in his ear.

Miracle! Last, accidental mercy! It was painless. Some procedural, highly specific anesthetic was in effect. With careful plunges, he obliterated the right inner ear and then thrust silence, with equal thoroughness, into the left. The slashing of the vocal chords followed, then the tendons in the back of the neck that hold it erect. He wished he were free to unstring knees and elbows, too, but it could not be. But blinded, with centers of balance lost, with only rough motor control—all these conditions should fetter the alien's escape, should it in the first place manage the reanimation of a bloodless corpse in which it had not yet achieved a fine-tuned interweave. Before he extinguished his eyes, he paused, the scalpel poised above his face, and blinked them to clear his aim of tears. The right, then the left, both retinas meticulously carved away, the yolk of vision quite scooped out of them. The scalpel's last task, once it had tilted the head sideways to guide the blood flow absolutely clear of possible effacement of the message, was to slash the external carotid artery.

When this was done, the old man sighed with relief and

laid his scalpel down. Even as he did so, he felt the deep inward prickle of an alien energy—something that flared, crackled, flared, *groped for* but did not quite find its purchase. And inwardly, as the doctor sank toward sleep—cerebrally, as a voiceless man must speak—he spoke to the parasite these carefully chosen words: "Welcome to your new house. I'm afraid there's been some vandalism—the lights don't work, and the plumbing has a very bad leak. There are some other things wrong as well—the neighborhood is perhaps a little *too* quiet, and you may find it hard to get around very easily. But it's been a lovely home to me for fifty-seven years, and somehow I think you'll stay. . . ."

The face, turned toward the body of Joe Allen, seemed to weep scarlet tears, but its last movement before death was to smile.

ACKNOWLEDGMENTS

"Glory" by Ron Goulart. Copyright © 1986 by Mercury Press, Inc. By permission of the author.

"Bug House" by Lisa Tuttle. Copyright © 1980 by Mercury Press, Inc. By permission of the author.

"Hand in Glove" by Robert Aickman. Copyright © 1978 by Mercury Press, Inc. By permission of the author's agent, Kirby McCauley, Ltd.

"Stillborn" by Mike Conner. Copyright © 1981 by Mercury Press, Inc. By permission of the author and his agent, Frances Collin.

"Balgrummo's Hell" by Russell Kirk. Copyright © 1967 by Mercury Press, Inc. By permission of the author.

"The Old Darkness" by Pamela Sargent. Copyright © 1983 by Mercury Press, Inc. By permission of the author.

"The Night of White Bhairab" by Lucius Shepard. Copyright © 1984 by Mercury Press, Inc. By permission of the author

"Salvage Rites" by Ian Watson. Copyright © 1986 by Mercury Press, Inc. By permission of the author.

"Test" by Theodore L. Thomas. Copyright © 1962 by Mercury Press, Inc. By permission of the author.

"The Little Black Train" by Manly Wade Wellman. Copyright © 1954 by Fantasy House, Inc. Copyright renewed 1982 by Mercury Press, Inc. By permission of Frances Wellman.

"The Autopsy" by Michael Shea. Copyright © 1980 by Mercury Press, Inc. By permission of the author.